Three N

"If the world could write by itself,
it would write like Tolstoy."
Isaak Babel

"Tolstoy's greatness lies in not turning the story
into sentimental tragedy… His world is huge and
vast, filled with complex family lives and great
social events. His characters are well-rounded
presences. They have complete passions: a
desire for love, but also an inner moral depth."
Malcolm Bradbury

"What an artist and what a psychologist!"
Gustave Flaubert

"The pure narrative power of his work is unequalled."
Thomas Mann

"Tolstoy is the greatest Russian writer of prose fiction."
Vladimir Nabokov

"The greatest of all novelists."
Virginia Woolf

ONEWORLD CLASSICS

Three Novellas

Leo Tolstoy

Translated by Kyril Zinovieff
and April FitzLyon

ONEWORLD
CLASSICS

ONEWORLD CLASSICS LTD
London House
243-253 Lower Mortlake Road
Richmond
Surrey TW9 2LL
United Kingdom
www.oneworldclassics.com

A Landowner's Morning first published in Russian in 1856
This translation first published by Quartet Books in 1984
Translation © Kyril Zinovieff, 1984, 2009

The Devil first published in Russian in 1911
This translation first published by Spearman & Calder in 1953
Translation © April FitzLyon, 1953, 2009

Family Happiness first published in Russian in 1859
This translation first published by Spearman & Calder in 1953
Translation © April FitzLyon, 1953, 2009

This revised edition first published by Oneworld Classics Limited in 2009

Reprinted February and August 2010

Printed in Great Britain by MPG Books, Cornwall

ISBN: 978-1-84749-125-1

Contents

Introduction to the 2009 Edition

The publication of these three stories in a single volume provides a rare opportunity for those interested in Tolstoy to see how he developed as a writer and, of course, also as a person. The stories in this volume were written over the course of more than half a century, from 1852 until 1909, a year before his death.

In the case of the first two – *A Landowner's Morning* and *The Devil* – we are presented with his attitude to peasants, an attitude which changed fundamentally from the first story, written in 1852 when serfdom still existed, to the end of the century, by which time serfs had been free for several decades. Emancipated in 1861, they were no longer the chattels of their landowners.

In *A Landowner's Morning*, Tolstoy views his peasants as objects dependent on their owner, who, in turn, feels direct responsibility for their welfare. He sets out to improve their lot in every way that he can, but it's as though they were pieces which he can move about on his chessboard, creatures whom he would like to help, but without feelings of their own which must be taken into account. He expects gratitude; they give him suspicion, mistrust. If he's offering it, then for that very reason there must be a catch in it and it will turn out not for their good but for his. So they categorically reject and entirely misunderstand his well-meant offers of improvement. It is interesting that, in his crestfallen despair, the idea of emancipation – of setting them free from him and free to trust him – never seems to enter his head.

In the second story, *The Devil*, written nearly fifty years later and long after the abolition of serfdom, emancipation has brought about a new situation. It is true that it does not result in a happier relationship; it ends in tragedy, whichever of the two endings you choose. But the story is now about two human beings, a man and a woman, emotionally involved. She is tempted by the material advantages and he by the sexual advantages on offer. The attitude of both may be reprehensible. But there is not doubt whatever that they regard each other, emotionally, as equals. He discovers that the relationship isn't purely sexual, as he had thought, that he isn't just "a stag" but in some sense a husband. He is possessed by her and she possesses him. That, indeed, is why there has to be a tragedy.

So Russia has changed fundamentally. And Tolstoy the person has changed with it. The third story takes us back to the early days of Tolstoy the writer. In *Childhood* (1852) and *The Sebastopol Stories* (1855–56), he was testing himself out as a realistic and objective describer. In *Family Happiness* (1859), we see him for the first time approaching the subject of marriage, which played such an important part in his great novels, *War and Peace* and *Anna Karenina*. He still deploys an almost photographic realism, but applies it now to the intimate, familial relationship of husband and wife, with the added challenge (for a male writer) of viewing it through the eyes of the wife. The novelist has taken an important step towards his great novels.

In this context, *The Devil* at first sight seems regressive – not so much because of its intense sexuality as because it represents what is in effect a retreat by Tolstoy the novelist, and a victory, at the end of his long life, for Tolstoy the didactic moralist. We can see it coming: in *Anna Karenina* (1877) and in *The Confession* (1879). It emerges, full-blown, in *Resurrection* (1899), where the meticulously observed story makes room for the homily. By the time we get to *The Devil*, Tolstoy is still the great observer, but he wants us to be perfectly sure of the moral message to be drawn from what he observes. *Resurrection* remains a novel – a very, very long one – in which the moral message is to some extent diluted. *The Devil* is stripped down, deliberately and brutally, into a short, edifying tale in which the reader has no escape and the author has completed his trajectory.

A Landowner's Morning

Translated by Kyril Zinovieff

Preface

This story was written nine years before the abolition of serfdom in Russia, at a time when the existence of serfdom was a subject of constant debate.

By this time, there were two main reasons why it was felt, both by the government and by the people as a whole, that the emancipation of the peasants was essential. One was moral: the sense of shame that a country which considered itself in terms of civilization on a par with Europe should still be practising a form of slavery that was medieval in origin and now indefensible. The second reason was rational and to an extent opportunistic: Russia, it was realized, could only compete with Europe economically if its industry was given the resources to develop along capitalist lines. This meant releasing the necessary labour and entrepreneurial energy locked up by an institution which placed much of the peasant population in thrall to its agricultural owners and landlords.

Even under serfdom, this was partly achieved by allowing peasants to "acquit" themselves of their obligations through a system of "quit-rent"; it was possible for a peasant to negotiate an arrangement under which, instead of working on the manorial land, he could choose to work on his own account – in towns and elsewhere – and to pay his owner in money instead of labour. (Tolstoy gives the example of the peasant family which had grown prosperous by becoming carters.) Many of the most enterprising peasants followed this route and the most successful were able to buy their freedom outright (some, indeed, were able to buy up their owners too). But these were the exceptions, and the system of "quit-rent" could not provide enough labour to supply nineteenth-century capitalism. Only emancipation could do that.

Tolstoy did not agree. He believed that on the whole peasants were not helped by education or by being given the freedom to choose; what they needed was material help to go on doing what they did, only better. It followed, though, that landowners for their part had the duty of improving to the best of their ability the standard of living of their peasantry and to help them both financially and materially.

When the story first appeared, in the December 1856 edition of the periodical *Otechestvennye Zapiski* (*Notes of the Fatherland*), Turgenev (in a letter to A.V. Druzhinin of January 1857) praised it as "masterly" for its "language, story-telling and characterization". But in the same letter he condemned the implication "running like a trace horse alongside": that to educate the peasantry as a whole, to improve their conditions of life, was a futile thing. This implication Turgenev found "unpleasant" and in conflict with his own principal concern at the time, which was to shine the most favourable light possible on the potential of the Russian peasant, so as to advance the arguments for emancipation.

The first version of *A Landowner's Morning* was started under a different title in 1852 when Tolstoy was twenty-four, more or less concurrently with *Childhood*. His original intention was to divide the novel into two parts. The first was to deal with peasants, the second with landowners. But the work proceeded slowly in spite of Tolstoy's satisfaction with it, and over four years later even the first part was not as complete as he would have liked. The second consisted merely of a short list of characteristics (mostly disreputable or, at least, unattractive) against some of which he put the names of persons he knew who were presumably to serve as models.

But there were many interruptions and other projects intervened. Tolstoy's original plan now appeared to him too ambitious. So he decided to recast his novel, making a novella or a long short story out of it, by drastically abridging it, retaining no more than the kernel of the idea that first inspired him – the attitude of peasants to landowners – and restricting the time of action to a single morning. As with almost all Tolstoy's writings, the story is based on personal experience and observation. The young landowner, Prince Nekhlyudov, is, of course, himself (he used that name later in other works, when modelling the principal character on his own personality), and the peasants all apparently bear a strong resemblance to those living on Tolstoy's family estate, Yasnaya Polyana. All that remained of the original novel was Nekhlyudov's letter to his aunt, setting out his somewhat vague, but idealistic plan of making his peasants happy, his aunts disillusioning, worldly-wise answer (both now in Russian instead of in French as in the original version) and Nekhlyudov's conversations with the peasants. All unnecessary details were eliminated and all traces of authorial presence removed. The narrative, thus freed from sententious and didactic expressions of the author's own opinions, was greatly improved.

The work of abridgement and alteration took Tolstoy a mere twelve days to complete, and he then conveyed the novella personally to the editor of the periodical. He himself never again referred to *A Landowner's Morning*. According to Vassily Botkin, a literary-minded tea merchant and friend of many Russian writers, including Turgenev and Belinsky, it "created no impression" on its publication. But several years later, when writing *War and Peace*, Tolstoy incorporated the lesson learnt by Nekhlyudov in his account of Prince Andrew's attempt to educate the peasants on his estate and improve their standard of living at his own expense. This attempt, says Tolstoy, "as has always happened and always will, merely strengthened their distrust of landowners [dislike of their masters]". (Tolstoy's alternative version is in square brackets.) For some reason, however, he excluded this sentence from the next draft of *War and Peace*, and it did not reappear in the final version.

Kyril Zinovieff

1

PRINCE NEKHLYUDOV was nineteen years old, and a third-year university student, when he arrived at his estate for the summer vacation to spend the whole summer there by himself. In the autumn he wrote, in his unformed childish writing, the following letter to his aunt, Countess Beloretskaya, who in his estimation was his best friend and the most intelligent woman in the world. The letter was in French and is here given in translation:

My dear aunt,
I have come to a decision which must affect the whole course of my life. I am leaving the university in order to devote myself to life in the country because I feel that I was born for it. For heaven's sake, my dear aunt, don't laugh at me. You will say that I am young; it may be true, perhaps, that I am still a child, but this does not prevent me feeling my vocation, wanting to do good and to love the good.

As I wrote to you before, I found my affairs here in very bad shape indeed. Trying to put them right again, I made a close study of them and discovered that the main evil consists in the quite pathetic poverty of the peasants, an evil which can be righted only through work and patience. If you could only see two of my peasants, David and Ivan, and the life they and their families lead, I am sure the mere sight of these two unfortunate people, more than anything I can say, will convince you that I am right in my intention. Is it not my direct and sacred duty to look after the happiness of these seven hundred men for whom I shall have to answer before God? Is it not a sin to abandon them, for the sake of pleasure or ambitious plans, to the whims of callous village elders and farm managers? And why seek in some other sphere opportunities for being useful and doing good, when such a noble and impressive duty lies immediately to hand? I feel it in me to become a good landlord – and in order to be one, as I understand it, there is no need for a university degree or official rank which you so much want me to have. My dear aunt, do not make ambitious plans for me; get used to the idea that I have chosen quite a special path, but one which is good and which will, I feel, lead me to happiness. I have thought a lot about my future duties, have written out rules of conduct for myself and, if only God grants me life and strength, I shall succeed in my enterprise.

Do not show this letter to my brother Vasya; I am afraid of his jibes. He is used to dominating me and I am used to obeying him. Vanya may not approve my intention, but he will understand it.

The Countess sent him the following letter in reply, here also translated from the French:

So far as I am concerned, my dear Dmitry, your letter proves nothing except that you have a very kind heart, and this I never doubted. But, dear friend, our good qualities do us more harm in life than our bad ones. I shall not tell you that you are doing a silly thing and that your behaviour distresses me, but shall try to convince you by persuasion alone. Let's reason it out, my dear boy. You say that you feel a vocation for life in the country, that you want your peasants to be happy and that you hope to be a good landlord. I must tell you, first, that we feel our vocation only after we have once made a mistake about it; second, that it is easier to achieve one's own happiness than the happiness of others; and third, that to be a good landlord you must be cold and stern, which you are not likely ever to become, though you try to pretend you are.

You consider your arguments to be irrefutable, and even take them to constitute rules of conduct, but at my age, my boy, people do not believe in arguments and rules, but only in experience. And experience tells me that your plans are childish. I am getting on for fifty and have known many worthy men, but I have never heard of a young man of good family and abilities burying himself in the country on the plea of doing good. You have always wanted to appear original, but your originality is nothing but excessive self-esteem. And, my friend, you had better choose the well-trodden paths – they lead quicker to success, and success, even if you don't need it as such, is essential to enable you to do the good you aspire to do.

The poverty of a few peasants is a necessary evil, or else an evil which can be remedied without forgetting one's duties to society, to *one's relations and to oneself. With your intelligence, your kind heart and your love of virtue, there is no career in which you would not succeed, but at least choose one which would be worthy of you and would do you credit.*

I believe in your sincerity when you say you are not ambitious, but you are deceiving yourself. Ambition is a virtue for someone of your age and your means, but it becomes ridiculous as well as a defect when a man can no longer satisfy this passion. And you will experience this if you do not change your intention. Goodbye, my dear Dmitry. I think I love you all the more for your absurd but noble and magnanimous plan. Do as you wish, but I must confess I cannot agree with you.

On receiving this letter, the young man considered it for a long time and, having finally decided that even a highly intelligent woman could err in her judgements, applied for a discharge from his university and settled down in the country for ever.

2

T HE YOUNG LANDOWNER, as he wrote to his aunt, had drawn up a set of rules for his estate management, and his entire life and work had to follow an hourly, daily and monthly timetable. Sundays were fixed for receiving petitioners – domestic servants and peasants – for visiting the households of poor peasants, and for giving them assistance with the agreement of the village commune which met every Sunday evening and had to decide how much assistance should be given and to whom. Over a year had passed in such activities and the young man was no longer quite a novice in either the practice or the theoretical knowledge of farm management.

It was a bright June morning when Nekhlyudov, having finished his coffee and read a chapter of *Maison Rustique*, put a notebook and a wad of banknotes in the pocket of his light raincoat, left the large country house with its colonnades and terraces, where he occupied one small room on the ground floor, and went along the unswept, overgrown paths of the old English-style garden, in the direction of the village which stretched out on either side of the main road.

Nekhlyudov was a tall, well-built young man with a mass of thick, curly brown hair, with bright, sparkling black eyes, a fresh complexion and red lips over which the first down of youth was only just beginning to appear. His gait and all his movements revealed strength, energy and the good-natured arrogance of youth. A motley crowd of peasants was coming back from church. Old men, young girls, children, women with their babies, all dressed in their Sunday best, were dispersing to their homes, bowing low to the squire and stepping out of his way.

Nekhlyudov stopped as soon as he reached the street, took the notebook out of his pocket and, on the last page, filled with his childish writing, he read the names of several peasants with comments. "Ivan Churis – asked for props," he read and went up to the gate of the second house on the right.

Churis's abode consisted of a crumbling log shack, rotting at the corners, sloping to one side and so sunk into the ground that a small window with a broken pane and a shutter torn off one of its hinges and one other window, stopped up with tow, were only just visible above the manure heap. A log-built passageway with a dirty threshold and a low door, another small log shack, even lower and more ancient than the passage, a gate and a wattle shed clustered next to the main building. All this had at one time or other been covered by a single uneven roof; now, however, rotting black thatch hung thickly only on the eaves, while laths and rafters were in places clearly visible. In the front of the yard was a well with ramshackle wooden sides, the remains of a post and pulley, and a dirty puddle which had been trampled by cattle and in which ducks were now splashing about. Two ancient willows, split, half-broken and with some straggly, pale-green branches stood beside the well. Under one of these willows – witnesses to the fact that someone at some time in the past had tried to make the place look a little more attractive – sat a fair-haired eight-year-old girl who was making another two-year-old girl crawl around her. A puppy was playing beside them but, on seeing Nekhlyudov, dashed headlong under the gate and barked furiously from there, a frightened, quivering bark.

"Is Ivan at home?" asked Nekhlyudov.

The elder girl seemed to freeze into immobility at this question and opened her eyes wider and wider without replying. The younger one opened her mouth and prepared to cry. A little old woman, in a tattered check skirt, tied low down with an old reddish belt, looked on from behind the door, but also said nothing. Nekhlyudov came up and repeated his question.

"He is, master," uttered the old woman in a quivering voice, bowing low and in a state of frightened agitation.

When Nekhlyudov, after greeting her, went through the passage into the small yard, the old woman rested her chin in her hand, came to the door and slowly shook her head without taking her eyes off the squire.

The yard had a poverty-stricken appearance. Here and there lay old, blackened, uncarted manure. Scattered about on the manure lay a rotting wooden block, a pitchfork and two harrows. A plough and a cart without a wheel and empty, useless beehives, piled on top of each other, were standing and lying in one corner of the sheds surrounding the yard. The roof over the sheds was almost entirely bare of thatch and one side of it had collapsed so that the front beams were no longer resting on the fork-posts but on the manure. Churis, using both the butt and the edge of his axe, was breaking down the wattle fence which had been crushed by the roof. Ivan Churis was a man of about fifty, below average height. The features of his suntanned, oblong-shaped face, framed by a light-brown beard streaked with grey, and thick hair of the same colour, were handsome and expressive. His dark-blue, half-closed eyes shone with intelligence and light-hearted good nature. When he smiled, his small shapely mouth, sharply defined under a scanty fair moustache, expressed a quiet self-confidence and a somewhat mocking indifference to the surrounding world. His rough skin, deep wrinkles, sharply defined veins on his neck, face and hands, unnatural stoop and crooked bandy legs revealed a life spent entirely in heavy work, well beyond his strength. His clothes consisted of white hempen trousers with blue patches on the knees and a dirty shirt of the same material, torn at the back and sleeves, with a tape by way of a belt worn rather low with a small brass key dangling from it.

"Good morning," said the squire as he entered the yard.

Churis looked round and then resumed his work. With one great effort he freed the wattle fence from under the roof, and only then stuck his axe into the wooden block and came out in the middle of the yard, adjusting his belt.

"A happy Sunday to you, your honour," he said, bowing low and then shaking back his hair.

"Thank you, my friend. I just came to have a look at your cottage and the way you live," said Nekhlyudov, shy and friendly as a child, examining the man's clothes. "Let's see what you wanted the props for – the ones you asked for at the general meeting of the commune."

"The props? Well, you know what props are for, your honour, sir. I wanted to prop things up a bit – you can see for yourself. The other day, for example, the corner there collapsed, but thank God the cattle were not in at the time. Everything here is hanging by a thread," said Churis, looking contemptuously at his thatchless, lopsided, crumbling sheds. "The rafters, now, and the gable-ends and the beams – just touch them, and they'll all fall apart; there won't be enough left for a piece of useful timber. And where can a man get wood nowadays? You know yourself."

"Well then, what do you want five props for, if one shed has collapsed and the others soon will? You don't want props, you want new rafters, new beams, new posts, that's what you want," said the squire, obviously showing off his knowledge.

Churis kept silent.

"In other words you need timber, not props. You should have said so."

"Of course I need it, but there's nowhere to get it from. I can't always go to the squire's house asking for it. Odd peasants we would be, the likes of us, if we all got into the habit of going to your house begging for all the stuff we need. But if you will be kind enough," he said, bowing and shuffling from foot to foot, "about those oak tops, I mean, lying about on your threshing floor, not being used for anything... I might change some, cut some up, and fix up something with the old stuff."

"How do you mean, the old stuff? You've just been saying yourself that all you have is old and rotten. There's one corner there, collapsed already; another may do so tomorrow and then another the next day. So if it's to be done at all, it must be done all anew; otherwise it's just wasted labour. Tell me, what do you think: can your place last out this coming winter without collapsing or can't it?"

"Who knows?"

"Yes, but what do you think – will it collapse or not?"

Churis thought for a minute.

"It should all collapse," he said suddenly.

"Well now, there you are! You should have said at the meeting that you need to have all the buildings rebuilt, and not just have a few props. I'd be glad to help you, you know…"

"I am very grateful to you, sir," replied Churis mistrustfully and without looking at the squire. "If you could only let me have about four beams and a few props I could fix things up myself, perhaps, and any bad timber could be used for struts in the cottage."

"But is your cottage in a bad state too?"

"The wife and I are expecting someone to be crushed any time," said Churis with complete indifference. "In fact, the other day a ceiling beam did crush my old woman."

"How do you mean – crushed her?"

"It just did, your honour. Came down with a whoosh across her back, so she lay as good as dead till night-time."

"Well, and has she recovered?"

"She has in a way, but she is always ailing. But then she's been ailing from birth, really."

"Are you ill?" Nekhlyudov asked the woman who was still standing in the doorway and who had immediately started groaning as soon as her husband mentioned her.

"It never leaves me – just here – it never does," she answered, pointing to her dirty, emaciated chest.

"Again!" said the young squire, shrugging his shoulders in annoyance. "Why then if you are ill didn't you go to the hospital? That's what the hospital was opened for. Haven't you been told of it?"

"We have indeed, sir, but there's just no time. It's work for the manor and work at home, and the children and I am all alone. There's no one to help us."

3

NEKHLYUDOV STEPPED INTO THE COTTAGE. The uneven, sooty walls in one corner of the room were hung with all kinds of rags and garments, while, in the opposite corner, they were literally covered with reddish cockroaches gathered round the icons and the bench. In the middle of this black, foul-smelling, fourteen-foot shack, there was a large crack in the ceiling which, in spite of struts in two different places, sagged so that it threatened to collapse at any moment.

"Oh, yes, the cottage is very bad," said the squire, looking closely at Churis, who did not seem eager to start a conversation on this subject.

"It'll crush us and it'll crush the children," began the woman in a tearful voice leaning against the stove under the *polati*.*

"Don't you start, now," said Churis sternly, and his moustache twitched, almost concealing a subtle, scarcely perceptible smile, as he turned to the squire. "I just can't think what to do with it, your honour, with the cottage, I mean. I put in struts and I put in boards, but there's just nothing can be done!"

"How can we spend the winter here? O-o-oh," said the woman.

"Well, of course, if we put up struts and a new beam in the ceiling," her husband interrupted her with a quiet, businesslike expression, "and changed some of the beams, we could perhaps live through the winter somehow. We could get along, only the struts would block up the cottage inside, that's the trouble. But if you so much as touch it, there'll be nothing left of it – not one sound splinter. It only holds together while it stands," he concluded, obviously very pleased that he had grasped that fact.

Nekhlyudov was both annoyed and pained that Churis should have brought himself to such a pass without applying to him sooner, for ever since his arrival he had never once refused to help the peasants and tried only to induce them to come straight to him with their troubles. He even had a feeling of anger against this man, shrugged his shoulders crossly and frowned. But the sight of the destitution surrounding him and, in the midst of that destitution, Churis's calm and self-satisfied appearance, turned his annoyance into a feeling of sadness as well as hopelessness.

"Now Ivan, why didn't you tell me before?" he remarked reproachfully as he sat down on the dirty, crooked bench.

"Haven't had the courage to, your honour," replied Churis with the same scarcely perceptible smile, shuffling from one black, bare foot to the other on the uneven earth floor, but he said it so boldly and calmly that it was hard to believe that he had not the courage to apply to the squire.

"We are only peasants, how would we have the courage?" whimpered the woman.

"Oh, stop it," said Churis, turning to her again.

"You can't live in this cottage; it's just nonsense," said Nekhlyudov after a short silence. "Now, this is what we'll do, old man…"

"Yes sir," replied Churis.

"Have you seen those brick cottages that I had built in the new village, the ones with hollow walls?"

"Of course I have," answered Churis, his smile revealing his teeth, still sound and white. "We even used to wonder a lot at the way they were being built – queer cottages. The kids used to laugh and say they might be storehouses, and the walls would be filled up against the rats. Fine cottages!" he concluded, shaking his head with an expression of scornful perplexity. "Just like prisons."

"Oh, yes, they are excellent cottages, dry and warm, and fires are not such a risk," said the squire, with a frown on his young face, evidently annoyed at the peasant's scorn.

"Can't say any different, your honour – fine cottages, they are."

"Well now, one cottage is quite ready. It is twenty-three feet square, with an entrance room and a storeroom, and is quite ready. I might let you have it at cost price; you'll pay me some day," said the squire with a self-satisfied smile he could not keep back at the thought that he was doing a good deed. "You will pull down your old one," he continued, "and use it to build a barn; the buildings in the yard we'll also move. The water there is excellent; I'll let you have virgin land for your vegetable plots, and all your land, all three fields of it, I'll let you have in one plot close by. You'll be really well off! Well, now, don't you like it?" asked Nekhlyudov, seeing that as soon as he mentioned resettlement, Churis froze into absolute immobility and no longer smiled as he looked down at his feet.

"It's as you please, your honour," he replied without raising his eyes.

The old woman came forwards, as if touched to the quick and was preparing to say something, but her husband forestalled her.

"It's as you please, your honour," he repeated firmly and yet resignedly, looking up at the squire and tossing back his hair, "but it's no life for us in that new village."

"Why?"

"You see, your honour, if you moved us there – we are bad enough here, but we'll never be any good. What good will we be there? And anyway a man couldn't live there, whatever you say."

"But why not?"

"We'll lose the little we have, your honour."

"But why couldn't a man live there?"

"What sort of a life is it out there? You judge for yourself: no one has ever lived there, untested water, no pasture. Our hemp here has been manured ever since anyone can remember, and there? And anyway what is there there? Nothing, the place is bare! No fences, no kilns, no sheds – nothing. We'll lose all we have, your honour, if you drive us out there, lose our all! The place is new, unknown…" he repeated thoughtfully, at the same time resolutely shaking his head.

Nekhlyudov tried to argue that resettlement would, on the contrary, be of great advantage to him, that the fences and sheds would be built, that the water out there was good and so on, but Churis's dull silence embarrassed him, and for some reason he felt that he was not speaking in the way he should. Churis did not argue back, but when the squire stopped, he smiled slightly and remarked that the best thing would be to settle the old house servants and Alyosha the fool in that village, so they could guard the grain.

"Marvellous, that would be," he remarked and gave a short laugh again. "There's no sense in it, your honour."

"What does it matter that the place is uninhabited?" insisted Nekhlyudov patiently. "This, after all, had also been an uninhabited place, but people are living in it now. And it'll be the same there. If you only went and settled there, you'd give a good example… You really should settle there…"

"Come now, your honour, sir, what comparison can there be?" answered Churis with some heat, as if frightened that the squire might make a final decision. "Here we are in the commune; it's a cheerful place, we're used to it; the road's near by, and the pond – the wife can wash the clothes and water the cattle, and all our peasant possessions are here and have always been: the threshing floor, and the vegetable plot for what it's worth, and the willows – those there, that my parents planted. My grandfather and father breathed their last here, and all I want is to live my life out in this place; I ask for nothing else. If you were to repair the cottage, sir, you'd make us very happy, but if not, we'd manage somehow in the old one till our days are over. Let us pray God for you till our dying day," he continued, bowing low, "don't turn us out of our home, sir!"

While Churis was speaking, louder and louder sobs came from under the *polati* where his wife stood, and when the husband said "sir" the wife unexpectedly thrust herself forwards and all in tears went down on her knees in front of the squire.

"Don't ruin us, master!" she wailed. "You are father and mother to us! How could we settle somewhere else? We are old people, and lonely. And have only God to depend on and you…"

Nekhlyudov jumped up from his bench and wanted to raise up the old woman, but she beat her head on the earthen floor in almost voluptuous despair and pushed away the squire's hand.

"What are you doing? Get up, please. If you don't want to go, you needn't. I shan't force you to," he said, waving them away and retreating towards the door.

When Nekhlyudov sat down on the bench again and silence in the cottage was restored, interrupted only by the whimperings of the woman who had once more retired under the *polati* and was wiping her tears with the sleeve of her smock, he understood what the tumble-down little hovel, the broken-down well with the dirty puddle, the rotting sheds and barns and the cracked willows in front of the crooked little window meant to Churis and his wife, and he felt depressed and sad somehow, and ashamed of something.

"Now, Ivan, how is it you didn't tell the commune last Sunday that you needed a cottage? I don't know how to help you now. I told you all at the first meeting that I have settled on the estate and have decided to devote my life to you, that I was ready to deprive myself of everything just to make you contented and happy, and I swear before God that I shall keep my word," said the young landowner, unaware that outpourings of this nature are incapable of earning anyone's trust, least of all that of a Russian who likes deeds, not words, and dislikes the expression of sentiments, however fine.

But the innocent young man was made so happy by the sentiment he was experiencing that he could not help pouring it out.

Churis, with his head to one side, was slowly blinking and was listening to his master with forced attention as we do to a man who must be listened to even though he does say things that are not quite nice and that do not concern us in the slightest.

"But, you know, I can't give everything to everyone who ever asks me for anything. If I never refused anyone who asks me for timber, I'd soon have nothing left myself, and I should not be able to give any to the man who really needs it. That's why I set aside some of the woodland for use as building timber to repair the peasants' buildings, and handed it over completely to the commune. The wood is no longer mine, but yours, it belongs to the peasants and I can no longer dispose of it. The commune can though, and does so as it thinks fit. You come to the meeting tonight; I shall tell the commune about your request, and if it decides to give you a cottage, all well and good, but I have no timber now. From the bottom of my heart I want to help you, but if you don't want to move, it is no longer my business, but the commune's. Do you understand me?"

"We are very grateful to you, sir," replied Churis, looking embarrassed. "If you'll oblige us with a little timber for the buildings here, we'll put things right. How can the commune help? Everyone knows…"

"You come, now."

"Very good. I'll come. Why shouldn't I? Only I shan't ask for anything from the commune."

4

THE YOUNG LANDLORD evidently wanted to put another question to Churis and his wife. He did not stir from the bench and looked in some hesitation now at Churis and now at the empty, cold unheated stove.

"Have you had your dinner?" he asked at last.

A mocking smile became visible under Churis's moustache, as if he found it funny that the squire should ask such a silly question. He made no answer.

"What dinner, master?" said the woman with a deep sigh. "We've had a bit of bread – that's all the dinner we'll get. We had no time to go gathering sorrel today, so I had nothing to make soup from, and what kvass there was I gave to the children."

"It's the hungry fast these days, your honour," Churis broke in, in explanation of the woman's words. "Bread and onions – that's all the food we peasants get. And yet I must consider myself lucky – my grain has lasted until now, thanks to you, sir, but most of our peasants here have no grain even. Onions failed everywhere this year. We sent to get some from Michael the gardener the other day, but he takes half a kopeck a bunch, so there's nowhere the likes of us can buy any. We haven't even been to God's holy church since about Easter, can't even afford to buy a candle for St Michael's icon."

Nekhlyudov had long known, not by hearsay and not because he took on trust what others said, but in actual practice, the extreme poverty in which his peasants lived. But this reality was so incompatible with the whole of his upbringing, his type of mind and way of life that unwittingly he kept forgetting it and every time he was, as now, vividly and tangibly reminded of it, he felt unbearably depressed and sad, as if tormented by the memory of an unexpiated crime he had committed.

"Why are you so poor?" he asked, giving expression to his thought in spite of himself.

"But what else could we be, your honour, sir? You know yourself what our land is like: clay and hummocks, and we must have brought God's wrath on ourselves – there's been no crops coming up since about the cholera year. And again, we have fewer meadows now and less arable. Some have been attached to the manor and added to its fields. I am a lonely old man... There are things I'd like to do, but I don't have the strength. The wife is ailing, and every year, almost, she gives birth to a girl; they must all be fed, you know. Here I am, toiling away, all by myself, and there are seven of us at home. It's a sin, I know, but I often think to myself if only God took some of them soon! It would make life easier for me and it would be better for them, too – better than suffering here..."

"O-oh," sighed the woman loudly as if in confirmation of her husband's words.

"Here's all the help I have," continued Churis, pointing to an unkempt flaxen-haired boy of about seven with a huge belly, who had just opened the door with a slight creak and come shyly into the cottage. He was staring at the squire with surprise from under his eyebrows and was holding on to Churis's shirt with both his little hands.

"This is all my help," continued Churis in ringing tones, stroking the child's fair hair with his rough hand. "Years to wait yet for him! But the work is too much for me now. It's not old age so much, it's my rupture is getting me down. When the weather is bad, I could scream with pain. I should have stopped working on the land long ago – too old for it. Look at Yermilov, Demkin, Zyabrev, all of them younger than me and yet they have stopped working on the land long ago. But I have no one to work for me, that's my trouble. We have to eat, so I struggle along, your honour."

"I should like to help you, I should really. But what can I do?" said the young squire, looking at the peasant with sympathy.

"How can you help, indeed? If a man has some land, of course he must work for the manor – we know that all right. I shall manage somehow till this youngster grows up. There is only one thing I would beg of you – let him off school. Only the other day the county council clerk came and said you wanted him to go to school, your honour. Let him off, your honour; there's no sense in him yet; he's young, got no understanding."

"No, old man," said the squire, "you may say what you like, but your boy has quite enough understanding, it's time he started school. I am only saying it for your own good. Just think – when he grows up and is head of the house and knows how to read and write and reads in church, things will go better in your home, with God's help," said Nekhlyudov, trying to express himself in a way which would make his meaning as clear as possible, but at the same time blushing and stammering for some reason.

"True enough, your honour, you don't wish us harm, but there's no one to stay at home when the wife and I are out in the fields working for the manor. He is only a small boy yet, but helps all the same – drives the cattle in, waters the horses. Anyway, small or not, he is a peasant after all." And Churis took the boy's nose between his thick fingers and made him blow it.

"All the same, you send him along when you are at home and when he has time – do you hear? Without fail."

Churis heaved a deep sigh and answered nothing.

5

"OH YES, and there is another thing I wanted to say to you," said Nekhlyudov. "Why hasn't your manure been carted yet?"

"What manure have I got, your honour, sir? Nothing to cart really. What's my livestock? A mare and a foal – that's all the livestock I have.

The heifer I gave to the inn-keeper last autumn when she was only a calf."

"But why, then, if you have so little livestock, did you sell your heifer as a calf?" asked the squire with surprise.

"But what could I feed her on?"

"Haven't you got enough straw to feed a cow? The others have enough."

"The others have well-manured land, but mine is just clay – can't do anything with it."

"Well then manure it, so it won't be all clay, and the land will yield grain and you'll have enough to feed your livestock on."

"But I have no livestock, so how can I have manure?"

"This is an odd vicious circle," thought Nekhlyudov, but was completely at a loss what to advise.

"And then again, your honour, it's not manure makes grain grow. God does it – just God," continued Churis. "Now last summer, for instance, we got six ricks off that field of mine that had no manure on it, but we only got a fistful off the one that had. It's all God," he added with a sigh. "Besides, our yard does not seem to suit livestock. They all die in it – have been doing so for the past six years. Last summer one heifer died, and I sold another. We had nothing to feed it with. And the year before a fine cow died. There was nothing the matter with her when we brought her in from the pasture. And then she reeled and staggered all of a sudden and there it was – all the steam came out of her. It's all my bad luck."

"Well, old man, to stop you saying you have no livestock because you have no fodder and no fodder because you have no livestock, here's something for you to buy a cow with," said Nekhlyudov, blushing as he took a wad of banknotes out of his breeches pocket and sorted it out. "Buy yourself a cow and may you have luck. And take the fodder from the threshing ground – I'll give orders. Mind you have a cow by next Sunday. I'll look in."

Churis took so long to stretch his hand out for the money while he smiled and shuffled that Nekhlyudov put it at the end of the table and blushed even deeper.

"We are greatly pleased with your kindness," said Churis with his usual, somewhat mocking smile.

The woman, standing under the *polati*, sighed deeply several times and seemed to be saying a prayer.

The young squire felt embarrassed; he got up hurriedly from his bench, went out into the passage and called Churis after him. The sight of the man he had done good to was so pleasant that he did not want to part from him too soon.

"I am glad to be helping you," he said, stopping at the well. "You can be helped because you are never lazy. I know you aren't. If you work I'll help you, and, God willing, you'll get straight."

"That's not the worry, sir – getting straight, I mean; all we can hope for is not becoming beggars," said Churis, his face suddenly assuming a serious, even stern expression as if very displeased that the squire should suppose he could ever get straight. "When my dad was alive my brothers and I lived with him and there was no want. But when he died and we broke up, all went from bad to worse. It's all from being alone."

"Why did you break up then?"

"All because of our wives, your honour. Your grandfather was no longer alive then, or we wouldn't have dared. There was real order then. He looked into everything himself, just like you. We shouldn't have dared to think of breaking up. Your grandfather would never let peasants get into bad ways, but after his death we had Andrei Ilich to manage us. A drunken man he was, God forgive him, and unreliable. We came to consult him once or twice. "The women make life impossible," we said. "Give us permission to live apart." Well, he had us thrashed a few times, but the women had their way in the end all the same, and we went off to live, each on his own with his wife. And you know what it is when a man lives apart from the others. Besides, there was no system in it. Andrei Ilich ruled us as he pleased. "See to it you have all that's needed," but where a man was to get it from, he never asked. Then the poll-tax was raised and we had to pay more dues on our produce, but we had less land and the crops failed. And when it came to reallocating the lands and he took our manured land – the old devil – and added it to the landlord's, he quite did us in. The death of us, he was. Your father, bless him, was a good landlord, but we saw him scarcely ever; he lived in Moscow mostly and of course we had to send produce there rather more often. Sometimes, when the roads disappeared in the spring or autumn and we had no fodder, we were still made to cart the stuff. The master can't do without, of course. We daren't resent that; only there was no system in it. Now that you let every peasant see you, your honour, we have become quite different, and the steward has become a different man. At least we know we have a master now. I can't tell you how grateful the peasants are to you, your honour. While you were a ward we had no real master; everyone was master; the guardian was master and Andrei Ilich was master and his wife was mistress, and the clerk from the police headquarters – he was master too. The peasants suffered much then. Very, very much indeed!"

Again Nekhlyudov felt something resembling shame or remorse. He raised his hat and went on his way.

6

"EPIFAN THE ODD WANTS TO SELL A HORSE," read Nekhlyudov in his notebook and crossed the street to Epifan's cottage. The cottage was carefully thatched with straw from the manor's threshing floor, and built of light-grey aspen wood – also from the manorial forest. It had windows, each with two red painted shutters, and a little porch with a roof over it and banisters made of deal, but of intricate design. The passage and outer portion of the cottage were also in excellent condition, but the general effect of ease and prosperity was somewhat spoilt by a barn with a half-finished wattle fence adjoining the gate and an open shed behind it. Just as Nekhlyudov was approaching the porch from one side, two women carrying a full tub slung on a pole were approaching it from the other. One of them was Epifan's wife, the other his mother. The former was a thickset, red-cheeked woman with an unusually well developed bosom and a broad, fleshy face. She wore a clean smock with embroidered sleeves and collar, an apron, similarly embroidered, a new woollen skirt, shoes, beads, and a smart, square head-dress embroidered with red cotton and spangles.

Her end of the pole did not sway, but rested firmly on her broad, solid shoulder. The slight strain noticeable in her red face, in the curve of her back and in the rhythmic movement of her arms and legs indicated extraordinary health and a man's strength. Epifan's mother, who was carrying the other end of the pole, was, on the contrary, one of those old women who seem to have reached the ultimate limits of old age and decrepitude, while remaining alive. Her bony carcass, dressed in a torn black smock and colourless woollen skirt, was bent so that the

on her back than on her shoulder. Her hands,
ngers holding the pole as if clutching on to it, were
brown colour and looked as if they could no longer
ooping head, with some rags bound round it, bore the
s traces of destitution and extreme old age. From under a
n   rehead, furrowed in all directions by deep wrinkles, two red
eyes,   protected by eyelashes, were staring dully on the ground. One
yellow tooth protruded from underneath a sunken upper lip and, as it
moved perpetually, it sometimes met the pointed chin. The folds on the
lower part of the face and throat looked like bags, swinging with every
movement. She breathed heavily and hoarsely, but her feet, bare and
deformed, kept up a measured, even tread for all that they seemed to
drag painfully along the ground.

7

THE YOUNG WOMAN almost collided with the squire, briskly set
down the tub, bowed shyly, then glanced at him from under her
brow with her sparkling eyes, and tried to conceal a slight smile with
the sleeve of her embroidered smock as she ran up the steps, her shoes
tap-tapping against them.

"You take the yoke back to Aunt Nastasya, Mother," she said,
stopping at the door and addressing herself to the old woman.

The modest young landowner looked attentively, if sternly, at the
pink-faced woman, frowned, and turned to the old one who, having
disengaged the yoke from the tub with her crooked fingers and hoisted
it on her back, was just about, in meek obedience, to go to the cottage
next door.

"Is your son at home?" asked the squire. The old woman, bent double
now with age and the effort of bowing, wanted to say something,
but suddenly put her hand to her mouth and broke into such a fit of
coughing that Nekhlyudov went into the cottage without waiting for
the answer. Epifan, who was sitting on a bench in the best corner,
rushed to the stove immediately he caught sight of the squire, as if
trying to hide from him, hastily shoved some object on the *polati* and,
his mouth and eyes twitching, flattened himself against the wall as if
to make way for the squire.

Epifan was a fellow of about thirty, lean and well built, with brown hair and a young, pointed little beard. He would have been fairly good-looking if it had not been for his shifty, brown little eyes peeping from under frowning eyebrows, and for the absence of two front teeth, immediately obvious because his lips were short and were constantly moving. He was wearing his best shirt with bright red gussets, striped linen trousers and heavy boots with wrinkled tops. Inside, Epifan's cottage was not as constricted and gloomy as Churis's, though it was just as stuffy, smelt of smoke and sheepskin coats, and was littered in the same untidy way with peasant clothes and implements. Two things stood out as somewhat odd: a small dented samovar standing on a shelf, and a black frame with in it the remains of dirty glass and the portrait of some general in a red uniform, hanging next to the icons. Nekhlyudov cast an unfriendly glance on the samovar, on the general's portrait and on the *polati*, where the tip of a brass-mounted pipe was sticking out from under some rags, and turned to the peasant.

"Good morning, Epifan," he said, looking at him straight in the eye.

Epifan bowed and muttered, "How do you do, ye'nour," mouthing the last word with particular tenderness. His eyes ran with lightning rapidity over the squire's whole figure, the cottage, the floor and the ceiling, without resting on anything; then he hastily went to the *polati*, pulled a coat off it and started putting it on.

"What are you dressing for?" said Nekhlyudov, sitting down on the bench and evidently trying to look at Epifan as sternly as possible.

"Oh, come now, ye'nour, it's only right I should, isn't it? We know, I think, how to behave…"

"I've come to ask why you should need to sell a horse, and how many horses you have and which horse you want to sell?" said Nekhlyudov drily, evidently repeating questions he had prepared in advance.

"I am very grateful to ye'nour that you have been good enough to visit a peasant like me," said Epifan, casting rapid glances on the general's portrait, the oven, the squire's boots and all other objects except Nekhlyudov's face. "I always pray God for ye'nour…"

"Why should you be selling a horse?" repeated Nekhlyudov, raising his voice and clearing his throat.

Epifan heaved a sigh, tossed his head (his glance again ran round the cottage) and, noticing a cat which lay quietly purring on the bench, yelled at it: "Out you get, you filthy brute," and hastily turned to the squire. "It's a horse, ye'nour, which is no good... If it were a good beast, ye'nour, I wouldn't be selling it, ye'nour."

"And how many horses have you got, in all?"

"Three horses, ye'nour."

"Any foals?"

"Of course, ye'nour. I have a foal too."

8

"COME AND SHOW ME YOUR HORSES. Are they in the yard?"

"Yes, ye'nour, sir. I did as I was ordered, ye'nour. I couldn't disobey ye'nour, could I now? Yakov Ilich told me yesterday not to let the horses out into the field. "The prince will look at them," he said. So I didn't let them out. I wouldn't dare disobey ye'nour."

While Nekhlyudov was coming out of the door, Epifan snatched the pipe from the *polati* and threw it behind the stove. His lips continued to twitch just as restlessly even when the squire was not looking at him.

A lean little grey mare was rummaging among some rotten straw in a shed. A two-months-old, long-legged foal, of some nondescript colour, with bluish legs and muzzle, never left her sparse, burr-covered tail. In the middle of the yard, with its eyes closed and its head pensively hanging down, stood a pot-bellied bay gelding, a good little peasant horse to all appearances.

"So these are all the horses you have?"

"No ye'nour sir. There's a mare there, too, and a little foal," answered Epifan, pointing to the horses which the squire could not help seeing.

"I can see them. Well, then, which one do you want to sell?"

"This one, sir, ye'nour," he answered, blinking and twitching his lips as he shook the skirt of his coat at the dozing gelding. The gelding opened its eyes and lazily turned its tail to him.

"It doesn't look old and it's a sturdy enough horse," said Nekhlyudov. "Would you catch it for me and show me its teeth? I'll see whether it's old."

"One man can't catch it alone, ye'nour. The animal is not worth a penny, but it's got a temper – in tooth and hoof, ye'nour," replied Epifan with a very cheerful smile, his eyes darting in all directions.

"Oh, nonsense! Catch it, I tell you."

For a long time Epifan smiled and shuffled, and only when Nekhlyudov cried angrily, "Well, what are you waiting for?" did he rush into the shed, bring out a halter and start running after the horse, frightening it and approaching it from behind instead of head-on.

The young squire evidently got tired of looking at this and, besides, he wanted, perhaps, to show his own skill. "Give me the halter," he said.

"Oh come now, ye'nour shouldn't really! Please don't…"

But Nekhlyudov came straight up to the horse's head, and suddenly seizing it by the ears bent it down with such force that the gelding, which proved to be a very quiet peasant horse, staggered and snorted as it tried to break loose. When Nekhlyudov noticed that it was quite unnecessary to apply such efforts and looked up at Epifan who never stopped smiling, the thought – the most humiliating that could be at his age – occurred to him that Epifan was laughing at him and regarded him as a child. He blushed, let go the horse's ears and without using the halter opened its mouth and examined its teeth: the eye teeth were sound and the double teeth full. This meant, as the young landowner had had time to learn, that the horse was young.

Epifan had in the meantime retired to the shed and, seeing that the barrow was not lying in its place, lifted and stood it up against the wattle fence.

"Come here," cried the squire with an expression of childish annoyance on his face and in a voice almost tearful with vexation and anger. "Now, is this horse old?"

"It certainly is, ye'nour – very old. About twenty years old, I should say. Some horses…"

"Shut up! You are a liar and a scoundrel, because an honest peasant wouldn't lie; he'd have no need to," said Nekhlyudov, choking back the angry tears that he felt welling up. He stopped, so as not to disgrace himself by crying in front of a peasant. Epifan, too, kept silent and, looking like a man who is just about to weep, sniffed and jerked his head slightly.

"And what will you plough with, when you sell this horse?" continued Nekhlyudov when he had calmed down sufficiently to speak in a normal voice. "You are specially sent out to work where no horses are needed, so that your horses could recover for the ploughing, and you want to sell the last you have! And even more important, why do you lie?"

As soon as the squire calmed down Epifan did too. He was holding himself straight and let his eyes run from one object to another as his lips continued to twitch.

"We'll drive out to work for ye'nour no worse than the next man."

"But how will you do it?"

"Don't you worry, we'll get ye'nour's work done," he replied, shooing away the gelding. "I wouldn't be selling it, now, would I, if I didn't need the money?"

"And what do you need the money for?"

"We have no bread, ye'nour, and, besides, I must pay back my debts to the other peasants, ye'nour."

"How do you mean – no bread? Why is it that others, with families, still have some, and you, with no family, have none? Where is it got to, then?"

"We've eaten it, ye'nour, and now there's not a crumb left. I shall buy a horse in the autumn, ye'nour."

"Don't you dare so much as think of selling your horse."

"But, ye'nour, how can we live then, if we have no bread and are not allowed to sell anything?" replied Epifan, turning away and twitching his lips. Then suddenly, looking at his master insolently, full in the face: "It means we're to starve to death."

"You be careful, man!" shouted Nekhlyudov, pale with anger and feeling a personal hatred for the peasant. "I shan't keep peasants like you, and you'll bear the consequences."

"As you wish, ye'nour," he replied, closing his eyes with an expression of feigned humility, "if I've failed to please you. But I don't think I can be accused of any vice. Of course, if ye'nour doesn't like me, you can do whatever you wish. Only I don't know what I am to be punished for."

"I'll tell you: because your sheds are unthatched, your manure is not ploughed in, your fences are broken, and you sit at home, smoking your pipe, doing nothing; because you don't give a crust of bread to your own mother who has handed over the whole farm to you, you let your wife beat her and behave in such a way that she came to me to complain."

28

"Oh, no, ye'nour, I don't even know what pipes are like," said Epifan looking embarrassed and hurt, mainly, it seemed, by the accusation of pipe-smoking. "You can always say anything about a man."

"There you are – lying again! I saw myself…"

"I wouldn't dare lie to ye'nour."

Nekhlyudov said nothing, but began pacing up and down the yard biting his lips. Epifan stood rooted to one spot and followed the movement of his master's feet without raising his eyes.

"Look here, Epifan," said Nekhlyudov in a childishly meek voice, stopping in front of the peasant and trying to hide his emotion. "You can't live like this – it'll be the end of you. Just you think: if you want to he a good peasant, give up your bad habits, don't lie, don't get drunk, have respect for your mother. I know all about you, you know. Look after your farm, instead of stealing wood from the state forest and going to the pub. There's nothing good about that, is there? If you need anything, come to me; ask straight out for whatever it is you want and tell me why you want it, and don't lie, but tell the whole truth, and I shall not refuse you anything I can possibly do."

"Oh, really, ye'nour, I can follow ye'nour's meaning well enough, I should say," replied Epifan with a smile, as if he fully understood the point of the squire's joke.

That smile and the reply deprived Nekhlyudov of any hope he had of touching the peasant's heart and setting him on the path of righteousness by expostulating with him. Besides, he felt all the time that it was unseemly for him, the man set in authority, to be expostulating with his peasant, and that all he was saying was not at all what he should have been saying. He bowed his head in sadness and went out into the passage. The old woman was sitting on the threshold and moaning loudly, as a sign of sympathy, it seemed, with the squire's words which she had overheard.

"Here's something to buy yourselves bread with," whispered Nekhlyudov, pressing a banknote into her hand. "Only buy it yourself and don't give the money to Epifan or he'll spend it on drink."

The old woman clutched at the door-post with a bony hand, to help herself up, and was about to thank the squire, but by the time she had got to her feet Nekhlyudov was already at the other end of the street.

9

"WHITE DAVID ASKED FOR GRAIN AND STAKES," was the next entry in Nekhlyudov's notebook after Epifan.

Nekhlyudov passed several cottages and was just turning down a lane when he met his bailiff Yakov Alpatych, who, seeing the squire from afar, took off his oil-skin cap, took out a silk handkerchief and began wiping his fat, red face.

"Put your cap on, Yakov! Put it on, I tell you…"

"Where have you been, your honour?" asked Yakov, shading his face with the cap and not putting it on.

"I've been to see Epifan the Odd. Why has he become like that, tell me?" asked the squire, continuing on his way down the street.

"Like what, your honour?" answered the bailiff, who had put on his cap and was smoothing his moustache as he followed the squire at a respectful distance.

"How do you mean 'like what'? He is a perfect scoundrel, lazy, a thief, a liar, ill-treats his mother, and is obviously such an inveterate scoundrel that he will never get better."

"I don't know, your honour, why he struck you that way."

"And his wife," the squire interrupted him, "seems to be a really horrid woman. The mother is dressed worse than any beggar, has nothing to eat, and she is all dressed up, and so is he. I simply don't know what to do with him."

Yakov became visibly embarrassed when Nekhlyudov spoke about Epifan's wife.

"Well, your honour," he began, "if he has let himself go like that, we must take measures. He is poor, certainly, like all one-man households, but he does keep himself in hand to a certain extent, unlike some others. He is intelligent, can read, too, and is quite an honest man, I think. He's always sent round to collect the poll-tax. He has been village elder, too, for three years while I was steward, and there were no complaints. In his third year your guardian decided to dismiss him, and he worked all right on the estate. Only he's taken to drink a little – that's because he had lived in town at the post station – but we should take measures. In the past, when he used to play up, we'd threaten him with a flogging and he'd come to his senses again; good for him and peace in the family. But as you don't want to use these measures, of course, I don't know what to do with him. He's let himself go badly, that's true enough. As a soldier he's no good either, because he has two teeth missing, as you've noticed. As a matter of fact, he's not the only one, I might tell you, to have lost all sense of discipline…"

"Don't you worry about that, Yakov," replied Nekhlyudov with a slight smile. "I've discussed this with you over and over again. You know what I think about it, and whatever you say to me I shall not change my mind."

"Of course, your honour, you know all about it," said Yakov, shrugging his shoulders and looking at the squire from behind as if what he saw boded nothing good. "And the old woman – there's no need for you to worry about her," he continued. "It's true, of course, that she brought up her children without a father to help her, and raised Epifan and married him off and all that, but then peasants, you know, always have it that way: when a mother or father give the farm to their son, it's the son and his wife that become masters then, and the old woman must earn her bread as best she can. They have, of course, no tender feelings, but that's always the way with peasants. And so, let me tell you, the old woman had no need to bother you. She's an intelligent woman and a good housekeeper, but why worry the squire about everything? All right – she had a tiff with her daughter-in-law, and the daughter-in-law may have given her a push. Women do that among themselves, and they should have made it up rather than worry you. As it is, you take everything too much to heart," said the bailiff, looking with some affection and condescension on the squire, who was striding silently up the street in front of him.

"Going home, sir?" he asked.

"No, to see White David or the Goat… what's his name?"

"Now, there's a lazy blighter for you, let me tell you. The whole of the Goat family is like that. I've tried everything – nothing helps. Yesterday I drove over the peasants' fields, and he hasn't even sown his buckwheat. What is one to do with people like that? The old man could at least have told his son, but he is just as lazy. Whether he works for himself or for the manor, it's always done just any old how. We did all we could, your guardian and me: sent him off to the police station and punished him at home – the way you don't like…"

"Whom? You don't mean the old man?"

"Himself, sir. Your guardian did it many a time, in front of the whole commune, too, and would you believe it, your honour? – no effect at all!

31

He'd just give himself a shake, and off he'd go, and it would all be just the same. And David, you know, behaves well and is no fool, doesn't smoke or drink, I mean," explained Yakov, "but, there you are, he is worse than any drunk. The only thing is if the army takes him, or else deport him, there's nothing else to do. The whole Goat family is like that; Matryushka, too, who lives in a cottage without a chimney, she belongs to their family, and is just as damn lazy. You don't need me, do you, your honour?" added the bailiff, when he noticed that the squire was not listening to him.

"I don't, you may go," replied Nekhlyudov absent-mindedly and went off to see White David.

David's cottage stood, crooked and lonely, at the very edge of the village. It had neither yard, kiln nor barn; only a few filthy cattle-sheds clung to one side of it; on the other side, brushwood and logs for building were lying in a heap. Tall green weeds grew where a yard had once been. There was no one near the cottage except a pig, which lay in the mud by the threshold and squealed.

Nekhlyudov knocked at a broken window, but, as no one answered, he went up to the entrance and shouted: "Hullo there!" But there was no reply to that either. He went past the entrance, glanced into the empty byres and went into the open cottage. An old red cock and two hens, jerking their ruffs and tapping with their claws, strolled about on the floor and the benches. On seeing a man they spread their wings and flew against the walls cackling desperately, while one of them jumped on the stove. The fourteen-foot cottage was entirely taken up by a stove with a broken chimney, a weaving loom, which had not been put away in spite of the summer, and a blackened table with a warped and cracked top.

Although it was dry outside, there was a dirty puddle at the threshold, formed by a leak in the roof and ceiling during previous rain. There was no *polati*. It was difficult to believe that the place was inhabited, so complete was the appearance of neglect and desolation presented by the cottage both outside and in. However, the cottage was inhabited by White David together with the whole of his family. At that very moment, despite the heat of the June day, David was lying fast asleep on top of the stove, curled up in one corner and wrapped up, head and all, in his sheepskin. The frightened hen, which had jumped onto the stove and had not yet calmed down, was strutting up and down David's back without waking him.

Seeing no one in the cottage Nekhlyudov was just about to leave when a long, juicy sigh betrayed the owner's presence.

"Hey, who's there?" cried Nekhlyudov.

There was another long-drawn sigh from the top of the stove.

"Who's there? Come down."

The squire's shout was answered by yet another sigh, a groan and a loud yawn.

"Come on then. What's the matter with you?"

Something stirred slowly on the stove. There appeared the hem of a worn-out sheepskin coat, down came one big foot in a tattered bast shoe, then another, and lastly the whole of White David became visible, sitting on the stove and rubbing his eyes glumly and lazily with his big fist. He slowly bent his head and yawned as he looked down into the cottage. On seeing the squire he quickened his pace somewhat, but was still so slow that Nekhlyudov had time to walk some three times from the puddle to the loom and back while David was climbing down from the stove. White David really was white: his hair, body and face were all exceedingly white. He was tall and very fat, but in the way peasants are fat, that is he did not just have a fat belly, but his whole body was fat. His stoutness, however, was somehow flabby and unhealthy. His rather handsome face, with its quiet, pale-blue eyes and broad, full beard, had a sickly look about it. It did not have a vestige of suntan or colour; the whole of it was of a pale yellowish tint, with a slight purple shadow under the eyes, and seemed bloated or swollen. His hands were podgy and yellowish like those of people suffering from dropsy, and covered with fine white hairs. His sleep had been so deep that now he could not fully open his eyes or stand without staggering and yawning.

"Aren't you ashamed of yourself," began Nekhlyudov, "sleeping in the middle of the day, when you should be building your outhouses, and when you have no grain?..."

As soon as David was able to shake off the last vestiges of sleep and realize that he was standing face to face with the squire, he folded his hands under his belly, hung his head, inclining it a little to one side, and did not stir a limb. He was silent, but the expression on his face and the whole attitude of his body said: "I know, I know; this isn't the first time I hear it. Come on then, beat me; I'll bear it if I must." He seemed to want the squire to stop talking, and hurry up and beat him, even slap his puffy cheeks hard, if only he would leave him in peace as soon as possible. Realizing that David did not understand him, Nekhlyudov tried to rouse the peasant out of his submissively patient silence by asking him various questions.

"Why, then, did you ask me for timber, if you leave it lying about for a whole month, and at the time when you have most leisure, too. Eh?"

David kept a stubborn silence and did not stir.

"Answer, can't you?"

David muttered something and blinked his white eyelashes.

"You must work, you know, my good fellow. How can you get along without work? By now, you see, you have no grain, and why? Because your land was badly ploughed the first time and was not ploughed again, and wasn't sown in time – all from laziness. You ask me for grain; well, of course I'll give you some, because you can't be allowed to starve to death, but you shouldn't behave like this, you know. Whose grain will I give you? Whose, do you think? You answer me: whose grain will I give you?" insisted Nekhlyudov.

"The landlord's," muttered David, looking up shyly and as if asking a question.

"And where does the landlord's grain come from? Just reason it out for yourself: who ploughed the land? and harrowed it? Who sowed and harvested the grain? The peasants – isn't that so? So you see, if the landlord's grain must be given away to the peasants, those who have worked most to grow it must be given most of it. But you've worked less – they complain about you on the estate, too – you've worked less than anyone, and you ask for the landlord's grain more than anyone else. Why should it be given to you and not to the others? After all, if we all lay on our backs like you and did nothing, we should all starve to death. One must work, my good fellow. It's no good otherwise. Do you hear me, David?"

"Yes, sir," he muttered slowly through his teeth.

10

JUST THEN THE HEAD OF A PEASANT WOMAN, carrying linen sheets on a wooden yoke, flashed past the window, and a moment later David's mother, a tall woman of about fifty, very young-looking and lively, came into the cottage. Her pock-marked and wrinkled face was not attractive, but her straight, firm nose, her thin, tight lips and keen grey eyes revealed intelligence and vigour. Her angular shoulders, flat chest, and lean arms and the well-developed muscles of her black, bare legs bore witness to the fact that she had long ceased to be a woman and was only a worker. She came briskly in, closed the door, pulled at her skirt and gave her son an angry look. Nekhlyudov wanted to say something to her, but she turned away from him and started crossing herself in front of a blackened wooden icon just visible behind the loom. Once this was over, she straightened her dirty, chequered head-kerchief, and bowed low to the squire.

"A happy Lord's day, your honour," she said. "God bless you, sir..."

On seeing his mother, David became visibly embarrassed, assumed an almost cringing position and hung his head even lower.

"Thank you, Arina," replied Nekhlyudov. "I have just been speaking to your son about your farm."

Arina, or Arina-Bargee, as the peasants nicknamed her when she was still unmarried, rested her chin on her right fist, supporting her right elbow with the palm of her left hand, and, without waiting for the squire to end, began to speak in such sharp and ringing tones that the whole cottage became filled with the sound of her voice, and from outside it might have seemed that several women's voices were speaking at once.

"What's the use of talking to him, sir? He can't even speak like a human being, you know. There he stands, the lout," she continued, contemptuously nodding her head at David's pathetic and massive figure. "What sort of farm have *I* got your honour, sir? We are paupers; you have no one worse off than us in the whole of the village. We do nothing for ourselves or for the manor – it's a disgrace. And it's all his doing. I bore him and reared him and fed him, could hardly wait for him to grow up. And now I've got him: wolfs his bread down all right, but I get about as much work out of him as out of that rotten log there. All he does is lie on the stove or else stand there and scratch his silly head," she said, imitating him. "If only you could put some fear into him, sir. I beg of you, now: have him punished, for God's sake, or send him off to be a soldier – there's no other way out. I can't cope with him any more, I can't really."

"Well now, David, aren't you ashamed of yourself, driving your mother to this state?" said Nekhlyudov reprovingly, turning to the peasant.

David did not stir.

"Now I could understand it if he was ailing," continued Arina, with the same vivacity and the same gestures, "but just look at him, as large as the mill chimney he is. You'd think there is enough of him to do some work, the bloated oaf. But no – all he does is to idle his time away, lying on the stove. And if ever he takes up anything, I'd sooner not look at it – the time he takes to get up and to move and all..." she said, drawling out her words and awkwardly turning her angular shoulders from side to side. "Now today, for example, my old man went to the forest to get some brushwood and told him to dig holes. But he didn't; didn't even pick up a spade..." She paused a moment. "He's been the death of me, he has, and me all alone in the world!" she suddenly shrieked, waving her arms and going up to her son with threatening gestures. "You bloated, lazy mug, may God forgive me!" (She turned away from him in mingled contempt and despair, spat and once again addressed the squire with the same animation and with tears in her eyes, still waving her arms about.) "I am all by myself, you know, sir. My old man is ailing and old, and isn't much use either, and I am by myself, all by myself. It's enough to crack a stone. I wish I were dead – that'd be the easy way out, the end of it all. He's worn me out, the scoundrel. I am right at the end of my tether, sir. My daughter-in-law worked herself to death, and I'll do the same."

11

"HOW DO YOU MEAN, worked herself to death?" asked Nekhlyudov incredulously.

"Died of overstrain, sir, honest to God she did. We got her from Baburino the year before last," she continued, suddenly changing her expression from one denoting anger to one that was tearful and sad. "She was a young, fresh-looking, quiet girl, sir. In her father's house she had her sisters-in-law to help her and she was well looked after and didn't know want. But when she came to us and discovered what our work was like – work on the manor, work at home and everywhere... There were just the two of us – her and me to do it all. I didn't care, I'm used to it, but she was pregnant, sir, and in pain. But she went on working beyond her strength, and strained herself, of course, the poor darling. In the summer, on St Peter's Day,* to her misfortune, she gave birth to a boy, but we had no bread, and ate what we could, sir, and there was pressing work to be done – and so her milk all dried up. It was her first child, we had no cow, and we are only peasants – how can we feed a child with a feeding bottle? Well you know how it is, women are silly, and her grief grew beyond anything. And when her baby died, she cried and cried and howled in sorrow, but the want and the work got worse and worse. She wore herself out during that summer, the poor darling, so that by Intercession* she was dead. It was he killed her, the beast!" she said, addressing herself again, in desperate fury, to her son. "There was something I wanted to ask you, your honour," she continued after a slight pause, dropping her voice and bowing.

"What is it?" asked Nekhlyudov absent-mindedly, still shaken by her story.

"He is still a young man, you know, and there isn't much work to be expected of me: alive today, dead tomorrow. How can he live without a wife? He'll be a bad worker for you. Think something out for us, sir."

"You mean you want to get him married? Well now, that's a good thing."

"Do us a favour; you are like a father and mother to us."

She made a sign to her son, and they both fell down on their knees in front of the squire.

"What are you grovelling at my feet for?" said Nekhlyudov, feeling vexed and raising her up by the shoulders. "Can't you say it without all this? You know I don't like it. Get your son married, by all means. I'm very glad if you know of a wife for him."

The old woman got up and began wiping her dry eyes with her sleeve. David followed her example and, after rubbing his eyes with a plump fist, continued to stand in the same patiently submissive posture, listening to what Arina was saying.

"There are suitable girls, of course there are! There's Vassily Mikheykin's girl, not a bad girl, but she won't marry him unless it's your will."

"Doesn't she want to?"

"No, sir, she won't marry him if it's by consent."

"What can I do then? I can't force her. Look for someone else, if not here, then in another village; I'll buy her out, only she must marry of her own free will. She can't be married off by force. There's no such law, and besides, it's a great sin."

"Eh, eh, sir, is it likely that anyone would marry him of her own free will, if she saw our life and our poverty? Even a soldier's wife wouldn't want to share such misery. What man would let us have his daughter? No one would, not if he was desperate, even. We are destitute, you know, beggars. 'They've as good as starved one girl to death,' he'd say, 'and they'd do the same with mine.' Who would give his daughter to us?" she added, shaking her head mistrustfully. "You reason it out for yourself, sir."

"What can I do then?"

"Think up something for us, sir," Arina repeated earnestly. "What are we to do?"

"But what can I think up? I can't do anything for you in this case."

"Who will think up something for us, if you won't?" said Arina, with bowed head, spreading out her hands in sad perplexity.

"Well now, the grain you asked for, I shall give orders to let you have some," said the squire, after a short pause in the course of which Arina kept sighing and David echoed her. "But I can't do anything more."

Nekhlyudov went out into the passage. Mother and son followed the squire, bowing to him as they did so.

12

"OH, I'M SO LONELY," said Arina with a deep sigh. She stopped and looked angrily at her son. David immediately turned away, dragged a fat foot in a huge, dirty bast shoe heavily across the threshold and disappeared through the opposite door.

"What am I do with him, sir?" continued Arina, addressing herself to the squire. You see yourself what he is like! He is not a bad man, doesn't drink, is gentle, too, and wouldn't hurt a child – it would be a sin to say any different; there's nothing bad about him. But God alone knows what has happened to him to make him his own worst enemy. He gets no joy out of it. Would you believe it, sir, my heart bleeds when I look at him and see how he suffers. He may not be up to much, but he is the child of my womb after all; I feel such pity for him, oh, the pity I feel... And it isn't as if he did something against me or his father or the authorities. He is a timid man, one might say, like a little child. How can he live a widower? Think up something for us, sir," she repeated, evidently anxious to efface the bad impression her invective might have made on the squire. "I've thought of this and I've thought of that, your honour, sir," she continued in a confidential whisper, "I can't imagine why he is like that. Bad men must have cast a spell over him – there's nothing else it could be." She remained silent for a while. "If the right man could be found, he could be cured."

"What nonsense you talk, Arina, how can a man have a spell cast over him?"

"Oh, my dear sir, they can cast such a spell over a man, he'd cease to be human for the rest of his life. As if there weren't many evil folk in the world. Out of spite, they might take a handful of earth from a man's footprint... or something like that... and make him unhuman for the rest of his life. Couldn't be easier, really. I was thinking: why shouldn't I go to Dunduk, the old man who lives in Vorobyovka: he knows all kinds of charms and herbs, and he takes away spells, and makes water flow from a cross. Perhaps he might help?" the woman was saying. "He would cure him, maybe."

"There's poverty and ignorance for you!" thought the young squire, his head bowed in sadness as he strode down the village. "What shall I do with him? He can't be left in his present situation, either for my sake or his own or because of the example to others," he was saying to himself, counting off these various reasons on his fingers. "I can't leave him in this situation, but how can I get him out of it? He is ruining all my best farming plans. So long as such peasants remain, my dreams will never be realized," he thought, feeling vexation and anger at the peasant for ruining his plans. "Deport him, as Yakov says, if he doesn't himself want to improve his lot, or have him conscripted? Certainly, he argued to himself, "I should be rid of him, at least, and should save a good worker from being conscripted."*

He was thinking of all this with pleasure, but at the same time he was vaguely aware in his own conscience that he was thinking with only one side of his brain and that it wasn't right. He stopped. "Wait a minute, what am I thinking of?" he said to himself. "Oh, yes. Conscript him, deport him. What for? He is a good man, better than many – and, besides, how do I know... Set him free?" he thought, no longer considering the question with one side of his brain, as previously. "This would be unfair, and, moreover, it would be impossible." But suddenly, a thought struck him which pleased him greatly; he smiled, with the air of a man who had solved a difficult problem. "Take him in as a servant," he said to himself, "look after him myself and use kindness, admonition and choice of occupation to accustom him to work and reform him."

13

"THAT'S WHAT I SHALL DO," said Nekhlyudov to himself with cheerful self-satisfaction and, remembering that he still had to visit a rich peasant, Dutlov, went off in the direction of a tall spacious cottage with two chimneys, standing in its own yard in the middle of the village. Just as he reached the cottage next to it, he met a tall, plainly dressed woman of about forty, coming towards him.

"A pleasant Sunday, sir," said the woman without a trace of shyness, stopping beside him and smiling affably as she bowed.

"Good morning, nurse," he replied. "How are you? I'm visiting your neighbour, you know."

"So I see, sir. A very good thing, too. But why don't you come in? My old man would be ever so pleased."

"All right, nurse, I will, and we'll have a chat. Is this your cottage?"

"It is, sir."

And the nurse ran on in front. Nekhlyudov followed her into the front passage and there sat down on a barrel and lit a cigarette.

"It's hot in there; let's sit out here, rather, and have a chat," he said in answer to the nurse's invitation to come into the cottage. She used to be his wet nurse, but was still a fresh-looking, handsome woman. Her features and particularly her large dark eyes bore a great resemblance to the squire's. She folded her hands underneath the apron and, boldly looking at him and constantly wagging her head, began to talk.

"Why do you want to see the Dutlovs, sir?"

"I want him to rent some of my land, about eighty acres, and start his own farm, and also buy a wood together with me. He has some money, you know, so why should it be lying idle? What do you think about that, nurse?"

"Well, why not? The Dutlovs are rich all right; I reckon he is the top man on the estate, sir," replied the nurse, wagging her head. "Last summer he built his cottage and yard buildings with his own timber

– didn't bother you. They must have about eighteen horses, apart from foals and colts. And when their cattle – cows and sheep – are being brought back from the field and the women are out in the streets driving them in, it's quite a sight to see them crowding the gateway. And then they have about two hundred beehives, or more perhaps. A very wealthy man, he is – has money, certainly."

"Do you think he has a lot of money?" asked the squire.

"People say – out of spite, perhaps – that the old man has quite a lot. However, he won't say so and won't tell his sons either, but he must have. Why shouldn't he go in for this wood business? Unless he is afraid of getting a reputation for wealth. About five years ago he went in for meadows in a small way, in shares with Shkalik, the inn-keeper, but Shkalik may have swindled him or something, and the old man lost about three hundred roubles. So he gave it up ever since. How can they help being well off, your honour, sir," continued the nurse. "They have three allotments, they are a large family, all of them workers, and the old man knows how to manage things, there's no denying it. He's had such good fortune in everything, people are amazed even; lucky with his harvests and with his horses and with his cattle and with his bees and with his children. He's married them all off now. He used to find wives for them among our own people, but now he married Ilya off to a free girl – bought her out himself. And she's turned out well, too."

"And are they all friends together?" asked the squire.

"When a house has a real head, there's never any quarrelling. Take the Dutlovs, now. Of course the daughters-in-law all snarl at each other at the oven from time to time – women always do. But while their father is here, the sons don't quarrel."

The nurse was silent for a moment.

"Now, they say, the old man wants to make his eldest son, Karp, head of the household. 'I'm old now,' he says. 'My job should be looking after the bees.' Well, Karp is a good man, a careful man, but all the same, he won't manage things as well as his father did. Hasn't got the brains."

"Well, then, Karp will perhaps want to take on the land and the woods, what do you think?" said the squire, anxious to obtain from the nurse all the information she had about her neighbours.

"I doubt it, sir," continued the nurse. "The old man hasn't told his son how much money he has. So long as he is alive and the money is in his house, the decision will always be his; besides, they go in for carrier work, mostly, with their horses."

"And the old man won't agree?"

"He'll be afraid to."

"But what will he be afraid of?"

"When a peasant is a serf, sir, how can he reveal how much money he has? He might be unlucky and lose all of it! He went into business with the inn-keeper, for example – and that was a big mistake. He couldn't go to law with him, how could he? And so the money was lost. And if it were his landlord, he'd just be ruined outright."

"Oh, that's what it is…" said Nekhlyudov and blushed.

"Goodbye, nurse."

"Goodbye, your honour, sir. Thank you kindly."

14

"HADN'T I BETTER GO HOME?" thought Nekhlyudov as he reached the gates of the Dutlov house, with a vague feeling of sadness and moral weariness.

At that moment the new deal gates opened before him with a creak, and a handsome, pink-cheeked, fair-haired lad of about eighteen, dressed like a stage-coach-driver, appeared in the gateway leading behind him three strong-legged, shaggy horses, still covered in sweat. He shook back his flaxen hair with a brisk movement of the head and bowed to the squire.

"Is your father at home, Ilya?" asked Nekhlyudov.

"He's in the apiary, behind the yard," replied the lad, leading the horses through the half-open gates one by one.

"All right, then, I'll keep to my intention, I'll make this proposal to him, I'll do whatever depends on me," thought Nekhlyudov and, after letting the horses through, he entered Dutlov's spacious yard. The yard had obviously been cleared of manure quite recently; the earth was still dark and damp and, here and there, and especially in the gateway, manure lay about in red, fibrous tufts. The yard and the high sheds were full of carts, ploughs, sledges, blocks of wood, barrels and all sorts of farm implements, all in good shape; pigeons flitted about and cooed in the shade under the broad, strong rafters.

The air smelled of manure and tar. In one corner, Karp and Ignat were fixing a new transom under a large iron-bound three-horse cart. Dutlov's three sons all looked very much alike. The youngest, Ilya, whom Nekhlyudov had met in the gateway, had no beard and was shorter, pinker and more smartly dressed than the two elder brothers. The second, Ignat, was rather taller and darker and had a pointed beard and, though he also wore boots, a coach-driver's shirt and a felt hat, did not have his younger brother's festive, carefree air. The eldest, Karp, was taller still. He wore bast shoes, a grey coat and a gussetless shirt, had a large red beard and looked not only serious but almost gloomy.

"Shall I send for Father, your honour?" he said, coming forwards and giving the squire a slight and awkward bow.

"No, I'll go and see him at the apiary myself and have a look at what he's done there. Also, I must speak to you," said Nekhlyudov, going off to the other side of the yard, so that Ignat should not hear what he was going to say to Karp.

The self-confidence and a certain pride characteristic of the whole manner of these two peasants, as well as what the nurse had told him, so embarrassed the young squire that he found it difficult to pluck up sufficient courage to speak to them about the proposed business. He felt guilty for some reason and it seemed to him easier to speak with one brother so that the other could not hear. Karp looked surprised at the squire taking him aside, but followed him.

"Look here," began Nekhlyudov with some hesitation, "I wanted to ask you, have you got many horses?"

"We could muster about fifteen, and there are foals as well," replied Karp, in his easy, unabashed way, scratching his back.

"Don't your brothers drive the mail coach?"

"We drive mail coaches with three troikas; Ilya has been away driving it. He is only just back."

"And does this pay? How much do you make by it?"

"Pay, your honour? Just about feeds us and the horses – and thank God for that."

"Why don't you go in for something else then? You could buy some woodland or rent land."

"Oh certainly, your honour, we could rent land if there was any handy."

"Now, this is what I want to propose to you – better than carrier work which only just feeds you. Why don't you, rather, rent some of my land, about eighty acres. I'll let you have the whole strip just beyond Sapovo, and you can start farming in a big way."

And Nekhlyudov, carried away by his plan for a peasant farm which he had often considered and rehearsed to himself, no longer hesitated as he explained to the peasant his proposal about the peasant farm.

Karp listened very attentively to the squire's words.

"We are very grateful to your honour," he said when Nekhlyudov stopped and looked at him expecting an answer. "It's not a bad plan, certainly. It's better for a peasant to work on the land than drive about, brandishing a whip, like. Getting about among strangers, seeing all kinds of people, the likes of us get corrupted. The best thing a peasant can do is to work on the land."

"Well, what do you think, then?"

"While Father is alive, what can I possibly think, your honour? It's for him to decide."

"Would you take me to the apiary? I'll talk to him."

"This way, please," said Karp, walking slowly towards the barn at the back. He opened a low gate leading to the apiary, let through the squire, closed it again, came back to Ignat and silently resumed his interrupted work.

15

NEKHLYUDOV HAD TO STOOP as he went through the low gate leading from the shady penthouse to the apiary behind the yard. The small space enclosed by a loosely woven, thatch-topped wattle fence was flooded by the hot, sparkling rays of the June sun. Golden bees were circling noisily round the hives, which were symmetrically disposed and roofed with pieces of board. From the gate, a path trodden out in the grass led to a wooden shrine in the middle of the plot, with a tin icon on it flashing in the sun. Several graceful young limes, their fuzzy crowns swaying above the thatched roofs of the neighbouring cottage and farm buildings, blended the soft rustle of their fresh, dark-green leaves with the hum of the bees. Short, sharp shadows thrown by the roofed fence, by the lime trees and by the board-topped hives fell on the fine, curly grass between the hives. The slight, stooping figure of an old man, hatless, grey-haired and with his bald patch glistening in the sun, could be seen at the door of the freshly thatched log shed. Hearing the creak of the gate, the old man looked round and, wiping the sweat off his suntanned face with the hem of his shirt, smiled a cheerful, gentle smile and came up to meet the squire.

It was so cosy, pleasant, quiet and light in the apiary; the figure of the grey-haired old man with his fine mesh of wrinkles radiating from the corners of his eyes, his bare feet thrust into some sort of wide shoes, waddling out with a smile of good-natured self-satisfaction to greet the squire in his own private domains, looked so artlessly affectionate that Nekhlyudov immediately forgot that morning's painful impressions and his favourite vision appeared to him in all its vividness. He already saw all his peasants just as rich and good-natured as old Dutlov and all of them smiling at him in affection and joy because to him alone they owed their wealth and happiness.

"Would you like a net, your honour? The bees are bad-tempered just now – they sting," said the old man, taking down from the fence a dirty canvas bag, attached to a wooden hoop and smelling of honey, and offering it to the squire. "The bees know me, and don't sting," he added with a gentle smile which practically never left his handsome, suntanned face.

"Well then I don't need it either. Tell me, are they swarming yet?" asked Nekhlyudov, also smiling, without knowing why.

"Hardly swarming, Dmitry Nikolaych, sir," replied the old man, showing some particular affection in thus addressing the squire by his Christian name and patronymic. "They're only just waking up. We've had a cold spring this year, you know."

"I've read in a book," began Nekhlyudov, trying to drive away a bee which had got into his hair and was buzzing right over his ear, "that if the combs are placed straight up, fixed to the laths, the bees swarm earlier. For this they make hives from board... with cross-pieces..."

"Don't wave your arms about, sir, the bees will get crosser," said the old man. "Hadn't you better have the net, perhaps?"

Nekhlyudov was in pain, but a childish vanity made him reluctant to admit it, and he again refused the net and continued to tell the old man about the construction of beehives of which he read in *Maison Rustique* and which, according to him, should lead to bees swarming twice as much, but the bee stung him on the neck, he lost the thread of his argument and stopped in the middle of it.

"True enough, Dmitry Nikolaych, sir," said the old man, looking at the squire with fatherly condescension, "true enough, they do write in books. But perhaps they've written it all wrong, so they could say: 'Let him do it the way we write, that'll give us a laugh.' That happens, too. How can you teach the bee where to build the comb? It goes the way it wants in the hive – sometimes across and sometimes along it. Have a look now," he added, unstopping one of the hives and peering into the aperture where bees were buzzing and crawling about on the crooked combs. "These here are young bees; their mind is on the queen, and they make the comb straight or sideways, whatever is most convenient for them according to the hive," said the old man, evidently carried away by his favourite subject and quite oblivious to the squire's predicament. "Today they're all coming back with their baskets full; it's a warm day today, you can see everything," he added, putting back the stopper and squeezing a crawling bee with a rag, and then brushing several bees off his wrinkled neck with the rough palm of his hand. The bees did not sting him; Nekhlyudov, on the other hand, could by now hardly contain his desire to run out of the apiary; the bees had stung him in three places and were buzzing all round his head and neck.

"Have you got a lot of hives?" he asked, retreating towards the gate.

"Whatever God's given," replied Dutlov with a little laugh. "You mustn't count them, the bees don't like it. Well now, your honour, I wanted to ask you, sir," he continued, pointing to some narrow hives standing at the fence, "about Joseph, the nurse's husband; you might speak to him; it's a bad way to behave towards neighbours in one's own village, it isn't right."

"How – bad?... oh, but they do sting!" replied the squire, with his hand already on the latch of the gate.

"Well, you see, never a year passes without him letting his bees out among my young ones. They ought to be getting better, but the strange bees rob them of their combs and take the honey out," said the old man, not noticing the squire's contortions.

"All right, later, in a moment..." mumbled Nekhlyudov, and, unable to bear the pain any longer, rushed out of the gate, trying to ward off the bees with both his hands.

"You ought to rub it with earth. It'll be all right," said the old man, following the squire out into the yard. The squire rubbed the place where he had been stung, blushed, glanced back at Karp and Ignat who were not looking at him, and frowned crossly.

16

THERE WAS SOMETHING I wanted to ask you about the boys, your honour," said the old man, feigning not to notice or genuinely not noticing the squire's black looks.

"What?"

"Well, you see, we are well off for horses, thank God, and we have a labourer, so we'll be all right for the work on the manor."

"Well, what then?"

"If you could be kind enough to let my boys pay quit-rent,* Ilya and Ignat could go carting with their three troikas all the summer; they might make a bit of money, perhaps."

"Where would they go?"

"It depends," chipped in Ilya, who had tied the horses up in the shed and had just come up to his father. "The Kadminsky fellows went to Romen with eight troikas and earned their keep, they say, and brought home about thirty roubles for each troika, besides. And in Odessa, too, they say, fodder is cheap."

"That's exactly what I wanted to speak to you about," said the squire, turning to the old man and trying to switch the conversation to farming as tactfully as possible. "Tell me please, is it more profitable to do carting than to do farming at home?"

"Much more profitable, your honour," Ilya chipped in again, shaking back his hair briskly. "There's nothing to feed the horses on at home."

"And how much will you earn in a summer?"

"Well now, in the spring, with fodder really expensive, we carted goods to Kiev, and then again in Kursk we loaded up with grain and took it to Moscow, and we earned our keep, and the horses got enough to eat, and we brought fifteen roubles in money back home with us."

"There's no harm in doing an honest job of work whatever it is," said the squire, again turning to the old man, "but I do think they could find another occupation. And besides the work is such that a young lad goes anywhere, sees all kinds of people, can get corrupted," he added, repeating Karp's words.

"What should us peasants work at if not carting?" replied the old man with his gentle smile. "On a good carting job, you'd feed yourself and feed the horses, and as to getting corrupted, it's not the first year, I must say, these lads of mine have been doing carting jobs. I used to go carting myself, and was never treated bad by anyone – only well."

"There's plenty of other work you could do at home – crops, meadows…"

"How could we, your honour?" Ilya broke in with some excitement. "We were born to it, know all the ins and outs of it, it's just the suitable job for us, the best job of all, your honour – going carting."

"Now, your honour, would you do us the favour of visiting our cottage? You have not been in our new place yet," said the old man, bowing low and winking at his son. Ilya raced into the cottage, and was followed by the old man, together with Nekhlyudov.

17

WHEN HE ENTERED THE COTTAGE the old man bowed again, brushed the dust off the bench in the front corner with the hem of his coat and said with a smile: "What may I offer you, your honour?"

The cottage had a chimney* and was spacious and provided with *polati* and bunks. The fresh aspen logs, with the moss between them only just recently withered, had not yet turned dark; the new branches and *polati* had not yet been worn smooth and the earthen floor had not yet been trodden down. A lanky young woman, with a long, dreamy face, Ilya's wife, was sitting on a bunk rocking a cradle with her foot. The cradle hung by a long pole from the ceiling. A small baby, his arms and legs spread out, was dozing in it, his eyes shut, his breathing so soft it was scarcely perceptible. Another woman, Karp's wife, thickset and pink-cheeked, her sleeves rolled up above her elbows, revealing her strong hands and arms suntanned to above the wrists, was shredding onions in a wooden bowl. A pock-marked pregnant woman was standing by the stove, shielding her face with her sleeve. It was hot in the cottage, both from the heat of the sun and the heat of the stove and there was a smell of freshly baked bread. The blond heads of two little boys and a girl, who had climbed on to the *polati* while waiting for dinner, were looking down at the squire with curiosity.

It gave Nekhlyudov great joy to see this prosperity, and yet for some reason he felt embarrassed in front of the women and children, who were all looking at him. He blushed as he sat down on the bench.

"Give me a small piece of hot bread, I like it," he said and blushed even more.

Karp's wife cut off a large piece of bread and served it to the squire on a plate. Nekhlyudov kept silent, not knowing what to say; the women also were silent; the old man was smiling gently.

"Really now, what am I embarrassed about? As if I were guilty of something," thought Nekhlyudov. "Why shouldn't I make this suggestion about the farm? How silly!" However, he still said nothing.

"Well now, Dmitry Nikolaych, sir, what have you decided about the lads?" said the old man.

"I would advise you not to let them go at all, but find work for them here," said Nekhlyudov, suddenly plucking up courage.

"You know what I have thought up for you? Go halves with me in buying a grove in the state forest, and some land too…"

The old man's gentle smile suddenly vanished. "How, your honour? Where will we get the money from to buy it with?" he said, interrupting the squire.

"I mean a small grove, you know, for about two hundred roubles," remarked Nekhlyudov.

The old man gave a short, cross laugh. "Oh certainly, if we had the money, why not buy it?" he said.

"Haven't you really got that money, though?" said the squire reprovingly.

"Oh, your honour, sir," replied the old man with sadness in his voice, looking round at the door, "we're lucky if we can keep the family alive; buying groves is not for us."

"But you have money; why should it just lie idle?" insisted Nekhlyudov.

Tremendous excitement suddenly overcame the old man; his eyes sparkled and his shoulders twitched.

"Evil men may have said this about me, perhaps," he began in a quavering voice. "But honest to God," he said with increasing animation and looking at the icon, "may my eyes pop, may I fall through the ground here and now if I have anything apart from the fifteen roubles Ilya has brought with him, and anyway I have to pay the poll-tax. You know yourself: we've built a cottage…"

"Well, all right, all right," said the squire getting up. "Goodbye, all of you."

18

"MY GOD, MY GOD!" thought Nekhlyudov, striding home along the shady alleys of his neglected garden, absent-mindedly plucking leaves and twigs on the way. "Were my dreams about the aim and duties of my life really nonsense? Why do I feel so depressed and sad, as if I am displeased with myself? And yet I used to imagine that once I had found the right path I should always experience the feeling of moral satisfaction which I had when these thoughts first occurred to me." And in his imagination he went back with extraordinary vividness and clarity to that happy moment a year ago.

He had got up very early one May morning, before anyone else in the house, and, in an agony of a repressed and unexpressed youthful emotion, strolled aimlessly out into the garden, and thence into the wood, and for a long time wandered about by himself surrounded on all sides by the vigour, the sap and the peace of nature, without a single thought, but overflowing with a feeling which he was unable to express. Sometimes, his youthful imagination would paint for him the voluptuous picture of a woman with all the charm of the unknown, and he thought that that was his unexpressed desire. But some other, loftier feeling said to him: "Not that," and impelled him to look for something else. Then his inexperienced, ardent mind, rising higher and higher into the sphere of abstract speculation, would, so it seemed to him, discover the laws of existence, and he would dwell on these thoughts with proud delight. But once again a loftier feeling would say: "Not that," and would impel him once again to resume his anguished search. Devoid of thoughts and desires, as always happens after a strenuous activity, he lay on his back under a tree, and gazed at the transparent morning clouds floating above him across the deep, infinite sky. Suddenly, for no reason, his eyes were filled with tears, and the obvious thought, which immediately occupied the whole of his mind and to which he clung with delight, occurred to him God alone knows how – the thought that love and goodness are truth and happiness, the only truth and the only possible happiness in the world. No loftier feeling said: "Not that." He half-rose and started to check the truth of this thought. "It is, it is so!" he said to himself with delight, measuring all his former convictions, all the phenomena of life up against the newly discovered and, as it seemed to him, entirely novel truth. "What nonsense it is, all that I knew, that I believed and that I loved," he said to himself. "Love, self-denial – that is the only true happiness, which is independent of chance," he repeated, smiling and waving his arms. Applying this thought to all sides of life, and finding confirmation for it both in life and in that inner voice which told him that this was *it*, he experienced a feeling of joyous emotion and ecstasy which was new to him. "And so, I must do good in order to be happy," he reflected, and the whole of his future rose up clearly in front of him, no longer in the abstract, but as a series of images representing a landowner's life.

He saw before him a vast field of action for a whole life which he would devote to doing good and in which he would, therefore, be happy. He had no need to look for a sphere of activity; it was there, ready for him. He had a direct duty: he had peasants... And what a pleasant and grateful task lay before him: "to influence this simple, receptive, unspoilt class of people, deliver them from poverty, give them prosperity, transmit to them the education which it is my good fortune to enjoy, reform their vices engendered by ignorance and superstition, develop their moral sense, force them to love good... What a brilliant, happy future! And in return for all this, I, who will be doing it for the sake of my own happiness, I shall enjoy their gratitude and shall see myself daily advancing towards my appointed goal. A wonderful future! How could I have failed to see it before?"

"And besides," he thought at the same time, "who prevents me from being happy myself in the love of a woman, in the happiness of family life?" And his youthful imagination painted an even more enchanting future. "I and my wife, whom I love as no one has ever loved anyone in this world, we both always live in the country, amid this peaceful, romantic nature, with our children, and our old aunt; we have our mutual love and our love for the children, and we both know that our purpose is to do good. We help each other to advance towards this goal.

I issue general instructions, give general and just assistance, set up farms, savings banks, workshops, and she, with her pretty little head, wearing a simple white dress which she lifts over her dainty little foot, walks through the mud to the peasant school, to the infirmary, to an unfortunate peasant who, in all fairness, does not deserve assistance, and everywhere she brings comfort and help... Children, old men, women adore her and regard her as some sort of angel, as Providence. Then she returns and tries to conceal from me that she has been to the unfortunate peasant and given him money, but I know it all and take her in my arms and tenderly kiss her charming eyes, her shyly blushing cheeks and her smiling rosy lips."

19

"WHERE ARE THESE DREAMS?" thought the young man now, as he was approaching his house after his visits. "For over a year now I have been seeking happiness along this track, and what have I found? True enough, I sometimes feel I can be satisfied with myself, but it is a dry, rational kind of satisfaction. Besides, it's not true; I am simply dissatisfied with myself. I am dissatisfied because I do not find happiness here, and long for, passionately long for, happiness. I have experienced no joy, and have by now cut myself off from everything that gives it. Why? What for? Who is the better for it? My aunt was right when she wrote that it was easier to find happiness than to give it to others. Have my peasants become richer? Have they become better educated or have they developed morally? Not in the least. They are no better off and I feel daily more and more depressed. If I could discern success in my undertaking, if I could discern gratitude... but no, I see a wrong kind of routine, vice, suspicion, helplessness. I am wasting the best years of my life in vain," he thought, and for some reason he remembered that his neighbours, so he had heard his nurse say, called him half-baked; that he had no money left in the estate-office; that his new threshing machine, invented by himself, had merely whistled to the general amusement of the peasants, without being able to thresh anything when it was started for the first time at the threshing floor in front of a large audience; that any day now he had to expect the arrival of county court officials to distrain his estate because he had become absorbed in various new undertakings and had failed to meet the payments on the mortgage. And suddenly, quite as vividly as earlier, he had visions of himself walking through the wood, dreaming of a landowner's life, so now he saw in his mind's eye his small student's room in Moscow where he had sat up late at night by the light of a candle, with his adored sixteen-year-old friend and fellow student. For about five hours on end they had read and tried to learn some boring notes on civil law and, having finished them, had sent for supper, split a bottle of champagne and discoursed upon the future in store for them. How entirely different the future had appeared to the young student. Then the future was full of joys, varied activity, brilliance and success, and was leading them both without any doubt to what they then thought was the greatest blessing in the world – fame.

"He is already on the way, well on the way along this road," thought Nekhlyudov about his friend. "And I…"

But by then he had reached the porch of his house, where about ten peasants and domestics stood waiting for the squire with various requests, and he had to turn from dreams to reality.

There was a tattered and dishevelled woman covered in blood, weeping as she complained that her father-in-law had allegedly wanted to kill her; there were two brothers who for the past ten years had been quarrelling over the division of their farm, and who were looking at each other with desperate hatred; there was, too, an unshaven, grey-haired domestic serf, with hands trembling from drunkenness, whom his son, the gardener, had brought to the squire with a complaint about his disreputable conduct; there was a peasant who had turned his wife out of the house because she had not worked the entire spring; and there, too, was his wife, a sick woman who sobbed and said nothing as she sat on the grass by the porch and showed her inflamed and swollen leg, roughly bandaged with some dirty rags…

Nekhlyudov listened to all the requests and complaints and, having given advice to some, settled the disputes of others and made promises to yet others, went to his room with a mixed feeling of weariness, shame, helplessness and remorse.

20

IN THE SMALL ROOM OCCUPIED BY NEKHLYUDOV stood an old brass-studded leather sofa, several armchairs of a similar design, an old-fashioned card table, inlaid, carved and mounted in copper, which stood open and had papers lying on it, and an open, old-fashioned, yellow-coloured English piano with worn, warped and narrow keys. Between the windows hung a large mirror in an old carved gilt frame. On the floor beside the table lay piles of paper, books and bills. Taken as a whole the room lacked character and had an untidy appearance, and this living untidiness formed a sharp contrast to the stiff, aristocratically old-fashioned arrangements of the other rooms in the big house. On entering the room Nekhlyudov threw his hat angrily on the table and sat down on the chair standing in front of the piano. He sat with his legs crossed and his head sunk in thought.

"Will you be having lunch, your honour?" said a tall, thin, wrinkled old woman in a mob-cap, a large shawl and a cotton dress.

Nekhlyudov glanced at her, but did not break his silence for a short while, as if trying to collect his thoughts.

"No, nanny, I don't want any," he said and relapsed into thought.

His nurse shook her head at him crossly and sighed. "Come now, Dmitry Nikolaych, what are you moping for? There are worse troubles than that; it'll pass, honestly it will."

"But I'm not moping. Where did you get that idea from, darling?" replied Nekhlyudov, trying to smile.

"You can't help moping, do you think I can't see?" said the nurse with some heat. "All by yourself, day in, day out. And you take everything to heart so, and see to everything yourself. And now you've almost stopped eating. Is it sensible? You might at least visit the town or the neighbours. As it is, who's ever seen anything like it? You are too young yet to grieve so much about everything. Excuse me, now, I'll sit down," continued the nurse, taking a chair near the door. "You've allowed people to lose all fear of you. Is that the way for masters to behave? There's nothing good about it. You're only ruining yourself, and spoiling the people. That's what our people are like; they have no understanding for this sort of behaviour, they haven't, really. You might at least go and see your aunt; it was true what she wrote…" said the nurse, trying to appeal to his conscience. Nekhlyudov felt sadder and sadder. His right elbow was resting on his knee and with that hand he touched, in somewhat desultory fashion, the keys of the piano. He produced some kind of chord, then another and another... Nekhlyudov drew up his chair, took the other hand out of his pocket and began to play. The chords he struck were sometimes unprepared, not quite correct even, often so commonplace as to be banal and revealed in him no musical talent whatsoever, but the occupation gave him a vague and melancholy pleasure. At every change of harmony he waited with bated breath to see what would come out of it and, whenever anything did come out, his imagination hazily supplied what was lacking. It seemed to him that he heard hundreds of melodies: a choir and an orchestra, consistent with his harmony. But his greatest pleasure he obtained from the increased play of his imagination which, patchily and in snatches but with an extraordinary vividness, showed him the most varied, mixed and absurd images and pictures stretching out of the past and into the future. Sometimes he saw the plump figure of White David, blinking in fright, with his white eyelashes, at the sight of his mother's black, sinewy fist, his round back and huge hands covered with white hairs, responding to torments and privations with nothing but patience and submission to fate. Then he saw his pert wet nurse, grown bold through life at the big house, and would for some reason imagine her going round the villages preaching to the peasants that they must hide their money from the landowners, and he unconsciously repeated to himself, "Oh yes, you must hide your money from the landowners." Then suddenly he saw the little blonde head of his future wife – who for some reason was in tears and overwhelmed by grief – resting on his shoulder. Then he saw Churis's kind blue eyes gazing tenderly at his only son, a little, pot-bellied child; he saw in him not just a son, but a helper and a saviour. "This is real love," whispered Nekhlyudov. Then he remembered Epifan's mother, remembered the patient and all-forgiving expression which, in spite of her protruding tooth and her ugly features, he noticed on her aged face. "Probably in the seventy years of her life I have been the first to notice this," he thought, and whispered "Strange!" while continuing unconsciously to finger the keys and listen to their sounds. Then he vividly recalled his flight from the apiary and the expression on the faces of Ignat and Karp, who evidently wanted to laugh, but pretended not to look at him. He blushed and involuntarily looked round at the nurse, who was still sitting by the door, looking at him with silent intensity and occasionally shaking her grey head. Now he suddenly saw a troika of sweating horses and the handsome, powerful figure of Ilya with his fair locks, his narrow blue eyes gaily sparkling, fresh colour in his cheeks and light down beginning to cover his lip and chin. He remembered how afraid Ilya had been of not being allowed to take up carting and how vigorously he had pleaded for the job so dear to his heart. And in his mind's eye he saw an early grey, foggy morning, a slippery highway and a long row of three-horsed carts, loaded high and covered by bast mats, with large black letters on them; thick-legged, well-fed horses, pulling uphill in a well-concerted effort, jingling their bells, bending their backs and pulling on the traces, trying to take a grip on the slippery surface of the road with the calkins* of their shoes. Towards them, coming swiftly down the hill, galloping mail coaches, their bells jingling and echoing far into the dense forest on either side of the road. "Oh-ho-ho!" cries the driver of the first coach in a childish voice, raising his whip above his head. He is wearing a felt hat with a brass number-plate on it.

Karp with his red beard and sullen expression strides heavily in his enormous boots by the front wheel of the first cart. On the second cart Ilya's handsome head peeps out from under the bast mat on the front seat where he has been pleasantly warming himself in the early-morning sun. Loaded with boxes, the three troikas rush past, wheels rumbling, bells jingling, men shouting; Ilya hides his handsome head under the mat again and falls asleep. And now evening comes, clear and warm. Timber gates creak open for the tired troikas crowding in front of the inn, and the high mat-covered carts bounce over the board laid in the gateway and disappear one after another into the spacious sheds. Ilya cheerfully greets the fair-faced, full-bosomed hostess, who asks: "Have you come from afar? And will there be many for supper?" and her eyes sparkle as she casts sugary glances on the handsome lad. And now, having seen to his horses, he goes into the hot, crowded house, crosses himself, sits down to a full wooden bowl and chats gaily with the hostess and the other men. And here, on the fragrant hay in the shed from which the open starry sky is just visible, is his place for the night – next to the horses, shuffling their feet and snorting as they shift the fodder in the wooden mangers. He comes up to the hay, turns towards the east, makes the sign of the cross over his broad, powerful chest, shakes his fair locks, says the Lord's Prayer, repeats 'Lord have mercy upon us' and falls asleep – the healthy, carefree sleep of a man who is strong and young. And now he dreams of cities: of Kiev with its saints and crowds of pilgrims, of Rome with its merchants and its goods, of Odessa and the blue sea far away with white sails upon it, and of Constantinople with its golden houses and Turkish maidens fair-bosomed and dark-browed. And thither he flies on invisible wings, flies freely and easily, further and further, and sees below him golden cities, bathed in dazzling radiance, and the blue sky with its many stars and the blue sea with its white sails, and he feels gay and glad to be flying further and further away…

"Glorious!" whispered Nekhlyudov to himself, and thought: "Why am I not Ilya?"

Notes

p. 14, *Polati*: A raised platform stretching from the stove to the opposite wall and used for sleeping on.

p. 36, *St Peter's Day*: 29th June.

p. 37, *Intercession*: Feast of the Intercession of the Virgin, 1st October.

p. 39, *worker... conscripted*: Under the law of the time the landowner had the right to select men from among his serfs for military service. This gave him the chance of retaining the best labour and getting rid of the worst.

p. 47, *quit-rent*: See page 3.

p. 48, *chimney*: The poorer cottages had a hole in the ceiling instead of a chimney.

p. 56, *calkins*: A calkin is a metal spike sometimes fitted on horse shoes to help the horse get a grip on slippery surfaces – analogous to a crampon for a mountaineer.

The Devil

Translated by April FitzLyon

Preface

TOLSTOY WROTE *THE DEVIL* in less than a fortnight, in November, 1889. It belongs, therefore, to the same period as *The Kreutzer Sonata*, *Resurrection* and *Father Sergius*. It was in these four novels that Tolstoy expressed his ideas about physical love and the social and moral evils for which he considered it to be responsible – a question which interested him deeply at that time. Although all four novels have this central theme in common, the treatment of the theme varies very considerably in each of them. In *The Kreutzer Sonata*, *Resurrection* and *Father Sergius*, solutions to the problem are offered – sometimes highly controversial solutions, as in *The Kreutzer Sonata* – but in *The Devil* Tolstoy does no more than state the problem, which he does with great force, probably owing to the semi-autobiographical nature of the book.

The existence of *The Devil* was a closely guarded secret because Tolstoy felt that the subject of the novel might offend his wife, and the manuscript was kept in St Petersburg in the house of a friend. In 1898, when Tolstoy was sending various miscellaneous manuscripts to his publisher in order to raise funds for the Dukhobors, he contemplated including *The Devil* with the other works he had chosen for publication. He read the manuscript through, but decided not to publish it. It was probably in 1909 that Tolstoy wrote the alternative version of the ending of the novel. In the spring of that year Countess Tolstoy found the manuscript, which had not previously attracted her attention because it had been transcribed by Tolstoy's disciples, Chertkov and I.I. Gorbunov-Posadov; however, seeing various corrections in the manuscript which Tolstoy had made in his own handwriting, she read it, and at once realized that it had been written by her husband. There was a scene of jealousy and tears on both sides, after which, he notes in his diary, they "both felt better". *The Devil* was finally published in 1911, after Tolstoy's death.

The Devil is not a *roman à clef* in the true sense, but many of the incidents and some of the characters in it are taken from life. In his diary Tolstoy at first referred to the book as *The Friedrichs Story*.

N.N. Friedrichs (or Fredericks) was a magistrate in Tula in the 1870s. He lived for some time with a peasant woman named Stepanida Munitzina, whose husband was a coachman in Tula. This liaison was of long standing and apparently based on mutual love, but in spite of it Friedrichs subsequently married a young girl of his own class with whom he was not in love. Three months after his marriage he shot and killed his mistress while she was working in a threshing barn. The motive for his crime was, it seems, his wife's jealousy. On medical evidence Friedrichs was acquitted, but his character changed fundamentally as a result of the murder, and he became deeply religious. In December, 1874, he was run over and killed by a train – whether his death was accidental or intentional was never established.[1]

Apart from using Friedrichs' story as a framework for his novel, Tolstoy also borrowed a number of details from it – the peasant woman's name, for instance, the manner and place of her death, and so on. But, as Tolstoy himself admitted, the novel contains much autobiographical material, and he really did no more than use Friedrichs' story as a peg on which to hang his own experiences.

Shortly before his death Tolstoy told his biographer, Biryukov:

In my youth I led a very bad life, and two incidents that occurred then particularly tormented me, and still torment me to this day. I am telling you this as my biographer, and I ask you to include it in my biography. These two incidents were: a liaison with a peasant woman from our village before my marriage – there is an allusion to this in my story *The Devil*. The second incident was the crime I committed against Gasha, a maidservant living in my aunt's house. She was a virgin, I seduced her, they turned her out, and she went to the bad.

---

1. For this information about Friedrichs I am indebted to N.K. Goudzi, who, so far as I am aware, was the first to publish it in 1936 in Moscow. His source of information was a letter from Friedrichs' sister. It had previously been believed that Tolstoy had invented the name of Friedrichs merely in order to conceal the autobiographical character of the story, and this was the view held in 1933 when *The Devil* was published in the Jubilee edition of Tolstoy's works.

The second incident that Tolstoy referred to was, of course, the origin of Nekhlyudov's seduction of Katyusha in *Resurrection*. The peasant woman with whom Tolstoy lived before his marriage was Axinya Bazykina. His relations with her made a great impression on him, and he remembered her all his life – he mentioned her in his diary when he was over eighty. His liaison with her continued for four years, and there are frequent references to her in his diary from 1858 when he first met her to 1868 – years after their liaison had been brought to an end by his marriage. For example, on 10th–13th May 1858, Tolstoy wrote: "A wonderful Whit Sunday. Caught a glimpse of Axinya. Very pretty. Waited in vain all these days. Today in the big old wood… Red suntan, eyes… I'm in love as never before in my life. Have no other thoughts. Am tormented. All my strength tomorrow." Periods of indifference, when he noted "Nothing but disgust" with Axinya, were followed by interludes of violent passion and perhaps genuine love, which made him confess to "the feeling no longer of a stag, but of husband to wife". This must have made a lasting impression on him, for some thirty years later he endowed Yevgeny in *The Devil* with precisely the same sentiments. Some fifty years later, only a year before his death, Tolstoy noted in his diary: "Looked at bare legs, and remembered Axinya, that she is still alive and, they say, Yermil is my son, and I don't ask her forgiveness, have not repented, don't do penance every hour, and presume to censure others!"

Unlike Liza, her counterpart in *The Devil*, Countess Tolstoy knew about her husband's liaison with Axinya – Tolstoy had given his wife his diaries to read before their marriage. There are several references to Axinya in Countess Tolstoy's diaries, and she was extremely jealous of her – in *The Devil* Tolstoy makes a reference to Liza's jealousy, but it does not play any part in the novel, and indeed, apart from jealousy, Liza and Countess Tolstoy appear to have nothing in common. Some months after her marriage Countess Tolstoy saw Axinya washing floors at Yasnaya Polyana together with another peasant woman – probably the origin of the spring cleaning episode in the novel – and noted in her diary pangs of ungovernable jealousy leading to a probably less than objective description of her husband's former mistress as "just a peasant woman, fat and white". In 1909, writing of *Who are the Murderers?* which she was then reading in manuscript, Countess Tolstoy wrote:

…it could be interesting. But the same old reproach – descriptions of peasant life. His relish at a woman's *full* bosom and a girl's sunburnt legs, all that once so strongly tempted him; the same Axinya, with shining eyes re-emerging almost unconsciously now, at the age of eighty, from the depths of his memory and the feelings of former years. Axinya was a peasant woman at Yasnaya Polyana, Lev Nikolayevich's last mistress before his marriage, and she is still living in the village. Somehow all this painfully came back to me.

Tolstoy's liaison with Axinya was not the only incident in his life which he incorporated in *The Devil*. In 1880, after his "conversion", when Tolstoy was sixty-four years old and already a world figure, he felt a strong physical attraction for a woman called Domna, the servants' cook at Yasnaya Polyana. Tolstoy described this in a letter to Chertkov, dated 24th July 1884:

I will tell you something which happened to me, and which I have not so far told to anyone else. I succumbed to sensual temptation. I suffered terribly, struggled against it, and felt helpless. And I felt that I would succumb at the first opportunity. Finally I committed the most abominable action; I arranged a meeting with her, and went to it. That day I was to give a lesson to my second son. I walked past his window into the garden, and suddenly he called to me and reminded me that we were to have a lesson that day – something he never did usually. I came to my senses and did not keep my appointment. It is obvious that God saved me. And He really did save me. But after that, did the temptation leave me? No, it still remained. And I again felt that I would be sure to fall. Then I confessed to a tutor who was living with us and told him not to leave me for a certain time, and to help me. He was a good man. He understood me, and followed me about as if I were a child. Later I also took steps to have this woman sent away, and I saved myself from sin – not from mental sin, but only from carnal sin – and I know that this was right.

The tutor referred to by Tolstoy – V.I. Alexeyev – has left his version of the story which adds nothing to it apart from a few picturesque details. Thus, after describing how Tolstoy asked him not to leave him for a time, Alexeyev continues:

We went out, and then he told me how almost every day, during his walks, he used to meet Domna, the servants' cook, how he began by silently following her for a few days, and this gave him pleasure... Then, as he followed her, he took to whistling to her; then he began to accompany her and talk to her, and finally he even made a date with her.

Alexeyev has left this portrait of Domna: "She was a young woman, employed as the servants' cook. I believe her husband was in the army. She was about twenty-two or twenty-three years old; I wouldn't call her pretty, but she had a strawberries-and-cream complexion, and was a tall, buxom, healthy and attractive young woman."

It will be seen from the foregoing remarks that *The Devil* is based on three separate sources, which Tolstoy blended to form an artistic whole. Friedrichs' story provided the framework for the plot and, notably, the ending of the novel. It is interesting that the second version of the ending (Stepanida's murder) which seems the less probable of the two, was actually based on fact. That Tolstoy drew a spiritual self-portrait when he described Irtenyev seems clear – physically, however, Irtenyev appears to be rather a portrait of Friedrichs, who was very short-sighted – a defect of Irtenyev's which is stressed in the novel. Tolstoy's liaison with Axinya before his marriage provided material for the description of Irtenyev's relations with Stepanida before *his* marriage – Tolstoy seems to have had a child by Axinya, for example. It is probable, too, that Stepanida was a portrait of Axinya rather than of Domna, with whom he never actually lived and who therefore could not have had the same physical hold over him that Axinya had, but there is no clear evidence on this point. The physical desire which Tolstoy, as a married man, felt for Domna and his spiritual struggles at that time clearly helped him to describe Irtenyev's similar spiritual conflict after his marriage. The part played by Alexeyev, the tutor, in Tolstoy's own life is transferred to Yevgeny's uncle in the novel. Many other lesser details in the novel are, of course, taken from all three sources.

April FitzLyon

"But I say unto you, that whosoever looketh on a woman to lust after her hath committed adultery with her already in his heart.

"And if thy right eye offend thee, pluck it out, and cast it from thee: for it is profitable for thee that one of thy members should perish, and not that thy whole body should be cast into hell.

"And if thy right hand offend thee, cut it off, and cast it from thee: for it is profitable for thee that one of thy members should perish, and not that thy whole body should be cast into hell."

Matthew 5:28–30

1

A BRILLIANT CAREER lay in store for Yevgeny Irtenyev. Everything about him indicated that he would have one. He had had an excellent home upbringing and he had brilliantly concluded his studies at the Law Faculty of St Petersburg University; his father, who had died not long before, had had the best possible social connections and Yevgeny had even started his work at the Ministry under the patronage of the minister himself. He had means, too; quite considerable means, even if uncertain. His father had lived both abroad and in St Petersburg and had given Yevgeny and his elder son, Andrei, who was in the Cavalier Guards, six thousand roubles a year each, and had himself squandered large sums together with their mother. He used to visit his estate in the summer only, when he would spend two months there, but he had taken no interest in its affairs and had left everything to his bailiff, in whom he had complete confidence, but who had not taken any interest in the estate either.

When the brothers began dividing up the property after their father's death, they found the debts to be so considerable that their lawyer advised them to keep only their grandmother's estate, valued at a hundred thousand roubles, and to renounce the rest of the inheritance. However, a neighbouring landowner who had had dealings with old Irtenyev – that is, had been his creditor, and had come to St Petersburg in connection with this – said that, in spite of debts, it would be possible to improve the business and still keep a considerable fortune. All they had to do was to sell the timber and some wasteland, devote themselves to the business, settle down in the country, and run the estate intelligently and economically. They could then keep Semyonovskoe, a veritable gold mine with its ten thousand acres of arable land, a sugar refinery, and five hundred acres of meadowland.

And so Yevgeny, who had visited the estate in the spring (his father had died in Lent), and had inspected it all, decided to retire, settle down in the country with his mother, and manage the business in order to try to keep the main estate. He made the following arrangement with his brother, with whom he was not on particularly good terms: he promised to pay him four thousand roubles, in exchange for which his brother renounced his share of the inheritance.

So Yevgeny did all this and, when he had settled down in the large house with his mother, he began to run the estate enthusiastically but carefully.

It is commonly thought that conservative-minded people are as a rule old, whereas innovators are young. This is not quite true. Conservative-minded people are most commonly young men – young men who want to live, but who neither think nor have time to think how to live and who therefore choose the old way of life as a model.

And thus it happened to Yevgeny. Having settled in the country, his dream and his ideal was to resurrect the way of life which had existed – not in his father's time, for his father had been a bad landlord, but in his grandfather's time. And he tried now, though of course with changes in tune with the times, to resurrect the general spirit of his grandfather's lifetime in the house as well as in the garden and on the estate – everything on a grand scale, prosperity for everyone around, order and contentment. A great deal of work was necessary in order to achieve this: he had to satisfy both the demands of his creditors and of the banks, and therefore to sell land and defer payments; he also had to obtain money with which to run the huge estate at Semyonovskoe with its ten thousand acres of arable land and the sugar refinery, either by employing outside workers or with his own men, and he had to make both the house and the garden look as if they were not neglected and decayed.

There was a great deal of work. But Yevgeny had a great deal of strength, both physical and spiritual. He was twenty-six years old, of medium height and strongly built, with his muscles developed by gymnastics; he was a full-blooded type with a high colour, glistening teeth and lips, and fine, soft, wavy hair. His only physical defect was his short sight, which he had himself made worse by wearing glasses, and he could now no longer dispense with pince-nez, which had already made little furrows above the bridge of his nose. Such was his physical aspect, while his spiritual side was of a kind that made people like him more the more they knew him. His mother, who had always loved him more than anyone else, made him, now that her husband had died, the centre of her whole life, let alone all her affections. But his mother was not the only one to love him in this way. His school and university friends had a special affection for him, but one mingled with respect. He affected strangers, too, in the same way. It was impossible not to believe him; it was impossible to conceive of deceit or untruth in connection with a face and, above all, eyes which were so open and honest.

In fact, his whole personality was of considerable assistance to him in business. A creditor who would have refused another, trusted him. A bailiff, an overseer or a peasant who would have deceived or played a dirty trick on anyone else, forgot to be deceitful under the pleasant impression made by contact with this kind, simple and, above all, frank man.

It was the end of May. Yevgeny somehow managed to settle his affairs in town, succeeding in freeing the wasteland from mortgage so that he could sell it to a merchant, and then borrowed money from that very same merchant in order to renew his stock – horses, bulls, carts and so on – as well as, and mainly in order to, build a farm, which represented an essential. The work began. Timber arrived, the carpenters were already at work, eight cart-loads of manure were brought up – but up till then everything hung by a thread.

2

IN THE MIDST OF ALL THESE WORRIES a circumstance arose which, although unimportant, nevertheless worried Yevgeny at the time. He passed his youth as all young, healthy, unmarried men do – in other words he had relations with all types of women. He was not a debauchee, as he was fond of saying, but neither was he a monk. However, he only indulged himself in this way in so far as it was essential for his physical health and freedom of mind, as he said. This had started when he was sixteen years old, and up till now everything had gone satisfactorily – satisfactorily in the sense that he had not indulged in debauch, had never lost his head, and had never caught any disease. In St Petersburg he had at first a seamstress, then she had gone to the bad and he had made other arrangements. And this side of his life had been so well provided for that it had not embarrassed him.

Then, after he had been living in the country for nearly two months, he did not quite know what to do about it. His involuntary continence was beginning to have a bad effect on him. Did he really have to go to town because of it? And where to? How? This was the only thing that worried Yevgeny Irtenyev, but, as he was convinced that it was essential for him and that he needed it, he really did begin to need it, and he felt that he was not free and that, against his will, his glances followed every young woman he saw.

He felt that it would not be right for him to live with a woman or a girl in his own home, on his own estate. He knew, from stories he had heard, that both his father and his grandfather had, in this respect, been quite different from other landowners of the time and had never had any dealings of that sort with serfs in their own homes, and he decided that he would not do that, but as time went on, as he felt himself to be more and more tied and imagined with horror what might happen to him in a small provincial town, and realizing that anyway there were no longer any serfs, he decided that it would be possible to come to some arrangement there. Only it must be done so that no one would know about it, and not for the sake of debauchery but just for his health's sake, he said to himself. Having made up his mind, he began to feel even more restless; while talking to the bailiff or to the peasants or to the carpenter he would involuntarily bring the conversation round to women and, if the conversation did touch on the subject of women, then he would try to keep it on that subject. As to women themselves, he stared at them more and more.

3

But it was one thing to decide this in his own mind, and quite another to put it into practice. It was impossible for him to approach a woman about it himself. Whom? Where? It had to be done through someone, but to whom could he turn?

It once so happened that he dropped in for a drink of water at the forester's hut. The keeper had been a huntsman of his father's. Yevgeny Irtenyev was chatting with him and the keeper began telling him old stories about hunting sprees. And it occurred to Yevgeny that it would be a good idea to arrange something here, in the forester's hut, or in the wood. Only he did not know how to set about it, or whether old Danila would be willing to undertake it. "Perhaps such a suggestion would horrify him, and I shall be disgraced, or perhaps he would quite simply agree to it." Thus he thought, listening to Danila's tales. Danila was telling him how they once had been camping in a field that belonged to the priest's wife, and how he had brought a peasant woman to a man called Pryanichnikov.

"I can," thought Yevgeny.

"Your Dad, God rest his soul, didn't go in for such nonsense."

"I can't," thought Yevgeny, but in order to find out he said: "How is it that you went in for such wickedness?"

"Why, what's bad about it? She was glad, and my Fyodor Zakharych was ever so pleased. I got a rouble. What do you expect me to do, after all? He was made of flesh and blood, too. Ate and drank like everyone else."

"Yes, I can say it," thought Yevgeny, and set about it straight away.

"You know," he felt himself blushing scarlet. "You know, Danila, I'm becoming a nervous wreck."

Danila smiled.

"I'm not a monk, after all – I'm used to it."

He felt that everything he said was silly, but was pleased Danila approved.

"Why, you should have said so long ago! Of course it can be arranged. You just tell me who it is you want."

"Oh, really, it's all the same to me. So long as she's not monstrously ugly, and is healthy, of course."

"I understand!" Danila broke in. He thought for a moment. "Oh, I know of a nice little bit," he began. Yevgeny blushed again. "A nice little bit. Just fancy! They married her off in the autumn," Danila began to whisper, "and he can't do anything. Ah, that's fair game for anyone."

Yevgeny even winced from shame.

"No, no," he broke in, "I don't need that sort of thing at all. What I need, on the contrary," (what did he mean by "on the contrary"?) "on the contrary, I just need someone healthy, and as little fuss as possible – a soldier's wife, or something…"

"I know. That means Stepanida's what you need. Her husband is away in town, she's just like a soldier's wife. And she's a fine, clean woman. You'll be pleased. And as a matter of fact, I said to her the other day 'You go…', but she…"

"Well, when then?"

"Well, tomorrow, if you like. Look: I'll go and get some tobacco and drop in there, and at dinner time you come along here or go to the bath-house, behind the vegetable garden. There's no one there. And anyway, after dinner everyone is asleep."

"All right, then."

On his way home Yevgeny began to feel terribly worried. "What will it be? What does it mean – a peasant woman? Perhaps something monstrous, frightful? No, they are lovely," he said to himself, remembering those at whom he had stared. "But what shall I say, what shall I do?"

For the whole of that day he was not himself, but the next day, at twelve o'clock, he went to the forester's hut. Danila stood at the doors and nodded his head silently but significantly in the direction of the wood. The blood rushed to Yevgeny's head, he felt his heart beat, and went towards the vegetable garden. There was no one there. He went to the bath-house – still no one; he looked inside, came out again, and suddenly heard the snapping of a broken branch. He looked round; she was standing in a thicket, beyond a little gully. He rushed there, through the gully which was full of nettles, but did not notice them. He stumbled, his pince-nez fell off his nose, and he ran up the hillock opposite. In a white embroidered blouse, a reddish-brown skirt, and with a bright red kerchief – there she stood, barefooted, fresh, sturdy, beautiful, timidly smiling.

"There's a path there – you should have gone round," she said. "I've been here a long time. Ever so long."

He went up to her and, looking round, touched her.

A quarter of an hour later they separated; he found his pince-nez, called in on Danila and, in answer to his question: "Are you satisfied, sir?", he gave him a rouble and went home.

He was satisfied. He had only felt shame at first, and then it had disappeared. And everything had been all right. All right, mainly, because he now felt light, calm, vigorous. He had not even looked at her very closely. He remembered that she was clean, fresh, not bad-looking, and simple, unaffected.

"Who is she, I wonder?" he said to himself. "Did he say she was a Pechnikov? Which Pechnikov can it be? There are two families of them, I believe. It must be the daughter-in-law of the old man, Mikhaila. Yes, probably that's the one. He has a son living in Moscow, I think. I'll ask Danila about it sometime."

From then on this formerly important unpleasantness of country life – involuntary continence – was eliminated. Yevgeny's freedom of mind was no longer destroyed, and he was free to devote himself to his work.

But the work which Yevgeny had undertaken was not at all easy; sometimes it seemed to him that he would not be able to hold out and that it would end by his having to sell the estate after all, that all his labours would be in vain and, worst of all, that it would be clear that he had not been able to stick it out, that he had not been able to go through with what he had undertaken. This worried him more than anything else. He had hardly succeeded in dealing with one difficulty somehow when another presented itself unexpectedly.

During all this time new and previously unknown debts of his father's kept turning up. It was clear that, in the last years, his father had borrowed indiscriminately, wherever he could. In May, at the time of the division of the property, Yevgeny had thought that at last he knew everything. But suddenly, in the middle of the summer, he received a letter which informed him that there was another debt of twelve thousand roubles due to a widow named Yesipova. There was no promissory note, only a simple IOU which, according to the attorney, could be disputed. But it never even entered Yevgeny's head that he might refuse to pay a genuine debt of his father's just because a document could be disputed. He only had to know for certain if it really was a genuine debt.

"Mamma! Who is this Valerya Vladimirovna Yesipova?" he asked his mother when they met, as usual, for dinner.

"Yesipova? She was grandfather's ward. Why?"

Yevgeny told his mother about the letter.

"I think she ought to be ashamed of herself. Your father gave her so much."

"But do we owe her anything?"

"Well, how shall I put it? There is no debt. Papa in his boundless kindness…"

"Yes, but did Papa consider it a debt?"

"I can't tell you. I don't know. I know how difficult it is for you, anyway."

Yevgeny saw that Marya Pavlovna did not know herself how to say it, and was, as it were, sounding him.

"This makes me realize that I must pay," her son said. "I'll go over and see her tomorrow, and I'll ask if it wouldn't be possible to defer payment."

"Oh, how sorry I am for you. But, you know, I think it would be the best thing to do. Tell her that she must wait," said Marya Pavlovna, obviously relieved and proud of her son's decision.

Yevgeny's difficulties were aggravated by the fact that his mother, who lived with him, did not understand them at all. All her life she had been accustomed to live on such a large scale that she could not even imagine her son's actual position, which was that any day they might find they had nothing left, that he would be obliged to sell everything and live and keep his mother on what he could earn, which, in his position, would be at the most two thousand roubles. She did not understand that the only way to save themselves from such a predicament was by cutting down every kind of expense, and therefore she could not understand why Yevgeny was so reluctant to spend anything on trifles, on wages for the gardeners and coachmen, on the servants, and even on food. In addition, like the majority of widows, she cherished a feeling of veneration for her deceased husband's memory – a feeling which was far from resembling what she had felt towards him when he had been alive – and she would not countenance the thought that anything which he had done might have been bad or could be changed.

With great difficulty Yevgeny kept up both the garden and the greenhouse with two gardeners, and the stables with two coachmen. Marya Pavlovna, however, naively imagined that by not complaining about the food, which was prepared by an old chef, and about the paths in the park, not all of which were kept clean, and because they only had one boy instead of footmen, she was doing everything that a mother could who was sacrificing herself for her son. Thus it was with this new debt, which Yevgeny saw as almost the final blow to all his undertakings, but which Marya Pavlovna saw only as an opportunity for showing Yevgeny's generosity. Also, Marya Pavlovna did not worry particularly about Yevgeny's material situation because she was convinced that he would make a brilliant match which would redeem everything. And he could make a very brilliant match. She knew of a dozen families who would be delighted if he married their daughter, and she wanted to arrange this as soon as possible.

4

Y EVGENY DREAMED OF MARRIAGE HIMSELF, only not in the same way as his mother did; the idea of making marriage a means of mending his affairs was abhorrent to him. He wanted to marry honestly, for love. He, too, looked attentively at the girls he met and knew, assessing their suitability, but his fate had not been decided. Meanwhile, his relations with Stepanida continued, and had even acquired the character of something established, which he had not at all expected. Yevgeny was so far from being a libertine, it was so unpleasant for him to carry on with this secret and – he felt – base affair, that he never felt at ease and, even after their first meeting, he hoped not to see Stepanida again, but it turned out that after a certain time he again fell prey to the same uneasiness which he ascribed to this. And this time his uneasiness was no longer impersonal; all the time his imagination was filled with those same black, shining eyes, the same low voice saying "Ever so long", the same smell of freshness and strength, the same high bosom lifting up the blouse, and all of this in the same walnut and maple thicket, flooded with bright light. Suppressing his feeling of shame, he again appealed to Danila, and again a meeting was arranged at midday, in the wood. This time Yevgeny looked at her more closely, and everything about her seemed to him attractive. He tried to talk to her, and asked about her husband. He was indeed Mikhaila's son and was a coachman in Moscow.

"Well, then, how do you?…" Yevgeny wanted to ask how it was that she was unfaithful to him.

"How do I what?" she asked. She was obviously intelligent and shrewd.

"Well how is it that you come and see me?"

"Oh, that!" she said cheerfully. "He's having his fun there, I suppose. Why shouldn't I?"

Obviously she was putting on an air of jauntiness and dash. And Yevgeny thought it charming. But all the same, he did not fix another meeting with her himself. Even when she suggested it in order to avoid acting through Danila, to whom she seemed to be unfriendly, Yevgeny did not agree. He hoped that this meeting would be the last. She attracted him. He thought that such intercourse was essential for him and that there was nothing bad in it, but in his heart of hearts there was a sterner judge who did not approve of it and who hoped that this would be the last time, or, if he did not hope this, at least he did not want to take an active part in this affair and arrange it next time for himself.

Thus passed the summer, in the course of which they saw each other about ten times, each time through Danila. Once it happened that she could not come because her husband had arrived, and Danila proposed another woman. Yevgeny refused with repugnance. Then her husband went away and the meetings continued as before, at first through Danila, though later Yevgeny named the time himself, and she would come with another woman, Prokhorova, as peasant women could not walk about alone. Once, at the very time arranged for their meeting, a family came to see Marya Pavlovna with the girl she had her eye on as a match for Yevgeny, and he simply could not escape. As soon as he could get away he made as if to go to the threshing floor and went round to the meeting-place by a path leading to the wood. She was not there. But, at the place where they usually met, wherever her hand had been able to reach, everything was broken – the wild cherry, the hazel bushes, even the young maple tree which was as thick as a stake. She had waited for him, become worried, then annoyed and, in play, had left him a reminder of herself. He stood there for a while, and then went to Danila to ask him to tell her to come the next day. She came, and was the same as usual.

So passed the summer. Meetings were always arranged in the wood, and only once, when it was nearly autumn, in the threshing barn in the back yard. It never even entered Yevgeny's head that this relationship had any significance for him. He did not even think about it. He gave her money, and that was all. He neither knew nor gave a thought to the fact that the whole village already knew about it and envied her, and that her sense of sin, under the influence of money and the interference of her family, had ceased to exist. It seemed to her that if people envied her, what she was doing must be all right.

"It's just necessary for my health," thought Yevgeny. "All the same, it's not a good thing, and although no one says anything, everyone, or at any rate a good many people, know about it. The woman she goes about with knows. And as she knows, she's probably told others about it, too. But what can I do? I'm behaving badly," thought Yevgeny, "but there's nothing to be done. Anyway, it won't be for long."

Yevgeny was disturbed mainly by the thought of her husband. At first, for some reason, he had imagined that her husband must be bad, and this somehow seemed partly to justify him. But then he saw her husband and was surprised. He was a fine, spruce young fellow, certainly no worse and probably no better than himself. At the first meeting after this he told her that he had seen her husband and how he had taken to him, and what a fine fellow he was.

"There's not another like him in the village," she said with pride.

This surprised Yevgeny and, after that, the thought of her husband troubled him even more. Once, when he happened to be at Danila's, Danila, who was talkative, said to him point-blank: "Mikhaila asked me the other day: 'Is it true that the master is living with my son's wife?' I said: 'I don't know. And anyway,' I said, 'better with the master than with a peasant.'"

"Well, and what did he say?"

"Oh, nothing, just said: 'You wait, I'll show her if I get to know of it.'"

"Of course, if her husband were to come back, I'd give it up," thought Yevgeny.

But her husband was living in town and for the time being their relationship continued.

"When I have to, I'll break it off, and nothing will remain of it," he thought.

And he never doubted it, because he was greatly occupied during the summer with many different things: setting up the new farm, the harvest, the building and, above all, the repayment of his debt and the sale of the wasteland. These were questions that absorbed all his thoughts, sleeping and waking. All that was real life, whereas his intercourse – he did not even call it a liaison – with Stepanida was something insignificant. It is true that when the desire to see her took him, it took him with such force that he could think of nothing else, but it did not last long; he would arrange a meeting and then again forget her for a week, sometimes for a month.

In the autumn Yevgeny often went to town, and there made friends with the Annensky family. The Annenskys had a daughter who had only just left school. And there, to the great distress of Marya Pavlovna, Yevgeny – as she said – sold himself too cheaply, fell in love with Liza Annenskaya, and proposed to her.

From that time his relations with Stepanida ceased.

5

IT IS IMPOSSIBLE TO EXPLAIN why Yevgeny chose Liza Annenskaya, just as it is never possible to explain why a man chooses one woman rather than another. There was an abundance of reasons, both positive and negative. One reason was the fact that she was not a very rich match, such as his mother would have made for him; another reason was that she was naïve and pathetic in her relationship with her mother, and also because she was not a beauty who took great care of her appearance, and yet she was by no means ugly. But the main reason was that their friendship began at a time when Yevgeny was ripe for marriage. He fell in love because he knew that he would get married.

At first Yevgeny simply liked Liza Annenskaya, but when he had decided that she was to be his wife, he experienced a much stronger feeling towards her; he felt that he was in love.

Liza was tall, thin and long. Everything about her was long; her face and her nose – not jutting out from, but going along her face – and her fingers, and her feet. Her complexion was very delicate, white, but a little sallow, touched with soft colour; her hair was long, blonde, soft and wavy, and she had beautiful, clear eyes, which were gentle and trusting. Yevgeny was particularly struck by her eyes and, when he thought of Liza, he saw her clear, gentle, trusting eyes before him.

Such was her physical appearance; he knew nothing about her spiritual side, but only saw her eyes, and it seemed as if they told him everything he needed to know – and this is what they told him: even when she had still been at school, from the age of fifteen onwards, Liza had continually fallen in love with every attractive man, and she was animated and happy only when she was in love. In exactly the same way, when she left school, she fell in love with Yevgeny as soon as she got to know him, and it was the fact that she was in love that gave her eyes the particular expression that so captivated Yevgeny.

During that very winter she had already been in love with two other young men at the same time, and she had blushed and been thrilled not only when they came into the room, but even at the mention of their names. But later, when her mother hinted to her that Irtenyev seemed to have serious intentions, she fell so much more in love with him that she became almost indifferent to the other two. When Irtenyev began visiting them, when, at balls and gatherings, he danced with her more than with others and obviously only wanted to know if she loved him – then her love for Irtenyev became morbid; she saw him in her dreams, whether she was asleep or awake in her dark room, and all the others ceased to exist for her. And when he proposed to her and had received her parents' blessing, when they had kissed and become engaged – then she had no other thoughts but for him, no other wishes than to be with him, to love him and to be loved by him. She was proud of him, and moved by him and by herself and by her love for him, and she felt ready to swoon and melt with love for him. The more he knew her, the more he, too, loved her. He had never expected to encounter such love, and it strengthened his feeling even more.

6

B EFORE SPRING he came to Semyonovskoe to look over the estate and to give orders, in particular concerning the house which was being redecorated for the wedding.

Marya Pavlovna was not pleased with her son's choice, but only because the match was not as brilliant as it might have been, and because she did not like Varvara Alexeyevna, his future mother-in-law. Whether she was a good or a bad woman she did not know and could not make up her mind, but the fact that she was not well-bred, not *comme il faut*, not, as Marya Pavlovna told herself, a *lady*, she had seen from their very first meeting, and this distressed her. It distressed her because she was accustomed to value breeding, knew that Yevgeny was very sensitive about it, and foresaw much distress for him because of it. She liked the girl herself. She liked her, mainly, because Yevgeny liked her. She had to love her. And Marya Pavlovna was quite ready to do so, and to do so perfectly sincerely.

Yevgeny found his mother gay and pleased. She was arranging everything in the house and was intending to go away herself as soon as he brought his young bride there. Yevgeny tried to persuade her to stay on, and the question remained undecided. As usual, in the evening after tea, Marya Pavlovna played patience. Yevgeny sat beside her, helping her. This was the time of their most intimate heart-to-heart conversations.

Having finished one game of patience and without starting another, Marya Pavlovna looked up at Yevgeny and, rather hesitantly, began thus: "Oh, I wanted to say something to you, Zhenya. You understand... I don't know... but generally speaking I wanted to give you some advice, that before you get married you must without fail put an end to all your bachelor affairs, so that nothing could worry you or – God forbid! – your wife. Do you understand me?"

And indeed, Yevgeny instantly understood that Marya Pavlovna was alluding to his relations with Stepanida, which had ceased in the autumn, and to which his mother, as lonely women do, attached far greater significance than they had, in fact, possessed. Yevgeny blushed, not so much from shame as from annoyance that the well-meaning Marya Pavlovna should meddle – lovingly, it is true – but meddle all the same in things which did not concern her and which she did not and could not understand. He said that he had nothing to hide and that he had always behaved in such a way that nothing could interfere with his marriage.

"Well, that's splendid, darling. You must not be offended at what I said, Zhenya," said Marya Pavlovna, getting embarrassed.

But Yevgeny saw that she had not finished and had not said what she wanted to say. And so it turned out. After a slight pause she began to tell him how, while he had been away, she had been asked to be godmother to... the Pechnikovs' child. Yevgeny now blushed crimson, no longer from annoyance or even shame, but from some strange sense of the importance of what was about to be said to him, an involuntary sense which did not at all agree with his reasonings. It came out precisely as he had expected. Marya Pavlovna, as if she had no other aim than conversation, told him that that year nothing but boys were being born – which probably meant a war. The Vasins and the Pechnikovs – the first child in both cases was a boy. Marya Pavlovna wanted to say this unobtrusively, but herself became embarrassed when she saw her son's red face and the nervous way in which he took off his pince-nez, tapped them and put them on again, and hurriedly lit a cigarette. She was silent. He was silent, too, and could not think of any way of breaking the silence. So that they both understood that they understood each other.

"Yes, when you live in the country the great thing is to be fair; there must not be any favouritism, the way it used to be with your uncle."

"Mother, darling," Yevgeny said suddenly, "I know why you are saying all this. You are worrying yourself for nothing. My future married life is sacred to me and I shall in no circumstances destroy it. As to what happened when I was a bachelor, that's all finished with. And I never took on any ties of any sort and no one has any claims on me."

"Well, I'm glad," said his mother. "I know what high standards you have."

Yevgeny took these words of his mother's as a well-deserved tribute, and was silent.

The next morning he was driving into town thinking of his fiancée and of everything under the sun except Stepanida. But, as if on purpose to remind him, as he was driving up to the church he began meeting people returning from it on foot and in carts. He met old Matvey with Semyon, children, young girls, and then two peasant women, one elderly and the other smartly dressed and wearing a bright red kerchief; there was something familiar about her. She was walking lightly, cheerfully, and carrying a baby in her arms. He drew alongside them, the older woman bowed to him, standing still in the old-fashioned way, but the younger woman with the child only inclined her head, and from beneath her kerchief there shone the familiar, smiling, gay eyes.

"Yes, it's her, but it's all over, and there's no need to look at her. And perhaps the child is mine," the thought flashed through his mind. "No, what nonsense. There was her husband, she used to go to him." He did not even stop to calculate. He was so certain that it had been necessary for his health, he had paid her money, and nothing more; no ties of any sort existed between him and her, there had been none, there could be none, and there should be none. It was not that he was smothering the voice of conscience – no, his conscience said absolutely nothing to him. And he did not once think of her again after his conversation with his mother and this meeting. Nor did he meet her again.

In the first week after Easter Yevgeny was married in town, and he and his young bride left immediately for the country. The house had been arranged in the way in which houses usually are arranged for the newly-wed. Marya Pavlovna wanted to leave, but Yevgeny, and especially Liza, coaxed her to stay. However, she moved into a wing of the house.

And so began a new life for Yevgeny.

7

HIS FIRST YEAR OF MARRIED LIFE was a difficult one for Yevgeny. It was difficult because his business affairs, which he had somehow contrived to lay aside during his engagement, now, after his marriage, all suddenly overwhelmed him.

He was unable to extricate himself from his debts. The summer villa was sold, the more urgent debts were paid, but more debts still remained and there was no money. The estate brought in a good income, but some of it had to be sent to his brother and some spent on the wedding, so there was no money, and the factory could not run and had to be closed. One way of extricating himself from this situation was to make use of his wife's money. Liza, as soon as she understood her husband's predicament, herself insisted that he should do so. Yevgeny agreed, but only on condition that the title deeds for half the estate should be made out in his wife's name. This is precisely what he did. Of course, he did not do this for the sake of his wife, who was hurt by it, but for the sake of his mother-in-law.

Business with its various fluctuations, success and failure following each other, was one of the things that poisoned Yevgeny's life during this first year. Another was his wife's ill health. In the autumn of this first year, seven months after their marriage, Liza had an accident. She was driving in a gig to meet her husband, who was returning from town, when a usually quiet horse played up and she was frightened and jumped out. Her jump was relatively fortunate – she might have been caught in the wheel – but she was already expecting a child. In the night her pains started, she had a miscarriage, and was unable to recover for a long time afterwards. The loss of the expected child, his wife's illness and the disorganization of his life resulting from it and, above all, the presence of his mother-in-law who had arrived as soon as Liza fell ill, made this year even more difficult for Yevgeny.

But, in spite of these difficulties, towards the end of the first year Yevgeny felt very cheerful. To begin with, his dearest wish, which was to restore his vanished fortune and resume his grandfather's way of life on a new basis, was being realized, even though the progress was difficult and slow. There was no longer any question of selling the whole estate to cover debts. The main estate, although it was made out in his wife's name, was saved, and if the beet crop would only sell well and for a good price, the present need and strain could, next year, be transformed into real prosperity. That was one thing.

Another was the fact that, no matter how much he had expected of his wife, he had never expected to find in her what he had, in fact, found: it was not what he had expected, but much better. The transports and raptures of lovers were absent, or were very unconvincing, however much he tried to bring them about, but what he did feel was something quite different, the feeling that life had not only become gayer and pleasanter, but easier to live. He did not know the reason for this, but it was so.

The reason for it was that she had decided as soon as they had become engaged that, of all the people in the world, there was but one Yevgeny Irtenyev, and he was on a higher level, more intelligent, purer, nobler than anyone else, and that therefore everyone was under an obligation to humour and serve this Irtenyev. But as it was impossible to make everyone do this, she must do it to the best of her ability herself. This she did, and therefore all her mental faculties were directed to finding out or guessing what he liked, and then doing it – no matter what it was nor how difficult it might be.

She had, too, something which makes up the principal charm of communion with a loving woman – she had, thanks to her love for her husband, a perception of his mind which amounted to second sight. She sensed – often, it seemed to him, better than he did himself – his very state of mind, every shade of feeling that he had, and acted accordingly. So she never hurt his feelings, but comforted him when he was depressed and encouraged him when he was happy. It was not only his feelings that she understood, but his thoughts, too. Even his thoughts on subjects which were most alien to her – such as those concerning agriculture, the factory, judgement of character

– she immediately understood and she could not only discuss these things with him in conversation, but was often, as he told her himself, a useful and irreplaceable adviser. She looked at everything – things, people, the whole world – only through his eyes. She loved her mother, but, as soon as she saw that Yevgeny did not like his mother-in-law's interference in their life, she at once took her husband's side, and with such determination that he had to check her.

In addition to all this, she had a great deal of taste and was tactful and, above all, calm. She never drew attention to what she did; results of her actions only were seen – that is, cleanliness, order and refinement always and in everything. Liza had at once understood what constituted her husband's ideal of life, and she tried to attain – and did attain – what he wished for in the running and order of the house. Their marriage lacked children, it is true, but there were hopes for this too. In the winter they went to Petersburg to see a gynaecologist, who assured them that she was perfectly well and could have children.

This desire too was realized. Towards the end of the year she became pregnant again.

The only thing which did not so much spoil as threaten to spoil their happiness was her jealousy – jealousy which she repressed, but from which she often suffered. Not only had Yevgeny no right to love anyone, for there was not a woman in the world worthy of him (she never asked herself if she was worthy of him or not), but for that very reason no woman could presume to love him.

8

THEY SPENT THEIR LIFE THUS: he always got up early in the morning, attended to his farm business, visited the refinery where some work was proceeding, and sometimes had a look at the fields. At ten o'clock he was back for coffee. Marya Pavlovna, an uncle who was living with them and Liza had coffee on the terrace. After some conversation – which was often very animated – over coffee, they separated again until lunch. They lunched at two o'clock, and afterwards they would go for a walk or a drive. In the evening, when he came back from the office, they had a late tea, and sometimes he would read aloud while she worked, or they would have some music, or, if they had guests, they would talk. When he went away on business he would write her a letter – and receive one from her – every day. Sometimes she would accompany him on his travels and this was particularly pleasant. On his and on her name-day visitors would come, and he liked to see how well she knew how to arrange everything so that everyone enjoyed themselves. He saw – and heard, too – how everyone admired the young and pretty hostess, and he loved her all the more for it. Everything was going very well. She took her pregnancy lightly and both of them began, with some diffidence, to make plans for bringing up the child. The ways and means of upbringing were all decided by Yevgeny, and all she desired was meekly to carry out his will. Yevgeny read a lot of medical books and intended bringing up the child according to all the rules of science. She, of course, agreed with everything and made preparations – sewed warm and cool coverings, and arranged the cradle. Thus came the second year of their marriage, and the second spring.

9

WHITSUN WAS APPROACHING. Liza was in her fifth month and, although she was being careful, was gay and active. Both mothers, hers and his, were living in the house under the pretext of protecting her and looking after her, but they only upset her with their bickering. Yevgeny was particularly busy with the farm and with a new method of processing sugar beet on a large scale.

Just before Whit Sunday Liza decided that the house ought to have a thorough spring clean, which it had not had since Holy Week, and summoned two extra daily women to help the servants wash the floors and windows, beat the furniture and carpets, and put on fresh covers. The women came in the early morning, put iron pots of water on to boil, and set to work. One of these two women was Stepanida, who had just weaned her little boy and who had begged the office clerk – with whom she was now carrying on – to let her have some cleaning work. She wanted to have a good look at her new mistress. Stepanida lived as she had always done, alone, without her husband, and was up to her old tricks; she was carrying on now with the young office clerk, just as she had done before with Danila, who had caught her stealing wood, and then later with the master. She never thought about the master at all. "He's got a wife now," she thought. "It would be fine to have a look at the mistress, they say her house is ever so well kept."

Since the time when he had met her with the child, Yevgeny had not seen her. She did not go out to daily work because of the child, and she rarely walked about the village. That morning, the day before Whit Sunday, Yevgeny got up early, at five o'clock, and rode off to a field on which phosphates were to be spread, and he had left the house before the daily women had arrived, while they were still busy with the stoves and boilers.

Yevgeny came back to lunch, happy, satisfied and hungry. He dismounted at the gate, handed his horse over to a gardener who was passing, and walked home hitting the tall grass with his whip and, as one often does, repeating a phrase he had said. The phrase which he was repeating was: "Phosphates will justify", but what they would justify and to whom he neither knew nor cared.

They were beating carpets on the lawn and had carried out the furniture.

"Good heavens! What a spring clean Liza has undertaken! Phosphates will justify... What a housewife! Yes, my little housewife," he said to himself, vividly imagining her in a white dressing gown and with her face beaming with joy, as it almost always was when he was looking at her. "Yes, I must change my boots, or else phosphates will justify, I mean it smells of manure, and my little housewife is expecting. And what is she expecting? Oh, a little Irtenyev, a new one, is growing up inside her," he thought. "Yes, phosphates will justify." And, smiling at his thoughts, he put his hand out to open the door of his room.

But before he had time to push the door open it opened itself, and he collided face to face with a peasant woman who was carrying a pail – her skirt tucked up, her legs bare, and her sleeves rolled high up her arms. He stood aside to let her pass; she stood aside too, rearranging her displaced kerchief with her wet hand.

"Go on, go on, I won't go in if it's wash..." Yevgeny began, and suddenly stopped as he recognized her.

Her eyes were smiling as she gaily glanced up at him and, pulling down her skirt, she went out.

"What nonsense is this? What's this?... It's not possible!" Yevgeny said to himself, frowning and shaking himself as if annoyed by a fly, and angry at having noticed her. He was angry at having noticed her, yet at the same time he could not take his eyes off her body, as she walked deftly and sturdily along, swaying slightly and showing her bare legs; he could not take his eyes off her arms, her shoulders, off the beautiful folds of her blouse, and her red skirt tucked high up over her white calves.

"What on earth am I looking at her for?" he said to himself, looking down so as not to see her. "Yes, well, anyway, I must go and get some other boots," and he turned back to go into his room, but he had not taken five steps when, without himself knowing why or at whose behest, he again looked round in order to see her once more. She was going round the corner, and at the same moment she, too, looked round at him.

"Oh, what am I doing?" he cried in his heart. "She may get ideas… She's probably got them already."

He went into his room, which was still wet from cleaning. Another woman, old and thin, was there, washing it. Yevgeny went on tiptoe through dirty pools to the wall where his boots were standing, and was just going out of the room when the woman went out too.

"That one has gone out, and the other one, Stepanida, will come – alone," a voice inside him suddenly insisted.

"Oh God! What am I thinking? What am I doing?" He seized his boots and ran with them into the hall, where he put them on, cleaned himself up, and went out on the terrace where both their mothers were already sitting at coffee. Liza had apparently been waiting for him, and came out on the terrace by another door at the same time as he did.

"Oh God! If she, who thinks I'm so honest, so pure, so innocent – if only she knew!" he thought.

Liza met him with a radiant face as she always did. But that day she somehow seemed to him particularly pale, yellow and long, and weak.

10

D URING COFFEE, as often happened, they had one of those conversations peculiar to ladies which had no logic in it whatever, but which was obviously held together by something, since it went on without interruption.

Both ladies were bickering, and Liza was skilfully navigating between them.

"I'm so disappointed that they didn't finish washing your room before you came back," she said to her husband, "but I would so much like it to be done thoroughly."

"Well, and what about you? Did you sleep after I left?"

"Yes, I did sleep. I feel quite all right."

"How can a woman in her condition feel all right in this unbearable heat, when the windows face the sun?" said Varvara Alexeyevna, her mother. "And without blinds or an awning, either. I always have an awning at home."

"Yes, but there's shade here from ten o'clock onwards," said Marya Pavlovna.

"That's just why one gets fever. From the damp," said Varvara Alexeyevna, not noticing that what she was now saying was in direct contradiction to what she had just said. "My doctor always used to say that one can never diagnose an illness without knowing the character of the patient. And he should know, because he is the best doctor, and we pay him a hundred roubles. My late husband didn't hold with doctors, but he never grudged me anything."

"How can a man grudge a woman anything when perhaps her life and the child's depend…"

"Oh well, when one has means, then the wife need not depend on her husband. A good wife gives in to her husband," said Varvara Alexeyevna, "only Liza is still too weak after her illness."

"Oh no, Mamma, I feel perfectly all right. Why didn't they give you any scalded cream, I wonder?"

"I don't want any. I can drink it with fresh cream."

"I asked Varvara Alexeyevna. She refused," said Marya Pavlovna, as if to justify herself.

"Oh no, I don't want any today" – and, as if to bring an unpleasant conversation to a close and yielding magnanimously, Varvara Alexeyevna turned to Yevgeny and said: "Well, have they spread the phosphates?"

Liza ran off to fetch the cream.

"I don't want any, I don't want any."

"Liza! Liza! Gently!" said Marya Pavlovna. "These quick movements are bad for her."

"Nothing is bad for one if one has peace of mind," said Varvara Alexeyevna, as if she was hinting at something, although she knew herself that her words could not hint at anything.

Liza came back with the cream. Yevgeny drank his coffee and listened morosely. He was used to these conversations, but their inanity irritated him particularly today. He wanted to think over what had happened to him, but this prattle prevented him from doing so. When she had finished her coffee Varvara Alexeyevna left, still in a bad mood. Liza, Yevgeny and Marya Pavlovna remained alone, and the conversation became simpler and pleasanter. But Liza, with the sensitivity of love, at once noticed that something was worrying Yevgeny and asked him whether something unpleasant had happened. He had not been prepared for this question and hesitated a little, before answering that there was nothing the matter. And this answer made Liza all the more pensive. That something was worrying him, and was worrying him very much, was to her as clear as the fact that a fly had fallen into the milk, but he did not tell her what it was that was worrying him.

11

AFTER LUNCH they all went their separate ways. Yevgeny, as usual, went into his study. He did not begin to read or to write letters; instead, he sat down and began to think, smoking one cigarette after another. He was terribly surprised and distressed by this unexpected appearance within him of the unworthy feeling from which he had considered himself to be free since his marriage. Since then he had not once experienced such a feeling either towards her, the woman that he used to know, or towards any woman other than his own wife. In his heart he had often rejoiced that he had freed himself from it, and then, suddenly, this coincidence, apparently so insignificant, had shown him that he was not free of it. He was tormented now, not because he was again a prey to this feeling, not because he desired her – he did not even want to think of that – but because the feeling was still alive in him and he had to be on the look-out against it. He had no doubt at all in his heart that he would suppress it.

He had one unanswered letter and a paper to draw up. He sat down at the writing table and set to work. Having finished it, and having quite forgotten what had been worrying him, he went out to visit the stables. And again, as if to make matters worse, no sooner had he come out on to the front steps than she appeared from round the corner, whether by accident or by design, and walked past him, swinging her arms and swaying as she went. Not only did she walk past, she ran past him as if she were playing with him, and caught up her friend.

The bright noon, the nettles, the back of Danila's hut, and her smiling face as she nibbled a leaf in the shade of the maple trees all rose up again in his imagination.

"No, I can't leave it at that," he said to himself and, after waiting till the women were out of sight, he went to the office.

It was the dinner hour, and he hoped to be in time to catch the bailiff. He was. The bailiff had just woken up. He stood in the office, stretching himself and yawning as he looked at the cowman, who was saying something to him.

"Vassily Nikolayevich!"

"Yes, sir?"

"I want a word with you."

"What can I do for you?"

"Well, finish what you are doing."

"Can't you bring it here?" Vassily Nikolayevich said to the cowman.

"It's heavy, Vassily Nikolayevich."

"What's this?" asked Yevgeny.

"Well, a cow has calved in the field. It's all right, I'll tell them to harness a horse. Tell Nikolai to harness Lysukha, and take the dray if there is nothing else."

The cowman went out.

"Well, you see," Yevgeny started, blushing and feeling that he was doing so. "Well, you see, Vassily Nikolayevich, when I was a bachelor I sowed some wild oats here... You heard about it, perhaps..."

Vassily Nikolayevich's eyes twinkled and, obviously feeling sorry for his master, he said: "Is it about Stepashka?"

"Well, yes. Well, it's like this – please, please don't take her on for cleaning work in the house. You understand, it's very unpleasant for me..."

"Oh, well, it looks as if that was Vanya's orders, the office clerk's."

"Well, please... Well, are they spreading the rest?" said Yevgeny, so as to cover his confusion.

"As a matter of fact, I'm just going up there now."

So that was that. And Yevgeny calmed down in the hope that, as he had not seen her for a year, he would not see her in the future either. "Besides, Vassily Nikolayevich will tell Ivan, the clerk, and Ivan will tell her, and she will understand that I don't want that sort of thing," Yevgeny told himself, and he was pleased that he had taken himself in hand and had told Vassily Nikolayevich, however difficult it might have been for him. "Yes, anything is better, anything is better than such doubt, such shame." He shuddered at the very memory of the crime he had committed in his thoughts.

12

THE MORAL EFFORT which he had made in order to overcome his shame and to tell Vassily Nikolayevich calmed Yevgeny. It seemed to him that it was all over now. And Liza noticed immediately that he was quite calm and even more cheerful than usual. "Probably the mothers' bickering annoyed him. It is hard, in fact, and especially for him with his sensitivity and his generous nature, to listen to such unfriendly insinuations about something or other; it's bad form," thought Liza.

The next day was Whit Sunday. The weather was beautiful, and the peasant women on their way to the wood to weave garlands stopped as usual at their master's house to sing and dance. Marya Pavlovna and Varvara Alexeyevna, elegantly dressed and carrying parasols, came out on the steps and went up to the dancers. They were accompanied by Yevgeny's uncle dressed in a Chinese frock coat; he was a flabby profligate and drunkard, and was staying in the house that summer.

As always, there was one multi-coloured, bright circle of young women and girls in the centre, while round it, from different sides, like planets and satellites that had broken away from it and were rotating round it, came now the girls holding hands, their new print dresses rustling, now the little boys, laughing at something and running backwards and forwards one after another, now the youths in blue and black coats and caps and red shirts, continually spitting out sunflower-seed husks, now the household servants or onlookers, watching the dancers from a distance. Both ladies went right up to the circle of dancers, and Liza followed them too, in a pale-blue dress and with ribbons of the same colour in her hair, and with broad sleeves which revealed her long white arms and angular elbows.

Yevgeny did not want to go out, but it was ridiculous to hide. He too went out on to the steps smoking a cigarette, exchanged greetings with some men and boys, and talked to one of them. Meanwhile the women were belting out a dance song with all their might, snapping their fingers and clapping their hands and dancing.

"The mistress wants you," said a lad, coming up to Yevgeny, who had not heard his wife call. Liza was calling to him to come and look at the dance, at one of the women who was dancing and particularly attracted her. It was Stepashka. There she was, broad, vigorous, rosy-cheeked and gay, wearing a yellow dress and a sleeveless velveteen jerkin and a silk kerchief. Probably she danced well. He saw nothing.

"Yes, yes," he said, taking off his pince-nez and putting them on again. "Yes, yes," he said. "I don't seem to be able to avoid her," he thought.

He did not look at her because he feared her attractiveness and, precisely, because what he had glimpsed of her had seemed to him to be particularly attractive. Besides, he had seen from a gleam in her eye that she had seen him, and that she had seen that he was admiring her. He stood there as long as was necessary for decency's sake and, as soon as he saw that Varvara Alexeyevna had beckoned to her and was saying something nonsensical and hypocritical to her, calling her 'dear', he turned and moved away. He moved away and went back to the house. He went so as not to see her but, once upstairs, he went to a window, and all the time the women were at the porch he looked and looked at her, drinking her in.

He ran downstairs, while no one could see him and, slowing down to a walking pace, came out on the balcony and lit a cigarette. He went into the garden as if he were going for a walk, following in the direction in which she had gone. He had hardly taken two steps in the alley when behind a tree, he glimpsed a velveteen jerkin on a yellow dress, and a red kerchief. She was going somewhere with another woman. "Where can they be going to?" he thought.

And suddenly, a violent feeling of lust scorched him and clutched at his heart. As if forced by some alien will, Yevgeny looked round and went towards her.

"Yevgeny Ivanovich! Yevgeny Ivanovich! I was coming to see you, sir," said a voice behind him, and Yevgeny, seeing old Samokhin, who was digging a well for him, recovered his senses. He turned round quickly and went to Samokhin. As he was talking to him, Yevgeny turned sideways and saw that Stepashka and the other woman had gone down, apparently, to the well, or pretended to go to the well, and then, after staying there a short time, ran off to join the dancers.

13

AFTER HIS CONVERSATION WITH SAMOKHIN, Yevgeny went back to the house with a heavy heart, just as if he had committed a crime. To begin with, she had understood him, she thought that he wanted to see her, and she desired it, and then, the other woman – Anna Prokhorova – obviously knew about it.

But the main thing was that he felt he was defeated, that he had no will of his own, but that there was another force which was moving him; that today he had been saved only by luck, and that if not today, then tomorrow or the day after he would nevertheless be damned.

Yes, damned – he could not see it in any other way. To be unfaithful to his young and loving wife, with a peasant woman in the village, for everyone to see, was not this damnation, terrible damnation after which it would be impossible to go on living any longer? No, he must, he must take steps against it.

"Oh God! Oh God! What must I do? Will I really be damned?" he said to himself. "Can't I really do something about it? Yes, I must do something about it. I mustn't think about her," he commanded himself. "Not think about her!" And he immediately began thinking about her and seeing her before him and seeing the shadow of the maple trees.

He remembered that he had read about a holy man who, when tempted by a woman on whom he had to lay his hand in order to heal her, had put the other hand into a brazier and burned his fingers. He remembered this. "Yes, I'm ready to burn my fingers rather than be damned." And, looking round to see that there was no one in the room, he lit a match and put his finger in the flame. "Well, think about her now," he said to himself ironically. It began to hurt him; he withdrew his sooty finger, threw the match away and laughed at himself. "What nonsense! That's not what I must do. But I must take steps not to see her – I must go away myself, or else have her sent away. Yes, have her sent away! I could offer her husband money to go away to the town or to another village. But people would find out, they'd talk about that. But still, anything's better than this danger. Yes, that's what I must do," he said to himself – and all the time kept his eyes riveted in her direction. "Where did she go to?" he asked himself suddenly. It seemed to him that she had seen him at the window, had glanced at him, taken some woman by the hand and gone towards the garden, vigorously swinging her arm. As a result of his thoughts, and without himself knowing why, he went to the office.

Vassily Nikolayevich, in a smart frock coat and his hair well oiled, was sitting at tea with his wife and a woman guest who was wearing a flowered kerchief.

"Could I have a word with you, Vassily Nikolayevich?"

"Yes, sir, of course. We've finished tea."

"No, it would be better if you could come outside a moment."

"Yes, certainly, just let me take my cap. Tanya, cover up the samovar," said Vassily Nikolayevich, going out cheerfully.

Yevgeny thought that he seemed a bit drunk, but there was nothing to be done and perhaps it was all to the good; he might sympathise more with his predicament.

"Vassily Nikolayevich, I've come about the same thing again," said Yevgeny, "about that woman."

"Why, what's the matter now? I gave orders that she was not to be taken on again on any account."

"Well, no, as a matter of fact I was thinking of something else, and I wanted to ask your advice about it. Would it be possible to send them away, to send the whole family away?"

"Where on earth could you send them to?" said Vassily, displeased and sarcastic, it seemed to Yevgeny.

"Well, I thought we might give them some money, or even some land at Koltovskoye – anything so long as she isn't here."

"But how can you send them away? Where can he go, with all his roots here? And anyway, why do you want to do it? What harm is she doing you?"

"Ah, Vassily Nikolayevich, you understand, it would be dreadful for my wife if she got to hear about it."

"But who would ever tell her?"

"Oh, but how can I live with a threat like that hanging over my head? And anyway, it's very difficult…"

"What are you worrying about, really? Let bygones be bygones and, anyway, who hasn't slipped up somewhere, sometime?"

"All the same, it would be better if she could be sent away. Couldn't you talk to her husband about it?"

"But there's nothing to talk about. Oh, Yevgeny Ivanovich, why do you worry yourself about it? It's all over and forgotten. All sorts of things happen, after all. Anyway, who will say anything bad about you now? After all, you're too highly placed."

"But you will mention something, all the same?"

"All right, I'll talk to him about it."

Although he knew in advance that nothing would come of it, this conversation calmed Yevgeny to a certain extent. Above all, he felt that worry had led him to exaggerate the danger.

It was not as if he had been going to a rendezvous with her. It would not have been possible, anyway. No, he had just gone for a walk in the garden, and she had just happened to run that way.

14

O<small>N THAT SAME WHIT SUNDAY</small>, after dinner, Liza was walking in the garden. She went into the meadow, where her husband was taking her to show her the clover. As she was crossing a little ditch, she stumbled and fell. She fell gently, on her side, but she groaned, and in her face her husband read not only fright, but pain. He wanted to help her up, but she pushed his hand away.

"No, wait a moment, Yevgeny," she said, smiling faintly and looking up at him from below with what seemed to him a guilty look. "I've only twisted my ankle."

"There now, I always say," Varvara Alexeyevna started. "How can one go about jumping over ditches in such a condition?"

"Really, Mamma, it's nothing. I'll get up in a minute."

She got up, with her husband's help, but at the same instant she went pale, and her expression showed alarm.

"No, I don't feel well," and she whispered something to her mother.

"Oh, goodness, what have you done? I said she mustn't walk," cried Varvara Alexeyevna. "Wait a moment, I'll send someone. She mustn't walk, she must be carried."

"You're not afraid, Liza? I'll carry you," said Yevgeny, putting his left arm around her. "Put your arm round my neck. That's right."

And stooping, he put his right arm under her legs and lifted her up. He was never afterwards able to forget the martyred and yet, at the same time, blissful expression on her face.

"It's heavy for you, darling," she said, smiling. "And there's Mamma, running – tell her she needn't!"

And she leaned towards him and kissed him. She obviously wanted her mother to see him carrying her.

Yevgeny shouted to Varvara Alexeyevna not to hurry, and that he would carry Liza back. Varvara Alexeyevna stopped, and began screaming more than ever: "You'll drop her, you're sure to drop her! You want to finish her off! You haven't any shame!"

"But I can carry her perfectly well."

"I don't want to see. I can't look on while you are killing my daughter." And she ran round a corner of the drive.

"Don't worry, it'll pass," said Liza, smiling.

"I only hope there won't be any after-effects, like the other time."

"No, I wasn't talking about that. That's nothing, I was talking about Mamma. You're tired – have a rest."

But although it was heavy for him, Yevgeny carried his burden back to the house with pride and joy, and did not hand her over to the maid and the chef, whom Varvara Alexeyevna had found and had sent to meet them. He carried her up to the bedroom and put her on the bed.

"Now, you go," she said, drawing his hand towards her and kissing it. "Annushka and I will manage."

Marya Pavlovna, too, came running from the wing. They undressed Liza and put her to bed. Yevgeny sat in the drawing room with a book in his hand, waiting. Varvara Alexeyevna walked past him with such a gloomy and reproachful look that he was terrified.

"Well?" he asked.

"Well? What's the use of asking? Just what you hoped for, probably, making your wife jump across moats."

"Varvara Alexeyevna!" he cried. "This is intolerable! If you want to torture people and poison their lives" – he wanted to say: "then go and

96

do it somewhere else", but he controlled himself. "Doesn't it hurt you to say it?"

"It's too late now."

And triumphantly shaking her mob cap, she went out of the door.

The fall had, in fact, been a bad one. Her leg had been awkwardly twisted, and there was a risk of another miscarriage. Everyone knew that there was nothing to be done, that she must simply lie quietly, but all the same they decided to send for the doctor.

"Dear Nikolai Semyonovich," Yevgeny wrote to the doctor. "You have always been so kind to us that, I hope, you will not refuse to come to my wife's help. She…" and so on. When he had written the letter, he went to the stables to arrange for the horses and carriage. One lot of horses had been prepared to fetch the doctor, and another lot to take him home. When a household is not on a grand scale all this cannot be done at once, but must be thought out. When he had seen to it all himself and sent off the coachman, Yevgeny returned home at about ten o'clock. His wife was in bed, and said that she felt perfectly all right, that she had no pain, but Varvara Alexeyevna was sitting by the lamp, which was shaded from Liza with some music, and was knitting a large red blanket with an expression which clearly said that after what had happened there could be no peace. And no matter what other people might do, she, at least, had done her duty.

Yevgeny saw this, but so as to appear as if he had not noticed, he tried to look cheerful and unconcerned, and recounted how he had collected the horses and how Kavushka, the mare, had been going splendidly harnessed on the off side.

"Yes, of course, it's just the time to try out a horse when help is needed. The doctor will probably be thrown into a ditch, too," said Varvara Alexeyevna, looking at her knitting from under her pince-nez and holding it right up to the lamp.

"Well, he had to be sent for somehow, and I did the best I could."

"Yes, I remember very well how your horses rushed me up to the porch."

This was a very old invention of hers, and Yevgeny now had the rashness to say that it had not been quite like that.

"It's not for nothing that I always say – and how many times I've told the prince, too – that the most difficult thing of all is to live with people who are untruthful, insincere; I can stand anything but that."

"After all, I'm the man who suffers most, if anyone does," said Yevgeny.

"Oh yes, one can see that!"

"What?"

"Nothing. I'm counting stitches."

At that time Yevgeny was standing by the bed. Liza looked at him, took his hand with one of her own moist ones that were lying on the blankets, and squeezed it. "Please put up with her for my sake. She doesn't prevent us from loving each other," her look seemed to say.

"It doesn't matter," he whispered, and he kissed her long, moist hand, and then her dear eyes, which she closed while he was kissing them.

"Is it really the same thing again?" he said. "How do you feel?"

"I'm terrified of saying it, in case I'm mistaken, but I feel that it is alive and will live," she said, looking at her stomach.

"Oh, it's terrifying even to think of."

In spite of Liza's insistence that he should go away, Yevgeny spent the night with her, falling asleep with one eye open and ready to wait on her. But she spent a good night, and if they had not sent for the doctor she might even have got up.

The doctor arrived at lunch time and, naturally, said that although repeated phenomena might, of course, cause apprehension, yet, strictly speaking, there was no positive indication, but as there was no negative indication either, one could assume, on the one hand, and of course one could assume on the other, too... And therefore she must stay in bed and, although he did not like prescriptions, yet all the same she must take this one and stay in bed. In addition he gave Varvara Alexeyevna a lecture on female anatomy, in the course of which Varvara Alexeyevna nodded her head significantly. When his fee, as usual, had been slipped into his hand, the doctor drove away, and the patient stayed in bed for a week.

15

YEVGENY SPENT MOST OF HIS TIME at his wife's bedside; he waited on her, talked to her, read with her and, most difficult of all, bore Varvara Alexeyevna's attacks without complaint, and even contrived to turn them into a joke.

But he could not stay at home all the time. First, his wife sent him away, saying that he would get ill if he sat with her all the time, and second, the estate was managed in a way that demanded his presence at every step. He could not sit at home, but spent his time in the fields, in the wood, in the garden, on the threshing floor – and everywhere, not only the thought, but the living image of Stepanida pursued him, so that he rarely forgot about her. But that was not so bad; he might, perhaps, have been able to repress this feeling, but what was far worse was the fact that, whereas formerly he had lived for months without seeing her, now he was continually seeing her and meeting her. She, obviously, had understood that he wanted to renew his relations with her, and she was trying to run into him. Nothing was said, either by him or by her, and so neither he nor she arranged a meeting outright; they just tried to come across each other.

One place where it was possible for them to run into each other was the wood, where the peasant women used to go with sacks to collect grass for the cows. Yevgeny knew this, and because of it he went past this wood every day. Every day he told himself that he would not go there, and every day it ended in him making his way to the wood and, hearing the sound of voices, he would stand still behind a bush and look with a sinking heart to see if it was her.

Why did he need to know if it was her? He did not know. If it had been her, and if she had been alone, he would not have gone to her – or so he thought; he would have run away. But he had to see her. Once, he did meet her; as he was going into the wood she came out of it with two other women, carrying a heavy sack full of grass on her back. A moment earlier, and he might perhaps have run into her in the wood, but now she couldn't possibly go back into the wood to him, in front of the other women. But although he acknowledged this impossibility, he still stood for a long time behind a hazel bush, at the risk of attracting the attention of the other women. Of course, she did not come back, but he had stood there waiting for a long time. And – heavens! – what charm she had in his imagination! And this was by no means the first time that he so imagined her, but the fifth, the sixth time. And the more often he did it, the more charm she acquired in his imagination. She had never seemed so attractive to him. And not only attractive; never had she so completely possessed him.

He felt that he was losing all self-control, that he was becoming almost insane. His sternness with himself had not weakened a jot; on the contrary, he saw all the loathsomeness of his desires, of his deeds even, for his walks in the woods were a deed. He knew that he only had to run into her somewhere, to touch her in the dark, if possible, and he would abandon himself to his feeling. He knew that he was only held back by his sense of shame – shame of other people, of her, and of himself. And he knew that he was seeking circumstances in which this shame would not be apparent – either the dark, or some contact which would smother shame with animal passion. And therefore he knew that he was a loathsome criminal, and despised and hated himself with all his soul. He hated himself because he was still refusing to yield; every day he prayed to God to give him strength and save him from perdition; every day he made up his mind never again to take another step, never to look at her, to forget her. Every day he invented means of ridding himself of this temptation, and he used those means.

But it was all in vain.

One of the means he had invented was continual occupation; another was strenuous physical labour and fasting; a third was calling up a clear mental picture of the shame that would overtake him when everyone found out about it – his wife, his mother-in-law, his servants. He would do all this, and would feel that victory was his, but then midday would come, the time of their former meetings and the time when he had met her with the grass, and he would go to the wood.

So passed five agonizing days. He only saw her from a distance, but did not meet her once.

16

LIZA SLOWLY RECOVERED, began to walk again and worried about the change which had taken place in her husband, which she did not understand.

Varvara Alexeyevna went away for a time, and the only stranger staying with them was Yevgeny's uncle. As always, Marya Pavlovna was at home.

Yevgeny was in this semi-insane state when, as often happens after June thunderstorms, there was torrential June rain which continued for two days. The rain made all work impossible – even manure was no longer carted because of the damp and dirt. All the peasants stayed indoors. The shepherds had trouble with their flocks, and finally drove them home. The cows and sheep went through the common and scattered in the farms. The women, barefoot and covered with kerchiefs, went splashing through the mud and rushed about searching for stray cows. Streams ran everywhere along the roads; all the grass and the leaves were covered with water; streams never ceased flowing from the gutters into bubbling pools. Yevgeny sat at home with his wife, whom he found particularly boring that day. She questioned Yevgeny several times on the reason for his bad mood, but he answered with annoyance that there was nothing wrong. She stopped asking him, but she was hurt.

They were sitting in the drawing room after lunch. His uncle was telling them, for the hundredth time, entirely untrue stories about his high-society friends. Liza was knitting a little coat and sighing, complaining about the weather and the pain in her back. His uncle advised her to lie down, and asked for some wine for himself. Yevgeny was terribly bored in the house. Everything was lifeless and boring. He was reading a book and smoking, but he did not understand what he was reading.

"Oh, I must go and see the rasping machine – they brought it yesterday," he said, and he got up and went out.

"You'd better take an umbrella."

"Oh no, I've got a leather coat. And I'm only going to the boiler house."

He put on his boots and his leather coat and went to the factory. But he had not gone twenty yards when he ran into her. She was coming to meet him with her skirt tucked up high over her white calves, and she was holding a shawl which was wrapped round her head and shoulders.

"What are you doing?" he asked, not recognizing her at first. When he did recognize her, it was too late. She stopped and looked at him for a long time, smiling.

"I'm looking for a calf. Where are you going to in this dreadful weather?" she asked, as if she saw him every day.

"Come to the hut," he said suddenly, not knowing himself why he said it. It was exactly as if someone else had said those words from inside him.

She bit at her kerchief so as to hold it on, indicated with her eyes that she agreed, and ran off in the direction in which she had been going – into the garden to the hut – whereas he continued on his way, intending to turn round behind a lilac bush and to go there, too.

"Oh, sir!" he heard a voice behind him. "The mistress is calling for you. She wants you to come for a minute."

It was Misha, their servant.

"Oh, God. You have saved me for the second time," thought Yevgeny, and went back to the house immediately. His wife reminded him that he had promised to take some medicine to a sick woman, so she asked him to take it.

While the medicine was being prepared, about five minutes elapsed. Then, when he went out taking the medicine with him, he did not dare go to the hut in case someone might see him from the house. But no sooner was he out of sight than he turned round immediately and went to the hut. In his imagination he already saw her in the middle of the hut, smiling gaily, but she was not there, and there was nothing in the hut to show that she had been there. He began to think that she had not come, that she had not heard or had not understood his words. He muttered them to himself under his breath, as if fearing that she might hear them. "Or perhaps she didn't want to come? Why should I think that she would throw herself at me like that? She has her husband; I'm the only one to be such a cad; I have a wife, and a good wife, and yet here I am running after someone else's." Thus he thought as he sat in the hut, which was leaking in one place and dripping from the thatch. "But what bliss it would be if she did come! Alone here, in this rain. If only I could have her in my arms, just once, and then come what may. Oh yes," he remembered. "If she was here, then I could see it by the imprint she's left on the ground." He looked at the path of trampled earth leading to the hut, where no grass grew, and the fresh trace of a bare foot was still imprinted on it. "Yes, she has been here. But now it's finished. I'll go straight to her, no matter where I see her. I'll go to her by night." He sat in the hut for a long time, and finally left it feeling worn out and defeated. He delivered the medicine, went home and lay down in his room, waiting for dinner.

17

BEFORE DINNER Liza came to see him. She was still trying to think what the reason for his bad mood could be. And so she told him that she was afraid he was displeased that they wanted to take her to Moscow for the birth of the child, but that she had now decided that she would stay at home and would on no account go to Moscow. He knew she was afraid of the actual delivery as well as of not giving birth to a healthy child, and he therefore could not help being touched by the ease with which she sacrificed it all out of love for him. Everything at home was so pleasant, so joyful and pure, but in his heart all was filthy, loathsome, horrible. The whole evening Yevgeny was tormented by his knowledge that, for all his sincere disgust at his own weakness, for all his firm resolve to put a stop to it, tomorrow would bring with it a repetition of the same thing.

"No, this is impossible," he said to himself, as he walked to and fro in his room. "Surely there must be some remedy against it? Oh God! What can I do?"

Someone knocked at his door, as foreigners do. This, he knew, was his uncle.

"Come in," he said.

His uncle had come as a self-appointed ambassador from his wife.

"You know, I do really notice a change in you," he said, "and I can see how it worries Liza. I can see that it's difficult for you to leave all the work that's already begun – and such fine work, too – but what's to be done, *que veux-tu*? I would advise you to go away for a bit. It'll be more peaceful, both for you and for her. And do you know, my advice is to go to the Crimea. There's the climate, and then there's a splendid doctor there, and you'll get there just for the grape season."

"Uncle," said Yevgeny suddenly. "Can you keep my secret, a terrible secret I have? A shameful secret!..."

"For Heaven's sake! Don't you trust me?"

"Uncle! You can help me. Not only help, you can save me," said Yevgeny. And the thought that he would disclose his secret to his uncle – for whom he had no respect – the thought that he would show himself to him in the most unfavourable light, that he would humble himself before him, pleased Yevgeny. He felt that he was loathsome, guilty, and he wanted to punish himself.

"Tell me, my boy. You know how fond I have become of you," said his uncle, obviously very pleased both that there was a secret and that it was a shameful one, and that he would be told of it, and that he might be of help.

"First of all I must tell you that I'm a blackguard and a cad, a scoundrel – that's it, a scoundrel."

"Come, come…" his uncle started, clearing his throat.

"Yes, I must be a scoundrel if I, Liza's husband, Liza's! – one has to know her purity, her love – if I, her husband, want to be unfaithful to her with a peasant woman!"

"But why do you want to? You haven't *been* unfaithful to her?"

"Yes – that is, I've as good as been unfaithful to her, because it did not depend on me. I was ready to do it. I was prevented, but I would now… I would now. I don't know what I would do."

"But, please, explain to me…"

"Well, it's like this. When I was a bachelor I was stupid enough to have relations with a woman here, from our village. That's to say, I used to meet her in the wood, in the field…"

"And was she pretty?" said his uncle.

Yevgeny winced at this question, but he needed external help so badly that he behaved as if he had not heard it, and went on.

"Well, I thought it was just like that, that I would break if off and it would all be finished. And I did break it off, before my marriage, and for nearly a year I didn't see her or think about her" – it seemed strange to Yevgeny to listen to himself, to listen to the description of his own state of mind – "then suddenly, I don't know why – really, sometimes one believes in witchcraft – I saw her, and a worm crept into my heart and is gnawing at it. I blame myself, and I understand the full horror of my action, that is, of what I might do at any minute, and yet I am ready to do it, and if I haven't done anything, it's only because God saved me. I was going to her yesterday, when Liza called me."

"What, in the rain?"

"Yes. I'm worn out by it, Uncle, and I've decided to tell you about it and to ask for your help."

"Yes, of course, it's not a good thing to do it on one's own estate. People will find out. I quite see that Liza is weak and that you must spare her, but why do it on your own estate?"

Once more Yevgeny tried not to hear what his uncle had said, and he came to the heart of the matter all the more quickly.

"But you must save me from myself. This is what I ask you to do. Today it was chance that prevented me from doing anything, but tomorrow, another time, I shall not be prevented. And she knows now. Don't leave me alone."

"Yes, you are right," said his uncle. "But are you really so much in love?"

"Oh, it's not that at all. It's not that, it's some kind of force that has seized me and holds me. I don't know what to do. Perhaps I'll become stronger, then…"

"Well, it all points to the same thing," said his uncle. "Let's go to the Crimea."

"Yes, yes, let's go, and while I'm with you I'll be able to keep you informed."

18

THE FACT OF ENTRUSTING HIS SECRET TO HIS UNCLE and, above all else, the pangs of conscience and shame that he had endured ever since that rainy day, sobered Yevgeny. They decided to go to Yalta in a week's time. During that week Yevgeny went to town to get money for the journey, worked at home and in the office, gave orders about his estate, and he felt cheerful again and close to his wife, and began to revive morally.

Thus, without once seeing Stepanida after that rainy day, he left for the Crimea with his wife. In the Crimea they spent two perfect months. Yevgeny had so many new impressions that it seemed to him as if all the past had been wiped from his memory. They met old friends in the Crimea and became even more friendly with them, and in addition they made new friends. Life there was a perpetual holiday for Yevgeny, besides being both useful and instructive. They made friends there with a former Marshal of Nobility of their own province, an intelligent, liberal-minded man who became fond of Yevgeny, taught him a great deal and gained his support. At the end of August Liza gave birth to a fine, healthy girl, and gave birth to her unexpectedly easily.

In September the Irtenyevs went home – four of them, including the baby and the wet nurse, as Liza could not feed the baby herself. Quite free from his former terrors, Yevgeny returned home a completely new and happy man. Having lived through all that husbands do live through at the birth of a child, he had grown to love his wife even more. The feeling which he had towards the baby when he took it in his arms was strange, new, and very pleasant – a ticklish feeling. There was something else new in his life now, too, apart from his work on the estate, for thanks to his friendship with Dumchin (the former Marshal of Nobility), a new interest had sprung up in his heart – an interest in local government problems, which was partly due to ambition and partly to a sense of duty. In October there was to be an extraordinary meeting, at which he was to be elected. After he came home he went once to town, and once to see Dumchin.

He never so much as spared a thought for his torments of temptation and moral struggle, and only with difficulty could he reconstruct them in his imagination. It all seemed to him as something like a temporary fit of madness into which he had been plunged.

He felt so free from all that that he was not even afraid to ask the bailiff about it at the first opportunity when they remained alone together. As he had already spoken to him about it he was not ashamed to ask him.

"Well, and is Sidor Pechnikov still not living at home?" he asked.

"No, he's still in town."

"And what about her?"

"Oh, she's a silly little thing! She's carrying on with Zinovy now. Quite a loose character she's become."

"Well, that's fine," thought Yevgeny. "It's amazing how little I care, and how I've changed."

19

ALL YEVGENY'S WISHES WERE FULFILLED. He had been able to keep the estate, the factory was a success, the beet crop was splendid and the profits were expected to be large; his wife had had a child with no trouble and his mother-in-law had gone away. And he was elected unanimously.

It was after his election, and Yevgeny was returning home from town. People congratulated him and he had had to thank them, and he had dined and drunk about five glasses of champagne. He now had quite new plans for life, and he thought about them as he was driving home. It was an Indian summer. The road was beautiful, the sun was bright. As he drove up to the house Yevgeny was thinking that, as a result of his election, he would have among the peasants just the position in which he would be able to serve them not just by farming, which provides work, but by direct influence. He was imagining how, in three years' time, his own and other peasants would judge him. "Like this one here," he thought, looking at a man and a woman who were crossing the road in front of him as he drove through the village. They stopped to let the carriage pass. The man was old Pechnikov, and the woman was Stepanida. Yevgeny looked at her, recognized her, and felt with joy that he remained completely unmoved. She was just as pretty as ever, but this did not affect him at all. He arrived home and his wife met him on the steps of the house. It was a beautiful evening.

"Well, can we offer you our congratulations?" said his uncle.

"Yes, they elected me."

"Well, that's splendid. We must celebrate."

The next morning Yevgeny rode over the estate, which he had been neglecting. A new threshing machine was working on the farm. While he was inspecting its work, Yevgeny walked among the peasant women, trying not to notice them. But no matter how he tried, he once or twice noticed the black eyes and red kerchief of Stepanida, who was carrying the straw. Once or twice he looked at her out of the corner of his eye and felt that again there was something, but could not quite realize what it was. Only on the following day, when he again rode over to the threshing floor at the farm and spent two hours there – quite unnecessarily – and let his eyes unceasingly fondle the familiar, beautiful figure of the young woman, did he feel that he was damned, utterly damned, irrevocably damned. Once more the same torments, once more all the horror and the terror – and there was no salvation.

And what he had expected did, in fact, happen to him. Without knowing himself how it came about he found himself in the evening of the very next day near her back yard, opposite her hay shed, where they had once met in the autumn. Pretending that he was going for a walk, he stopped there and smoked a cigarette. A neighbouring woman saw him and, as he was walking back, he heard her saying to someone: "Go on, he's waiting for you, I'll be bound, standing there. Go on, you fool!"

He saw a woman – it was her – run to the shed, but by then it was impossible for him to turn back because a peasant had just met him, and he went home.

20

WHEN HE WENT INTO THE DRAWING ROOM everything seemed strange and unnatural. He had got up in the morning still feeling cheerful and resolved to give her up, to forget, not to allow himself to think. But for some reason, not only did the morning's work fail to interest him, but he even tried to get rid of it. What had formerly seemed important to him and had given him pleasure had now lost all significance. He tried, unconsciously, to free himself from his business affairs. He felt that he must be free in order to thrash it out, to think it over. And he did get rid of his work, and remained alone. But as soon as he was alone he went off to wander about the garden, in the wood. And all those places were besmirched by memories, memories which held him in their grip. He realized that he was walking in the garden, and told himself that he was thinking something over, whereas he was not thinking about anything, but was frantically, unreasonably waiting for her, waiting for her to understand by some miracle how much he desired her, waiting for her to come there, or somewhere where no one would see, or to come to him at night, perhaps, when there would be no moon, and no one, not even she herself, would see, and on such a night she would come to him, and he would touch her body...

"So I *did* break it off when I wanted to!" he said to himself. "So I lived with a clean, healthy woman for my health's sake! Oh no, she obviously can't be trifled with like that. I thought that I had taken her, but it was she who took me; she took me and never let me go. Why, I thought that I was free, but I was not free. I deceived myself when I got married. It was all nonsense, deceit. Since I began to live with her I've experienced a new feeling, the true feeling of a husband. Yes, I *had* to live with her.

"Oh yes, there are two lives open to me: one is the life that I have started with Liza; service, the estate, the child, people's respect. If that is the life I want, then it is essential that she, Stepanida, should not be here. She must be sent away, as I said, or she must be destroyed, so that she would no longer be here. And the other life – that's here, too. Take her away from her husband, give him money, forget the shame and scandal, and live with her. But in that case there must be no Liza or Mimi (the child). No, the child wouldn't matter after all, but Liza must not be here, she must go away. If only she could find out about it, curse me, and go away. If she could find out that I have been unfaithful to her with a peasant woman, that I am a deceiver, a cad. No, that would be too dreadful! That's impossible. Oh, but perhaps it might happen," he went on thinking, "it might happen. Liza might get ill, and die. She might die, then everything would be lovely.

"Lovely! Oh, what a scoundrel I am! No, if anyone dies, it must be her. If she, Stepanida, were to die, what a good thing it would be.

"Oh yes, that's how people poison or kill their wives or mistresses. That's the way to do it – take a revolver and go and call her, and then, instead of an embrace, a bullet in the chest, and it's all over.

"She must be a devil! A real devil. It is, after all, against my will that she took possession of me.

"Kill someone? Yes. There are only two ways out: to kill my wife or to kill her. Because it's impossible to live like this.* Impossible. I must think it out and plan it. What will happen if things go on as they are?

"What will happen is that I shall tell myself again that I don't want her, that I'll give her up, but I shall only say it, and in the evening I shall go to her back yard again, and she will know it, and she will come. And either people will find out and tell my wife, or I shall tell her myself, because I can't lie to her. I can't live like that. I can't. It will be found out. Everyone will find out, even Parasha and the blacksmith. Well, then, how can I live like that?

"I can't. There are only two ways out: to kill my wife, or to kill her. Though still... Ah, yes, there is a third way: to kill myself," he said aloud, under his breath, and suddenly it made his flesh creep. "Yes, myself; then I wouldn't have to kill them." He felt terrified, precisely because he felt that only this way out was possible. "I have a revolver. Shall I really kill myself? That's something I never thought I should do. How strange it will be."

He went back to his own room, and immediately opened the cupboard which contained the revolver. But he had scarcely opened it when his wife came into the room.

21

H E THREW A NEWSPAPER over the revolver.

"Again the same," she said with alarm, as she looked at him.

"The same what?"

"The same terrible expression that you used to have before, when you didn't want to tell me. Zhenya, darling, tell me what the matter is. I can see you are suffering. Tell me, and you'll feel better. Whatever it may be, anything is better than this suffering of yours. Why, I know that it's nothing bad."

"You know?"

"Tell me, tell me, tell me. I won't let you go."

He smiled pathetically. "Tell you? No, that's impossible. And anyway, there's nothing to tell."

Perhaps he would have told her, but at that moment the nurse came into the room to ask if she could take the child out for a walk. Liza went to dress the child.

"So you will tell me? I'm just coming."

"Yes, perhaps…"

She could never forget the smile full of suffering with which he said this. She left the room.

Hurriedly, stealthily, like a bandit, he seized the revolver and drew it from its holster. "Yes, it's loaded, but that was a long time ago, and one cartridge is missing. Well, come what may."

He pressed it to his temple, almost hesitated, but no sooner did he think of Stepanida, of his decision not to see her, of the struggle, the temptation, the fall, of yet another struggle, than he shuddered with horror. "No, this is better." And he pressed the trigger.

When Liza ran into the room – she had only just come down from the balcony – he was lying face-downwards on the floor, the black, warm blood was gushing from the wound, and the corpse was still twitching.

There was an inquest. No one could explain or give reasons for the suicide. It never even entered his uncle's head that the reason had anything to do with the confession which Yevgeny had made to him two months previously.

Varvara Alexeyevna assured everyone that she had always foretold it – it had been obvious when he argued. Neither Liza nor Marya

Pavlovna could understand at all why it happened. Yet, all the same, they did not believe the doctors who said that he had been insane. They could not possibly agree with this, because they knew that he had been a great deal saner than hundreds of people of his acquaintance.

And indeed, if Yevgeny Irtenyev was insane, then all men are just as insane – and of those that are insane the most undoubtedly so are those who see signs of madness in other people which they do not see in themselves.

19th November 1889
Yasnaya Polyana

Alternative Ending of The Devil

...he said to himself and, going up to the table, he took a revolver from the drawer, inspected it – one cartridge was missing – and put it in his trouser pocket.

"My God! What am I doing?" he suddenly cried and, folding his hands, he started to pray.

"Oh Lord, help me, deliver me. Thou knowest that I do not want to do something wicked, but I cannot fight alone. Help me," he cried, crossing himself before the icon.

"But surely I can control myself; I'll go and walk for a bit and think things over."

He went out into the hall, put on a fur coat and galoshes and went out. Unconsciously his steps led him past the garden along the field path, to the farm. At the farm the threshing machine was still droning and he could hear the shouts of the boys driving it. He went into the threshing barn. She was there. He saw her at once. She was raking the corn together and, as she caught sight of him, she ran swiftly through the scattered ears of corn, looking pert and gay, her eyes laughing. Yevgeny did not want to look at her, but could not help it. He only came to when she disappeared out of sight. The bailiff reported that they were now threshing grain that had deteriorated in store, and that, consequently, it took longer and the output of grain was smaller. Yevgeny went up to the drum, which was knocking now and again as the badly spread sheaves went through it, and asked the bailiff if there were many sheaves that were spoiled like that.

"It should be about five cart-loads."

"Well, then..." Yevgeny started, and did not finish what he was saying. She had come up to the drum, raking the wheat-ears from under it, and scorched him with her laughing gaze.

That gaze spoke of the gay, light-hearted love between them, of how she knew that he desired her, that he had come to her in the barn, and that she, as always, was ready to live and enjoy herself with him, with no thought for any conditions or consequences. Yevgeny felt himself in her power, but did not want to surrender.

He remembered his prayer and tried to repeat it. He started to say it to himself, but immediately felt that it was useless. One thought alone now dominated him entirely: how to arrange a meeting with her so that no one else would notice?

"If we finish this today, may we start a new rick, or shall we wait till tomorrow?" asked the bailiff.

"Yes, yes," Yevgeny answered, and involuntarily moved after her, towards the pile of wheat-ears which she and another woman were raking together.

"Am I really unable to control myself?" he said to himself. "Am I really damned? Oh God! But no, there is no God. There's a devil. And she is it. But I don't want it, I don't want it. A devil, yes, a devil."

He went right up to her, drew the revolver out of his pocket and once, twice, three times shot her in the back. She ran and fell on the pile of chaff.

"Oh, Lord! Heavens! What's all this?" the women screamed.

"No, I didn't do it by accident. I killed her on purpose!" shouted Yevgeny. "Send for the police."

He walked home and without saying anything to his wife he went up to his study and locked the door.

"Don't come to me!" he shouted through the door to his wife. "You'll find out all about it!"

An hour later he rang the bell, and said to the servant: "Go and find out if Stepanida is alive."

The servant had already found out everything, and said that she died an hour ago.

"Very well. Now leave me alone. When the police or the magistrate come, tell me."

The police and the magistrate came the next morning, and Yevgeny, after taking leave of his wife and child, was taken to prison.

He was tried. It was in the early days of trial by jury.* He was recognized as temporarily of unsound mind and condemned only to religious penance.

He spent nine months in prison and one month in a monastery.

He began to drink while he was still in prison, went on doing so in the monastery, and returned home a weak, irresponsible dipsomaniac.

Varvara Alexeyevna assured everyone that she had always foretold this – it had been clear when he argued. Neither Liza nor Marya Pavlovna could understand why it had happened at all, and yet did not believe what the doctors said, that he was insane, a psychopath. They could not agree with this, because they knew that he was saner than hundreds of people of their acquaintance.

And indeed, if Yevgeny Irtenyev was insane when he committed his crime, then everyone is insane – and the most insane are undoubtedly those who see signs of madness in others which they do not see in themselves.

Notes

p. 109, *like this*: The alternative version of the ending starts here.
p. 114, *early days... jury*: A reference to the extreme leniency with which the early juries in Russia exercised their functions.

Family Happiness

Translated by April FitzLyon

Preface

IT IS NOT KNOWN PRECISELY WHEN Tolstoy began to write *Family Happiness*, but he was working on it in 1858, and the novella was first published in 1859 in the first two April issues of the periodical *Russkiy Vestnik (Russian Messenger)*; it is, therefore, an early work.

Like almost all Tolstoy's novels, *Family Happiness* has an autobiographical character. In a letter to his biographer, Biryukov, dated 27 November 1903, Tolstoy wrote: "then, most important of all, there was something really serious – Valerya Arsenyeva. She is still alive, married a Volkov, and is living in Paris. I was almost engaged to her (*Family Happiness*) and there are a lot of bundles of letters which I wrote to her."

Valerya Vladimirovna Arsenyeva was born in 1836 and died in Basel in 1909. Tolstoy met her in 1856 – her parents' estate, Sundakova, was not far from Yasnaya Polyana – and fell in love with her. Her daughter told P. Pavlov in 1926[1] that they finally parted company because Valerya refused to accept the conditions which Tolstoy attached to his proposal of marriage: twenty years' quiet seclusion in the country.

There are a few similarities between Tolstoy and Valerya and Sergey Mikhailovich and Masha in the novel. For example, Tolstoy was eleven years older than Valerya, was guardian to her little brother, and they lived on neighbouring estates. But it cannot be said that the story is based on Tolstoy's relationship with Valerya, for they were never married, and *Family Happiness* is the story of a marriage. It seems rather that Tolstoy wrote the novella in order to prove to himself that, if he had married Valerya, the marriage would probably not have been a success. Tolstoy's attitude to the book seems to confirm this theory. While he was writing it he was most enthusiastic about it, and described it as "a poem", but when he had finished it he disliked it intensely and was even reluctant to have it published. It seems probable that, by the time the book was finished, Tolstoy had already lost interest both in Valerya – who was already married to someone

---

1. See *The Slavonic Review*, January 1929.

else by then – and in the ideas which had originally prompted him to write the story.

Family Happiness was not received with particular enthusiasm when it was first published, although two discerning critics – Apollon Grigoryev and V.P. Botkin – thought highly of it. A contemporary critic said scathingly that mothers could certainly give *Family Happiness* to their daughters without fearing any ill effects, which shows to what an extent the novel was misunderstood. It seems nowadays that Tolstoy's subtle description of how marriage can transform the dreams of youth into the grey, everyday relationship of habit described at the end of the book was hardly encouraging reading for unmarried girls at a time when marriage was supposed to be the be-all and end-all of an educated girl's existence. Critics found the end of the story "unsatisfactory". Translators, both French and English, apparently thought the last paragraph unsatisfactory too, so they changed it. In one case, at least, a translator not only changed the character of the book with a single sentence, but also altered the influence which the book had on subsequent writers. F.W.J. Hemmings, in *The Russian Novel in France, 1884–1915* (OUP, 1950), describes the influence which Tolstoy's ideas – and more particularly his ideas on family life – had on certain French writers, especially on Paul Margueritte and Edouard Rod. In order to illustrate this point, Hemmings quotes the last paragraph of *Family Happiness* in the following version; the name of the translator is not stated:

The old (romantic) feeling stayed among those sweet memories to which there is no returning, and a new feeling of love for my children and for the father of my children marked the start of a new existence differently happy, and which I am still enjoying, *convinced that the reality of happiness is in the home and among the unsullied joys of family life.*

The words in italics were not written by Tolstoy, who left the reader having to make up their own mind whether the title of the book was – or was not – ironical.

Family Happiness is written in the first person, from the heroine's point of view – a difficult feat for a young man, not yet married. Tolstoy had an uncanny ability to get under the skin of his characters, and his subtle description of a young girl's emotions before and after marriage is masterly. Yet it is a depressing fact that Tolstoy, who could analyse feminine psychology and women's problems in marriage so subtly on paper, was quite incapable of seeing the woman's point of view in real life; his own marriage was a tragedy for this very reason. He remained an unrepentant anti-feminist to the end of his days, despite the fact that by 1910, when he died, public opinion, particularly in Russia, had become much more sympathetic to women and to female emancipation. Although, in *Family Happiness*, it is Masha and Masha's problems and feelings which come to life and ring true, Tolstoy himself identified with her husband. Yet, as V.P. Botkin pointed out when the novel was first published, "despite the repulsive puritanism in the book, the presence of a great talent continually makes itself felt".

April FitzLyon

1

K ATYA, SONYA AND I spent the whole winter by ourselves in the coun-try; we were in mourning for my mother, who had died in the autumn.

Katya was an old friend of the family, the governess who had brought us all up and whom I remembered and had loved ever since I could remember myself. Sonya was my younger sister. We spent a gloomy and depressing winter in our old house at Pokrovskoye. The weather was cold and windy so that snowdrifts swept up higher than the windows, which were almost always frosted and dimmed; we hardly went anywhere the whole winter. We had few visitors, and those that did come brought no gaiety or joy to our house. They all had long faces and talked in low voices as if afraid of waking somebody, they did not laugh, but would sigh and often – as they looked at me, and particularly at little Sonya in her black dress – they would weep. Death still seemed to make itself felt in the house; the grief and horror of death lingered in the air. Mamma's room was locked; every time I went past it on my way to bed I felt terrified, and yet something drew me to look into that cold and empty room.

I was then seventeen; in the very year of her death Mamma had wanted to move to town to bring me out. The loss of my mother was a great grief to me, but I must confess that this grief was partly enhanced by the feeling that I was young and pretty – as everyone told me – and that, for the second winter in succession, I was uselessly killing time in the seclusion of the country. Towards the end of the winter this feeling of depression, induced by solitude as well as simple boredom, grew so much that I seldom left my room and never even opened the piano or picked up a book. When Katya tried to persuade me to occupy myself in some way, I replied: "I don't feel like it, I can't," but in my heart I asked: "What for? What's the use of doing anything when my best years are being uselessly wasted?" And tears were the only answer to this question.

I was told that I had grown thinner and was losing my looks at that time, but even this did not interest me. What for? For whom? It seemed to me that the whole of my life must be spent in that lonely backwater and helpless depression from which, alone, I had neither the strength nor even the will to escape. As the end of winter approached Katya began to worry about me, and decided to take me abroad at all costs. But to do this we needed money, and we scarcely knew what my mother had left us; we were daily expecting our guardian, who was supposed to come and look into our affairs.

In March our guardian arrived.

"Thank goodness!" Katya said to me, as I wandered aimlessly about like a shadow, with nothing to do, without any thoughts or wishes. "Sergey Mikhailovich has arrived. He has sent to enquire about us, and would like to come to dinner. Pull yourself together, Mashechka," she added. "Whatever will he think of you otherwise? He used to be so fond of you all."

Sergey Mikhailovich was a near neighbour of ours and, although much younger than my father, had been a friend of his. Apart from the fact that his arrival changed our plans and made it possible for us to leave for town, I had been accustomed to love and respect him since childhood. When Katya advised me to pull myself together she guessed that I should mind appearing in an unfavourable light to Sergey Mikhailovich more than to any of our other friends. Besides, although like everyone else in the house from Katya and Sonya – his god-daughter – down to the last coachman, I loved him from habit; for me he had a special significance because of a remark which Mamma had once made in my presence. She had said that she hoped for just such a husband for me. Then this idea had seemed extraordinary to me and even unpleasant; my ideal was quite different. I imagined my hero as thin and spare, pale and sad; whereas Sergey Mikhailovich was no longer in his first youth, was tall and thickset and, it seemed to me, always cheerful. But in spite of this, these words of my mother's took root in my imagination and, even six years before, when I was eleven years old and he used to say *tu* to me, when he would play with me and call me his "little violet", I sometimes asked myself – not without alarm – what I would do if he should suddenly want to marry me.

Sergey Mikhailovich arrived before dinner, for which Katya had prepared spinach sauce and a special cream pudding. From the window I saw him drive up to the house in a small sleigh, but as soon as he reached the corner I hurried into the drawing room, wanting to pretend that I was not expecting him at all. However, when I heard the clatter of feet in the hall, his loud voice and Katya's footsteps, I could contain myself no longer and went out to meet him. He was talking loudly and was smiling, holding Katya's hand. When he saw me he stopped, and looked at me for a few minutes without greeting me. I began to feel uncomfortable, and felt myself blushing.

"Ah! Can it really be you?" he said in his resolute and simple way, holding out his arms and coming towards me. "How can one change so much! Where's the violet now? It's a rose you've turned into!"

He took my hand in his own large one, and squeezed it warmly and so hard that it almost hurt. I thought he would kiss my hand and I bent towards him, but he only squeezed my hand again and looked me straight in the eyes, steadily and cheerfully.

I had not seen him for six years. He had changed a great deal: he had become older and swarthier, and had grown side-whiskers which did not suit him at all, but his simple manner was the same, it was the same strong-featured, frank and honest face with bright, intelligent eyes and the same kind, almost childish smile.

In five minutes he had ceased to be a guest and had become one of the family to all of us, even to the servants who particularly welcomed his arrival, as was shown by their eagerness to be of service to him.

He did not behave at all like the neighbours who visited us after Mamma's death, and who felt obliged to sit with us silently and with tears in their eyes; on the contrary, he was talkative and cheerful, and did not mention Mamma at all, so that at first his indifference seemed odd to me, and even out of place on the part of such a close friend. But later I understood that it was not indifference but sincerity, and I was grateful for it. Later on in the evening, Katya sat in her old place in the drawing room and poured out the tea, as she had done in my mother's time; Sonya and I sat beside her; old Grigory found a pipe of Papa's and brought it to Sergey Mikhailovich, who paced up and down the room as in the old days.

"What a lot of terrible changes this house has lived through, when one thinks of it!" he said, standing still.

"Yes," said Katya with a sigh, putting the lid on the samovar; she looked at him, and was already on the verge of tears.

"You, I think, can remember your father?" he said, turning to me.

"Very slightly," I replied.

"How well you would have got on with him now!" he said quietly and thoughtfully, looking at my forehead. "I loved your father very much!" he added, even more quietly, and it seemed to me that his eyes shone.

"And now God has taken her too!" said Katya, and at once put her napkin on the teapot, brought out her handkerchief, and burst into tears.

"Yes, this house has seen terrible changes," he repeated, turning away. "Sonya, show me your toys," he added after a moment, and went into the drawing room. When he had gone I looked at Katya with my eyes full of tears.

"He is such a good friend!" she said.

And indeed I somehow felt warmed and comforted by the sympathy of this man, a stranger, and yet so kind.

Sonya's squeals and the sound of his romping with her came from the drawing room. I sent him some tea; we heard him sit down at the piano, and he started to bang the keys with Sonya's little hands.

"Marya Alexandrovna!" I heard him call. "Come here and play something!"

I was pleased that he addressed me in such a friendly and peremptory way; I got up and went to him.

"Here, play this," he said, opening the Beethoven album at the *adagio* of the sonata *quasi una fantasia*. "Let's see how you play," he added, and took his tea to a corner of the room.

I felt for some reason that I could neither refuse him nor make the excuse that I played badly; I sat down obediently at the piano and began to play as best I could, although I feared his judgement, for I knew that he loved and understood music. The *adagio* was in keeping with the spirit of reminiscence which had been evoked by the conversation at tea, and I think I played it quite well. But he would not let me play the *scherzo*. "No, you don't play this well," he said coming up to me. "Leave this, but the first wasn't bad. You're musical, I think." This moderate praise made me blush from sheer happiness. It was so strange and pleasant that he, a friend and equal of my father's, should be speaking to me seriously, as one grown-up to another, no longer treating me as a child as he had formerly. Katya went upstairs to put Sonya to bed, and we remained together in the drawing room.

He told me about my father, about how they had become friends, and of the good times they had had together when I was still in the schoolroom and playing with toys, and in his stories my father for the first time appeared to me as a simple and lovable man, such as I had never known him until then. He also asked me what I liked, what I read, and what I intended to do, and gave me his advice. He no longer seemed to me a humorist and a gay wag who would tease me and make toys for me, but a serious person, simple and affectionate, to whom I felt drawn and for whom I had involuntary respect. I felt happy and at ease, yet at the same time, in spite of myself, I was conscious of a certain tension while talking to him. I weighed every word I said; I was so anxious to be worthy of his love for my own sake and not to win it only – as I had done so far – because I was my father's daughter.

When she had put Sonya to bed, Katya rejoined us, and she complained to him about my listlessness, which I had not mentioned.

"She didn't tell me the most important thing!" he said, smiling and reproachfully shaking his head at me.

"What is there to tell?" I said. "It's very boring, and anyway it will pass." I now really thought that my depression would pass, that it had already passed, that, indeed, it had never existed.

"It's a bad thing not to be able to stand solitude," he said. "Are you really a grown-up young lady?"

"Of course I'm a young lady," I replied, laughing.

"No; a young lady who is only alive so long as she is admired, but as soon as she is alone lets herself go and finds no delight in anything, is not a real young lady: everything for show and nothing for herself."

In order to say something I said: "You've got a fine opinion of me!"

"No!" After a moment's silence he continued: "You're not like your father for nothing. You have *something*..." and his kind, attentive, way of looking at me once more flattered and pleasantly disconcerted me.

It was only then that I noticed that, in spite of having what seemed at first sight a cheerful face, he had his own particular way of looking at one; direct to begin with, but increasingly attentive and somewhat sad.

"You mustn't and you can't be bored," he said. "You have your music, which you appreciate, books, study, your whole life is in front of you, and you must prepare yourself for it now, or else you will regret it later. In a year's time it will already be too late."

He spoke to me as a father or an uncle, and I felt that he was constantly restraining himself from speaking to me as an equal. I was hurt that he should consider me beneath him, and at the same time I was pleased that he should think it necessary to try to be something different just for me.

For the rest of the evening he talked business with Katya.

"Well, goodbye, dear friends," he said, getting up and taking my hand.

"When shall we see you again?" Katya asked.

"In the spring," he replied, still holding my hand. "I'm going to Danilovka now" – our other estate – "I'll see how things are and do what I can there, then I'll go to Moscow on my own business, and then, in the summer, we shall see something of each other."

"Shan't we really see you all that time?" I said sadly, and indeed, I already hoped to see him every day: I suddenly felt miserable and afraid that my depression would return. I must have revealed this by my look and tone of voice.

"You must study more – and don't mope," he said in a way which seemed to me too cold and forthright. "And in spring I will set you an examination," he added, letting go my hand and not looking at me.

In the hall, where we were standing to see him off, he hurriedly put on his fur coat, and again avoided looking at me. "There's no point in him trying like that!" I thought. "Does he really think I like it so much when he looks at me? He's a good man, a very good man... but that's all."

However, that evening Katya and I stayed awake very late and talked, not of him, but of how we would spend the coming summer, of where and how we would live in the winter. The dreadful question: what for? no longer arose in my mind. It seemed both simple and obvious that one must live in order to be happy, and my future appeared very happy. It was as if life and light had suddenly flooded our gloomy old house at Pokrovskoye.

2

IN DUE COURSE SPRING CAME. My former depression had left me, and was succeeded by the dreamy melancholy of springtime, full of ill-defined hopes and longings. Although I no longer spent my time as I had done at the beginning of winter, but now gave lessons to Sonya, played the piano and read, I would often go out into the park and wander for hours along its avenues, or sit on a bench and give myself up to heaven knows what thoughts, what wishes and hopes! Sometimes, too, I would sit up all night at my window, especially on moonlit nights, and sometimes I would slip on a jacket and would steal out into the garden unbeknown to Katya, and would run through the dew to the pond, and one night I even went as far as the field and walked all round the garden by myself.

Looking back, I find it hard to remember and to understand the dreams which then filled my imagination. Even when I do recall them, I find it difficult to believe that those were really my dreams, so strange were they and so far removed from life.

At the end of May Sergey Mikhailovich returned from his travels, as he had promised.

The first time he came to see us he arrived in the evening, when we were not expecting him at all. We were sitting on the terrace, and were just about to have tea. The garden was already covered in green, and nightingales had made their homes in the overgrown flower bushes for the whole of June. The tops of the flowery lilac bushes around us were strewn with white and mauve, with flowers just starting to bloom, and the foliage of the birch avenue was transparent in the setting sun. The terrace lay in a cool shade, and a heavy dew covered the grass. From the yard beyond the garden came sounds of the day drawing to its close, the sound of the cattle being driven in; Nikon, the village simpleton, rode along the path in front of the terrace with a barrel, and the cool stream of water from the watering-can made dark circles in the freshly dug earth round the dahlias and their supports. On the terrace the shining, well-polished samovar stood boiling on the white tablecloth in front of us, and there were pretzels and cakes and cream for tea. Katya, with her podgy hands, was busily washing the cups. I was hungry after bathing, and without waiting for tea I was eating bread with thick, fresh cream. I was wearing a gingham blouse with open sleeves, and my wet hair was tied up in a handkerchief. Katya was the first to see him through the window.

"Ah! Sergey Mikhailovich!" she said. "We were just talking about you!"

I stood up, and wanted to go and change, but he caught me as I reached the door.

"Oh, one doesn't stand on ceremony in the country," he said, looking at the handkerchief round my head and smiling. "You don't mind being seen like that by Grigory and really I am just another Grigory so far as you are concerned." But it seemed to me that, even as he was speaking, he was looking at me in a way that Grigory would never have looked at me, and I felt uncomfortable.

"I won't be a minute," I said, as I left him.

"What's wrong with you as you are?" he called after me. "Just like a young peasant woman!"

"How strangely he looked at me," I thought as I hurriedly changed upstairs. "But anyway, thank goodness he's come; it will be more cheerful now!" I glanced at the mirror, ran gaily downstairs and, without concealing my haste, went out panting onto the terrace. He was sitting at the table and telling Katya about our affairs. Judging from what he was saying, our finances were in an excellent state; now we should only have to spend the summer in the country, and then we could either go to St Petersburg for the sake of Sonya's education, or go abroad.

"If only you could come abroad with us!" said Katya. "We shall be quite lost there by ourselves."

"Ah, if only I could go round the world with you!" he said, half in jest and half in earnest.

"Well, why not?" I said. "Let's go round the world!"

He smiled and shook his head.

"And what about my mother? What about my business?" he said. "But anyway, that's beside the point. Now, tell me what you've been doing all this time. You haven't been moping again?"

When I told him that while he had been away I had been busy and had not been bored, and when Katya confirmed what I said, he praised me and gave me encouragement both by what he said and by the way he looked at me, as if I was a child and as if he had a right to do so. I thought it essential to tell him, frankly and in great detail, all the good things that I had done, and to make a clean breast of everything which might displease him, as if at confession. It was such a lovely evening that when tea had been cleared away we remained on the terrace; I was so interested in the conversation that I never noticed how, little by little, the human sounds around us had died away. The scent of flowers grew stronger, heavy dew moistened the grass, in a nearby lilac bush a nightingale trilled and, on hearing our voices, became silent again; the starry sky seemed to envelop us.

I only noticed that it was getting dark when a bat suddenly flew noiselessly under the canvas awning of the terrace and fluttered round my white handkerchief. I squeezed myself against the wall and wanted to cry out – but the bat escaped from under the awning as silently and swiftly as it had come, and was lost to view in the dusk of the garden.

"How I love your Pokrovskoye," he said, interrupting the conversation. "I'd love to spend my life just sitting here on this terrace!"

"Well, why not?" said Katya. "Go on sitting here!"

"Ah! Go on sitting here!" he said. "Life doesn't sit still."

"Why don't you get married?" said Katya. "You'd make a splendid husband."

"Why? Because I like sitting still?" and he laughed. "No, Katerina Karlovna, it's already too late for you and me to marry. People have long since ceased to consider me eligible. I fully agree with them, and I can assure you that I feel all the better for it."

It seemed to me that somehow he said this with a kind of unnatural enthusiasm.

"What a thing to say! Thirty-six years old, and your life finished!" said Katya.

"Yes, it certainly is," he continued, "and all I want now is to sit still, whereas for marriage something else is needed. There, ask her what she thinks," he added, nodding at me. "Those are the people who should be married off, and you and I will wish them joy."

There was suppressed sadness and strain in his voice as he said this, which he could not hide from me. He was silent for a moment; neither Katya nor I said anything.

"Why, imagine," he continued, turning in his chair, "imagine if I, by some unfortunate fluke, were suddenly to marry a seventeen-year-old girl like Mash... like Marya Alexandrovna. It's an excellent example, I'm very glad it's happened like that – it's the best possible example."

I laughed, and could not understand at all what he was so glad about, and what it was that had happened.

"Now, tell me the truth, hand on your heart," he said, turning to me jokingly, "wouldn't you consider it a misfortune if you joined your life to that of an old, spent man who wants to sit still, whereas you have who knows what urges and desires?"

I felt uncomfortable and was silent, not knowing what to answer.

"Why, I'm not proposing to you," he said, laughing, "but tell me truthfully – is that the sort of husband you dream about when you walk along the garden paths alone in the evenings? And wouldn't it be a misfortune?"

"Not a misfortune…" I began.

"But anyway, not a good thing," he finished my sentence for me.

"No, but perhaps I may be mistak—"

But he interrupted me again.

"There, you see, she's absolutely right, and I am grateful for her frankness, and very glad that we've had this conversation. Besides, it would be the greatest misfortune for me," he added.

"What an odd man you are! You haven't changed a bit," said Katya, and left the terrace to give orders for dinner to be served.

We were both silent after Katya had left us, and, around us, all was silent too. Only the nightingale poured out its song over the garden, unhurriedly and calmly as nightingales do in the night, and no longer spasmodically and hesitantly as they do in the evening, and, for the first time that night, far away from the bottom of the ravine, another nightingale gave it an answering call. The one near us fell silent, as if listening for a minute, and then the sound of its even, clear trill came again, sharper and tenser than before. And there was majestic calm in those voices as they resounded in their own nocturnal world, a world alien to us. The gardener went to his bed in the greenhouse, and we could hear the sound of his thick boots on the path grow fainter in the distance. Down the hill, someone whistled shrilly twice, and then all was silent once more. A leaf stirred with scarcely a sound, the awning of the terrace fluttered, and a fragrant scent hovered in the breeze and flooded the terrace. After what had been said the silence made me feel uncomfortable, but I did not know what to say. I looked at him. In the dusk his bright eyes looked back at me.

"It's fine to be alive!" he said.

For some reason, I sighed.

"What?"

"It's fine to be alive!" he repeated.

We again became silent, and again I felt uncomfortable. I was thinking all the time that I had distressed him by agreeing that he was old, and I wanted to console him, but did not know how to do it.

"Well, goodbye," he said, getting up. "My mother is expecting me to supper; I've scarcely seen her today."

"But I wanted to play you a new sonata," I said.

"Another time," he said – coldly, it seemed to me.

"Goodbye."

I was now even more certain that I had hurt him, and felt sorry. Katya and I saw him off as far as the porch, and stood looking at the road along which he had disappeared. When the sound of his horse's hooves had died away I went round to the terrace, and again looked at the garden, into the dewy mist full of night sounds, and for a long time I stood there and saw and heard all that I wished to see and hear.

He came to see us again – a second and then a third time – and the awkwardness which had arisen because of our strange conversation vanished completely, and never again made itself felt. All through the summer he would visit us two or three times a week; I grew so accustomed to him that if ever he failed to visit us for some time my loneliness weighed on me, I became annoyed with him and felt that he was behaving badly in leaving me to myself. He treated me as if I were a young man with whom he was on particularly friendly terms, questioned me, provoked the frankest and most intimate discussions, gave advice, encouraged me, and would sometimes scold and restrain me. But, in spite of his constant efforts to keep on my level, I felt that, besides the part of him that I understood, there remained a whole alien world into which he did not consider it necessary to admit me, and it was this, above all, which maintained my respect for him and which attracted me to him. From Katya and the neighbours I knew that, besides looking after his old mother with whom he lived, and managing his estate, and besides his duties as our guardian, he had some sort of local government duties which were causing him a great deal of unpleasantness, but what he thought about all this, what were his convictions, his plans, his hopes, I could never find out from him. As soon as I brought the conversation round to his affairs he would frown in his own particular way, as if to say: "Come now, why should you bother about that?", and would change the subject. At first this used to offend me, but later on I became so used to the fact that we only discussed things which concerned me that I came to regard this as quite natural.

Another thing which annoyed me at first, but which I appreciated afterwards, was his complete indifference and almost contempt for my appearance. He never, either by word or look, so much as hinted to me that I was pretty, but on the contrary, would make a wry face and laugh when people complimented me on my looks in front of him. He even liked to find fault with my appearance, and to tease me about it. The fashionable hairstyles and dresses in which Katya liked to dress me up for smart occasions only provoked his mockery – which hurt kind Katya's feelings and, at first, disconcerted me. Katya, having decided in her own mind that I was attractive to him, could not understand at all how he could fail to like seeing a woman who attracted him appearing at her very best. I, on the other hand, soon understood what he wanted. He wished to believe that I was devoid of affectation and, once I had understood this, not a shadow of affectation did, in fact, remain in my dresses, my hairstyles, my movements, but then its place was taken by the very obvious affectation of simplicity, at a time when I could not yet be simple. I knew that he loved me, but whether as a child or as a woman I did not yet ask myself; I prized this love, and feeling that he considered me to be the best girl in the world, I could not but wish that this illusion should remain with him. And I deceived him involuntarily, but in deceiving him, I became better myself. I felt that it was better and more worthy to show the best side of my nature rather than that of my body. It seemed to me that he at once sized up my hair, my hands, my face, my habits – whatever they were, good or bad – and knew that I could not add anything to my external appearance, apart from a desire to deceive. But he did not know my inner self, because he loved it and because at that time it was growing and developing, and in that I could – and did – deceive him. How simple my relations with him became once I had understood this! My groundless confusion and constraint of movement left me completely. I felt that, no matter how he saw me, full face or in profile, sitting or standing, with my hair up or down – he knew all of me and, it seemed to me, was pleased with me as I was. I believe that if, contrary to his habits, he were to have told me, as others did, that I had a beautiful face, I would not even have been pleased. But how glad and happy I would feel when, after some remark I had made, he would look at me steadily and say in a voice charged with emotion to which he would try to give a jesting tone: "Yes, oh yes, you have *something* about you. I must say, you're a fine girl!"

And why did he reward me in this way, filling my whole heart with pride and joy? Because I had said that my heart was warmed by old

Grigory's love for his granddaughter, or because reading poetry moved me to tears, or because I had said that I preferred Mozart to Schulhoff. And it amazed me with what an extraordinary flair I guessed then what was good and what one should like, although at that time I had as yet no idea of what was good and what one should like. Many of my former tastes did not please him, and it was enough for him to show me, by a twitch of his eyebrow or a glance, that what I wanted to say displeased him; he had only to make his own particular, woeful and very slightly contemptuous expression, for me to think that I no longer liked what I had liked before. It sometimes happened that he just wanted to give me his advice about something, and I would feel that I already knew what he was going to say. He would look into my eyes as he asked me something, and his look would draw whatever thought he desired out of me. All my thoughts, all my feelings at that time were not my own, but were all his thoughts and feelings which suddenly became mine, which entered into my life and illuminated it. Without noticing it at all, I began to look at everything with different eyes: at Katya, at our servants, at Sonya, and at myself and my occupations. Books, which I had formerly read only in order to kill boredom, suddenly became one of my greatest pleasures in life – and only because we discussed books and read them together, and because he would bring them for me. Helping Sonya with her studies, giving her lessons, I used formerly to consider as onerous tasks which I forced myself to carry out only out of a sense of duty; he came to one of the lessons, and it became a joy for me to watch Sonya's progress. Before it had seemed an impossible task to learn a whole piece of music, but now, knowing that he would listen to it and, perhaps, praise me, I would play one passage forty times over, so that poor Katya would stop her ears up with cotton wool – but I was never bored. I phrased the same old sonatas somehow quite differently now, and they sounded quite different and much better. Even Katya, whom I loved and knew as well as I knew myself, changed in my eyes. Only now did I understand that she was under no obligation to be mother, friend and slave to us as she, in fact, was. I understood all the unselfishness and devotion of that loving creature, I understood all I owed to her, and I loved her all the more. He taught me, too, to look at the people who worked for us – at the peasants, at the servants and girls – in quite a different way. Ridiculous as it may seem, I had lived amongst these people for seventeen years, and yet had remained more alien to them than I was to people whom I never saw; I never once realized that they had loves and desires and regrets, as I had. Our garden, our woods, our fields which I had known for so long, suddenly became new and beautiful to me. He was right when he said that there was only one undoubted happiness in life – to live for others. It seemed strange to me then, and I did not understand it, but the truth of this imperceptibly entered my heart. He opened up a whole life of joy in the present, changing nothing in my life and adding nothing to it – apart from adding himself to every impression. Everything which had silently surrounded me since childhood suddenly came alive. It was enough for him to appear, for all things to begin speaking to me, vying with each other to attain my innermost heart, and filling it with happiness.

During that summer I would often go upstairs to my room and lie down on the bed, and instead of the former nostalgia of spring and desires and hopes for the future, anxiety for my present happiness would envelop me. I could not fall asleep, and would get up and sit on Katya's bed and tell her that I was completely happy – which, when I think of it now, it was quite unnecessary to tell her, for she could see it for herself. But she would tell me that she, too, needed nothing, that she, too, was very happy – and she would kiss me. I believed her, for it seemed to me so essential and just that everyone should be happy. But Katya could think of sleep as well, and would even sometimes pretend to be annoyed and would drive me off her bed and fall asleep; whereas I would lie awake for hours analysing the reasons for my happiness. Sometimes I would get up and say my prayers again, praying in my own words to thank God for all the happiness which He had given me.

It was quiet in the room; only Katya breathed sleepily and evenly, the clock ticked near her, and I would turn round and whisper words to myself, or I would make the sign of the cross over myself and kiss the cross hanging round my neck. The doors were closed, the windows were shuttered, a fly or gnat would stir and buzz somewhere. I felt that I never wanted to leave that little room, I did not wish for morning to come, I did not want the spiritual atmosphere surrounding me to dissolve. I felt that my dreams, my thoughts and prayers were live creatures, living there in the darkness with me, flying round my bed and standing over me. And every thought was his thought, and every feeling his feeling. I did not know then that this was love; I thought that one could have this feeling at any time, for no reason.

3

O NE DAY, AT HARVEST TIME, I went into the garden after dinner with
Katya and Sonya to our favourite bench in the shade of the lime
trees by the ravine, from which there was a view of the wood and fields.
Three days had passed since Sergey Mikhailovich had visited us, and
that day we were expecting him, especially as our bailiff had told us
that he had promised to come across the fields. At about two o'clock
we saw him on horseback, riding through a field of rye. Katya ordered
peaches and cherries – which he liked very much – to be brought and,
lying down on the bench, she looked at me with a smile and began to
doze. I broke off a crooked, flat branch of lime with sappy leaves and
bark that moistened my hand and, as I fanned Katya with it, I went
on reading, frequently stopping to look at the path through the field
by which he should arrive. Sonya was building a summer-house for
her dolls at the foot of the old lime tree. The day was hot and still, it
was very close, and dark clouds were piling up and growing darker;
ever since morning a storm had been gathering. I was tense, as always
before a storm. But after midday the clouds began to thin out round
the edges, the sun emerged in a clear sky; only in the distance a faint
roll of thunder could be heard, and an occasional flash of lightning
sent pale zig-zags down to earth, cutting through a heavy cloud which
spread over the horizon and merged with the dust on the fields. It was
clear that the storm would disperse that day – at any rate where we
were. Along the road, parts of which could be seen beyond the garden, an endless succession of high carts loaded with sheaves slowly
creaked along, while towards them empty carts rattled fast, making
the legs of the peasants sitting on them shake and their shirts flap. The
thick dust was not carried away, and did not settle, but hovered over the
fence between the transparent foliage of the garden trees. Further off,
in the field where the threshing was taking place, the same voices and
squeaking wheels could be heard, the same yellow sheaves which had
been slowly moving past the fence were there flying through the air,
and before my eyes oval houses were growing, with pointed roofs and
with the figures of peasants swarming on them. In front of us, in the
dusty field, carts were moving too, the same yellow sheaves were there,
and the same sounds of carts, of voices and songs reached us from afar.
At one end of the field the expanse of stubble was gradually growing,

streaked through with balks overgrown with wormwood. The brightly coloured dresses of the women could be seen a little further down to the right in the unsightly and entangled mown field, as the women bent down and gesticulated, binding the sheaves, and the entangled field was becoming clearer, and beautiful sheaves were being stacked on it close to each other. It was as if suddenly, before my eyes, summer was turning to autumn. Dust and heat lay everywhere, except on our favourite spot in the garden. From every side, in the dust and heat of the burning sun, came the clamour of the labouring folk as they walked and moved about.

Katya was snoring so peacefully under her white cambric handkerchief on our cool bench, the cherries shone so juicily and black on the plate, our dresses were so fresh and clean, the water in the jug shone with such rainbow lights in the sunshine, and I – I had such a sense of well-being. "What can I do?" I thought. "Can I help being happy? But how can I share my happiness? How and to whom can I give my whole self, and all my happiness?..."

The sun had already set behind the top of the birch avenue, dust was settling on the field, the air became clearer and more luminous in the slanting light, the clouds had quite dispersed; from behind the trees the tops of three new hayricks could be seen on the threshing floor, and the peasants climbed down from them; carts bumped along, obviously for the last time, peasant women with rakes on their shoulders and binding-twine in their belts were going home, singing loudly, but Sergey Mikhailovich had still not come, although I had long ago seen him riding below the hill. Suddenly his figure appeared in the drive at the side from which I was least expecting him – he had skirted the ravine. His face was gay and radiant; he took off his hat and came towards me with quick steps. Seeing that Katya was asleep he bit his lips, shut his eyes and walked on tiptoe; I noticed at once that he was in that special mood of reasonless gaiety which I loved so much in him and which we called "wild delight". He was just like a schoolboy freed from his studies; his whole person, from top to toe, radiated content, happiness and childish high spirits.

"Good evening, young violet, how are you? Well?" he said in a whisper, coming up to me and shaking my hand. "I'm in great form," he said, in answer to my question. "I feel thirteen years old, and want to play horses and climb trees!"

"In wild delight?" I said, looking at his laughing eyes and feeling that this "wild delight" was being communicated to me.

"Yes," he answered, winking and suppressing a smile, "only why hit Katerina Karlovna on the nose?"

I had not noticed that, as I was looking at him and still waving the branch, I had knocked the handkerchief off Katya and was brushing her face with the leaves. I laughed.

"And she'll tell us that she wasn't asleep," I said in a whisper, as if so as not to wake Katya, but not at all for that reason: I simply enjoyed talking to him in a whisper.

He moved his lips, teasing me, as if I had spoken so quietly that it was impossible to hear a word. Catching sight of the plate of cherries, he seized it stealthily and, going up to Sonya under the lime tree, he sat down on her dolls. Sonya was annoyed at first, but he quickly made it up with her by racing her at eating cherries.

"Would you like me to have some more brought?" I said. "Or shall we go and get some ourselves?"

He took the plate, sat the dolls on it, and the three of us went to the cherry cage. Sonya ran after us, laughing and holding on to his coat, trying to make him give back the dolls. He gave them to her, and became serious as he turned to me.

"Of course you're a violet!" he said, still in a whisper, although there was no longer any fear of waking anyone. "As soon as I saw you, after all the dust and heat and work, I smelt a violet. And not a scented violet, you know, but that first, rather dark one which smells of snow and spring grass."

"Well, is everything going all right on your estate?" I asked him, so as to cover the joyful confusion which his words had produced.

"Splendidly! These people are splendid, everywhere. The more you know them, the more you love them."

"Yes," I said. "Just before you came today I was watching their work from the garden, and suddenly I felt ashamed that they have to work, and I'm so fortunate, so…"

"Don't treat that lightly, my dear," he interrupted me, suddenly looking into my eyes gravely, but tenderly. "That is something sacred. God forbid that you should boast about it!"

"But I only say this to *you*."

"Mm, yes, I know. Well, how are the cherries?"

The cage was locked, and none of the gardeners was about (he had sent them all to work in the fields). Sonya ran off to fetch the key, but without waiting for her he climbed up one corner of the cage, lifted the net, and jumped down on the other side of the wall.

"Do you want some?" I heard him call. "Give me the plate."

"No, I want to pick them, too. I'll go and fetch the key," I said. "Sonya won't find it."

But at the same time I wanted to see what he was doing there, how he looked, how he moved, when he supposed no one was looking at him. And then, at that moment, I simply did not want to lose sight of him for a minute. I ran on tiptoe through the nettles round the cage to the other side where the wall was lower, and standing on an empty tub so that the wall was at waist-level, I bent over into the cage. I looked round the interior of the cage, with its old, bent trees and their broad-toothed leaves under which juicy black cherries hung down stiffly and heavily and, pushing my head under the net, saw Sergey Mikhailovich from under the crooked branch of an old cherry tree. He probably thought I had gone away, and that no one could see him. Hatless, and with his eyes closed, he was sitting in the fork of an old cherry tree and was carefully rolling a lump of resin into a little pellet. Suddenly he shrugged his shoulders, opened his eyes and smiled, muttering something. The word he said and his smile were so unlike him that I began to feel ashamed of spying on him. It seemed to me that he was saying: "Masha!" "It's not possible," I thought. "Dear Masha!" he repeated, more quietly now and yet more tenderly. But this time I heard these two words quite distinctly. My heart began to beat fast, and an exciting, almost forbidden joy suddenly seized me, so that I gripped the wall with my hands to prevent myself falling and giving myself away. He heard me move, turned round in alarm, and suddenly looked down and blushed, went crimson like a child. He wanted to say something to me, but could not do so, and he blushed more and more. However, he smiled as he looked at me. I smiled, too. His whole face beamed with joy. This was no longer a fond old uncle and mentor, this man was my equal, loving and fearing me as I feared and loved him. But suddenly he frowned, his smile and the sparkle in his eyes vanished, and he turned to me coldly, once more like a father, as if we had been doing something wrong, and as if he had come to his senses and advised me to do the same.

"Climb down now – you'll hurt yourself," he said. "And tidy your hair – just look what a sight you are!"

"Why does he pretend? Why does he want to hurt me?" I thought, vexed. And at the same instant I had an irresistible urge to disconcert him again and to test my power over him.

"No, I want to pick the cherries myself," I said, and catching on to the nearest branch, I swung my legs over the wall. He had no time to catch me before I jumped on the ground inside the cage.

"What silly things you do do!" he said, blushing again and trying to cover his confusion with an air of annoyance. "You might have hurt yourself. And how are you going to get out of here?"

He was even more confused now than before, but this time his confusion no longer gave me pleasure but frightened me. I, too, became confused and, blushing and trying to avoid him, not knowing what to say, I started to pick cherries, although I had nowhere to put them. I reproached myself, regretted what I had done, was frightened, and felt that, by this act, I had ruined myself for ever in his eyes. We were both silent, and both felt uncomfortable. Sonya, running up with the key, got us out of this awkward situation. For a long time after this we did not speak to each other, but only to Sonya. When we got back to Katya, who assured us that she had not been asleep but had heard everything, I ceased worrying, and he tried to regain his patronizing and fatherly tone – but this tone was no longer very convincing and did not deceive me. I now vividly recalled a conversation which we had had a few days before.

Katya had been saying how much easier it was for a man to love and to express his love than it was for a woman.

"A man can say that he is in love, but a woman can't," she said.

"But I don't think a man should say he loves someone, either; nor can he," he said.

"Why not?" I asked.

"Because it will always be a lie. Is there really anything new in the fact that a man loves someone? As if, as soon as he says it, something clicks, bang – he is in love. It is as if, as soon as he pronounces this word, something extraordinary must happen, there should be some omen, all the trumpets should sound at once. It seems to me," he continued, "that people who solemnly pronounce the words: 'I love you', either deceive themselves or, even worse, deceive others."

"But then, how can a woman tell if someone loves her, if he doesn't say so?" asked Katya.

"That I don't know," he answered. "Each person has his own way of saying it. And if there is feeling, then it will always express itself. When I read novels I always imagine the puzzled expression of Lieutenant Strelsky or Alfred when they say 'I love you, Eleonora!', thinking that something extraordinary will happen – and nothing happens, either to her or to him; they have just the same eyes and noses, and everything is just as it was before."

Even then, I had felt that this jest contained something serious which concerned me, but Katya would not allow heroes in novels to be treated lightly.

"Paradoxes all the time!" she said. "Now, tell me honestly, have you yourself never told a woman that you love her?"

"I've never said it, and I never went down on bended knee either!" he answered, laughing. "And I never will."

"There is no need for him to tell me that he loves me," I thought now, vividly remembering this conversation. "He loves me, I know. And all his efforts to appear indifferent won't convince me to the contrary."

He did not say much to me all that evening but, in each word he said to Katya or to Sonya, in every movement and look of his, I saw love, and never doubted it. I only pitied him and felt sorry that he should still find it necessary to conceal it and to feign indifference when it was all so obvious, and when it would have been so easy and simple to be quite impossibly happy. But the fact that I had jumped into the cherry cage to him worried me, as if it had been a crime. I kept thinking that this would make him lose all respect for me, and that he was angry with me.

After tea I went to the piano, and he followed me.

"Play something. I haven't heard you for a long time," he said, catching me up in the drawing room.

"That's just what I wanted to do... Sergey Mikhailovich!" I said, suddenly looking at him straight in the eye. "You're not angry with me?"

"Why?" he asked.

"Because I disobeyed you after dinner," I said, and blushed.

He understood what I meant, shook his head and laughed. He looked as if he felt he ought to scold me but did not have the strength to do so.

"Let's forget about it, we're friends again," I said, sitting down at the piano.

"Of course!" he said.

The large, high room was lit only by two candles on the piano; the rest of the room was in semi-darkness. The light summer night looked in through the open windows. All was quiet but for the occasional squeak of Katya's footsteps in the dark drawing room, and his horse, tied up outside the window, snorted and beat the burdocks with its hooves. He was sitting behind me, so that I could not see him, but everywhere – in the semi-darkness of the room, in the sounds, in my own self – I felt his presence. His every look and movement, although I could not see them, were echoed in my heart. I played Mozart's sonata-fantasia, which he had brought for me and which I had studied with him and for him. I was not thinking at all of what I was playing, but I believe I played well and I was under the impression that he liked it. I felt the delight that he was experiencing and, without looking at him, I felt his gaze fixed on my back. Without stopping the unconscious movement of my fingers, I quite involuntarily looked round at him. His head was silhouetted against the light background of the night. He was sitting, leaning his head on his hand, and was looking at me intently, his eyes shining. I smiled, seeing his look, and stopped playing. He smiled, too, and nodded reproachfully at the music to make me go on. When I had finished playing, the moon had become lighter and had risen higher and, apart from the weak light of the candles, another, silvery light came into the room through the windows and fell on the floor. Katya said I should be ashamed of myself for stopping at the best place and that I had played badly, but he said that, on the contrary, I had never played so well as I had today, and he started to walk through the rooms – through the ballroom, into the dark drawing room, and back again into the ballroom – looking at me each time and smiling. And I smiled too, and even felt like laughing for no reason at all, as if pleased at something or other which had only just occurred. Every time he disappeared through the door I hugged Katya, who was standing next to me by the piano, and kissed her on my favourite spot – on her puffy neck under her chin; as soon as he returned I would make a seemingly serious face and could hardly keep back my laughter.

"What has happened to her today?" Katya said to him.

But he did not answer and only laughed at me; he knew what had happened to me.

"Look, what a night!" he said from the drawing room, stopping in front of the balcony door which was open on to the garden.

We came up to him, and it was indeed a night such as I have never seen since. The full moon stood over the house behind us, so that it was out of sight, and half the shadow of the roof, of the pillars and of the terrace awning lay aslant *en raccourci** on the sandy drive and on the lawn. The rest of the garden was light, and bathed in silver dew and moonlight. The shadows of the dahlias and their supports lay aslant one side of the wide flower-bed which, all light and cold, its uneven gravel glinting, receded into the mist and the distance. From beyond the trees could be seen the light roof of the greenhouse, and a growing mist was rising from the ravine. The lilac bushes were already somewhat bare, and the branches showed white; all the flowers were sprinkled with dew, and could be distinguished from one another. In the avenues light and shade were so blended that the avenues seemed no longer to be trees and paths, but transparent houses, shimmering and trembling. To the right, in the shadow of the house, all was black, indifferent and fearful. But because of this the fantastically spread crown of the poplar tree stood out all the more brightly; strangely enough, it remained there, and had not flown off somewhere far away into the receding, bluish sky.

"Let's go out for a walk," I said.

Katya agreed, but said that I must put on my galoshes.

"I don't need them, Katya," I said. "Sergey Mikhailovich will give me his arm."

As if this could prevent me from getting my feet wet! But then this was quite understandable to all three of us, and not a bit odd. He never used to give me his arm, but now I took it myself and he did not think it strange. The three of us came down from the terrace. The whole of that world, the sky, the garden, the air were not those that I knew.

As I looked ahead down the avenue through which we were walking, I had the impression that we would not be able to go any further, that the world of the possible ended there, that all this must be fixed for ever in all its beauty. But we did move forwards, and the magic world of beauty moved apart to let us through, and there too, it seemed, was our familiar garden, the trees and paths and dry leaves. And we really

144

did walk along the paths, trod on the circle of light and shade, the dry leaves did rustle under our feet, and a fresh wind brushed my face. And it really was him, striding evenly and quietly by my side, carefully holding my hand, and it really was Katya walking beside us with squeaking boots. And it must have been the moon in the sky, shining on us through the motionless branches...

But with every step the magic wall closed in behind and in front of us, and I ceased to believe that we could go any further, I ceased to believe in anything that existed.

"Oh! A frog!" said Katya.

"Who says this, and why?" I thought. But then I remembered that it was Katya and that she was afraid of frogs, and I looked at the ground. A little frog jumped and stood stock-still in front of me, and I could see its little shadow on the light clay of the path.

"You're not afraid, are you?" he said.

I looked at him. One lime tree was missing in the avenue at the spot where we were – I could see his face clearly. It was so fine and happy...

He said: "You're not afraid?", but I heard him say: "I love you, my darling girl." "I love you, I love you!" his look and his hand repeated, and the light and the shade and the air and everything repeated it too.

We went round the whole garden. Katya walked beside us taking short steps and breathing heavily because she was tired. She said it was time to go back, and I was sorry, so sorry for her, poor thing. "Why doesn't she feel the same as we do?" I thought. "Why isn't everyone young and happy, like this night, and like him and me?"

We went home, but he did not leave for some time, although the cocks were crowing, everyone in the house was asleep, and his horse beat its hooves on the burdocks more and more often and snorted under the window. Katya did not remind us that it was late, and we sat up until three o'clock in the morning without ourselves realizing it, and talking of the most trivial things. The cocks had already crowed for the third time and dawn was already breaking when he left. He said goodbye as usual, and did not say anything special, but I knew that from that day he was mine and that I would not lose him now. As soon as I had realized that I loved him, I told Katya everything. She was glad, and touched that I had told her about it, but she, poor thing, was able to fall asleep that night, whereas I walked up and down the terrace for a long time, went into the garden and down the same avenues that I had walked with him, recalling to mind every word and every movement. All that night I did not sleep, and for the first time in my life I saw the sunrise and the early morning, and never again have I seen such a night or such a morning. "Only why doesn't he just tell me that he loves me?" I thought. "Why does he think up all sorts of difficulties, and call himself an old man, when it is all so simple and wonderful? Why does he waste precious time which, perhaps, we shall never have again? He should say 'I love you', say it in so many words, 'I love you'; he should take my hand, bend his head over it and say 'I love you'. If only he'd blush and look embarrassed, and then I'd tell him everything. And I won't even say anything, just put my arms around him and hold him to me, and weep. But what if I am wrong – suppose he doesn't love me?" I thought suddenly.

This feeling frightened me. God knows where it could lead me. I remembered his confusion – and my own – in the cherry cage when I jumped down to him, and I was worried and felt heavy-hearted. Tears flowed down my cheeks and I began to pray. And a strange thought, a hope, came to me and calmed me; I decided from that day to do penance and prepare myself to take Communion on my birthday, and on that day to become engaged to him.

Why or how this should happen, I had no idea, but from that very minute I believed in it and knew that it would be so. Day had already dawned and people were getting up when I returned to my room.

4

IT WAS THE FAST OF THE ASSUMPTION, and so no one in the house was surprised at my intention of doing penance at the time.

He did not come to see me all that week, and I was not only not surprised or alarmed or angry with him, but was actually glad that he did not come, and did not expect him to arrive until my birthday. Every day during the course of the week I got up early and, while the horse was being harnessed for me, I would walk alone in the garden, going over in my mind my sins of the day before, and thinking out what I should do that day so as to be satisfied with it and avoid sinning. It then seemed so easy to me to be without sin. It seemed that all I had to do was just make a little effort. The horses would arrive, I would get into the carriage either with Katya or with a maid, and we would drive the two miles to the church. Each time I entered the church I remembered to pray for everyone, "entering therein in fear of God", and I would try to keep just this in mind as I went up the two steps overgrown with grass into the porch. At that time there would be not more than ten people – peasant women and servants – doing penance in the church; I tried to respond to their greetings with painstaking humility and would go myself to the candle box to take candles from the old churchwarden, an ex-soldier, and set them up – which seemed to me a heroic deed. Through the centre doors of the iconostasis could be seen the altar covering, which had been embroidered by Mamma, and over the iconostasis stood two angels with stars, which had seemed huge to me when I was a little girl, and a dove with a yellow halo which used to interest me then. In the choir the font was visible, dented with age, in which I had so often seen our servants' children being baptised, and in which I had been baptised myself. The old priest would come out in a chasuble which had been made out of my father's funeral pall, and he would conduct the service in exactly the same voice in which, ever since I could remember, mass had been said in our house, and as it had been said at Sonya's christening, at the requiem for my father, and at my mother's funeral. The same quavering voice of the sacristan would be heard in the choir, and the same old woman, whom I always remembered seeing in church at every service, stood bent by the wall, looking with tears in her eyes at the icon in the choir, pressing her clasped fingers to her faded shawl and muttering something with her toothless mouth. No longer did all this merely arouse my interest, nor was it memories alone that made it dear to me; now all this was great and sacred in my eyes and seemed full of deep meaning. I listened to every word of the prayers which were read and would try to answer them with feeling, and if I did not understand them I would ask God to enlighten me, or would invent my own prayers in place of those which I did not quite hear. While the prayer of repentance was being read I would remember my past, and that childish, innocent past seemed so black to me in comparison to the limpid state of my soul that I would weep and be horrified at myself, but at the same time, I felt that all this would be forgiven and that, if I should be guilty of still greater sins, then repentance would be all the sweeter. When, at the end of the service, the priest would say: "The blessing of the Lord be with you", it seemed to me that I instantly experienced a feeling of physical well-being which had been communicated to me. It was as if some sort of light and warmth suddenly filled my heart. The service would come to an end, the priest would come up to me and ask if and when he should come to us to serve Vespers, but I would thank him, touched that he should want to do this – for me, as I thought – and would tell him that I would walk or drive over to church myself.

"You want to give yourself the trouble, do you?" he would say.

And I would not know what to answer, so as not to commit the sin of pride.

When I went to mass I always sent the horses back if Katya was not with me, and would go home alone on foot, bowing low with humility to everyone I met and trying to find occasion to be of help, to give advice, to make a sacrifice of myself, to help lift a load, to nurse a child, to make way for people and to be splashed with mud. Once I heard the bailiff tell Katya that Semyon – a peasant – had come to ask for planks to make a coffin for his daughter and for a rouble for the wake, and how he had given it to him. "Are they really so poor?" I asked. "Very poor, madam – they haven't even any salt," the bailiff answered. Something made my heart ache, and at the same time I was almost glad to hear what he said. I told Katya that I was going for a walk, and then ran upstairs, took all my money (it was not much, but it was all I had), made the sign of the cross, and went alone across the terrace and the garden to Semyon's cottage, which was on the outskirts of the village. Unnoticed by anyone, I went and put the money on the window sill and knocked on the window. Someone came out of the cottage and called out to me, the door squeaked, and I ran home like a criminal, shivering with cold and fear. Katya asked me where I had been and what was the matter with me, but I did not even understand what she was saying, and did not answer her. Suddenly it all seemed so petty and trivial to me. I shut myself up in my room and walked up and down it alone for a long time, not able to do anything or think of anything, nor able to take stock of my feelings. I pictured the joy of the whole family, the words they would use to discuss who had put the money there, and I was sorry I had not given them the money myself. I thought, too, of what Sergey Mikhailovich would say if he were to find out about my action, and was glad that no one would ever find out about it. I was filled with such joy, I myself and everyone else seemed so wicked to me, and I thought of myself and of everyone with such meekness that the thought of death came to me as a vision of happiness. I smiled and prayed and wept, and at that moment I loved everyone in the world, including myself, with passionate warmth. Between the services in church I read the Gospels, and their meaning became increasingly clear to me, and the story of the divine life simpler and more touching, and the depth of feeling and thought which I found in His teaching more terrible and impenetrable. On the other hand, how clear and simple everything seemed to me when, getting up from reading this book, I would once more contemplate and reflect on life surrounding me! It seemed so difficult to lead a bad life, and so simple to love everyone and to be loved. Everyone was so kind and gentle with me; even Sonya, to whom I continued to give lessons, was quite different; she tried to understand and please me and not to annoy me. Everyone behaved to me as I myself behaved. As I tried to recall any enemies of whom I had to ask forgiveness before confession, I could only remember one girl, a neighbour that I had laughed at a year ago in front of guests, and who had ceased visiting us in consequence. I wrote her a letter in which I acknowledged my guilt and asked for her forgiveness. In her answering letter she herself asked forgiveness and forgave me. I wept for joy, reading these simple lines in which I then saw such deep and moving feeling. My nurse burst into tears when I asked for forgiveness. "Why are they all so kind to me? What have I done to deserve such love?" I asked myself. Involuntarily I remembered Sergey Mikhailovich, and thought of him for a long time. I could not do otherwise, and never even considered it a sin. But now I thought of him not at all as I had done on that night when, for the first time, I realized that I loved him; I thought of him now as I thought of myself, unconsciously linking him with every thought about my own future. His overwhelming influence, which I experienced in his presence, completely disappeared in my imagination. I felt that I was now his equal and, from the heights of my spiritual mood, I completely understood him. Everything in him which before had seemed strange was now clear to me. It was only now that I understood why he said that happiness only came from living for others, and now I entirely agreed with him. I felt that, together, we would be so infinitely and serenely happy. And what came to my mind was neither journeys abroad, nor society, nor social glitter, but an entirely different, quiet family life in the country, with constant self-sacrifice, with constant love for each other, and with the constant consciousness of an ever gentle and helping Providence.

I took Communion, as I had intended, on my birthday. That day, when I returned from church, I was filled with such complete happiness that I was afraid of life, afraid of every impression, of anything which could destroy this happiness. However, no sooner had we got out of the carriage at the porch, than a familiar cabriolet thundered over the bridge, and I saw Sergey Mikhailovich. He wished me many happy returns of the day, and we went into the drawing room together. Never since I had known him had I been so calm and self-possessed in his presence as I was that morning. I felt that there was a whole new world within me which he did not understand, and which was above him. He must have understood the reason for this, and he was especially tender and gentle and devoutly respectful to me. I wanted to go to the piano, but he locked it and hid the key in his pocket.

"Don't spoil your mood," he said. "You are now filled with music which is better than any in the world."

I was grateful to him for this, and at the same time a little annoyed that he had too easily and clearly understood all that was in my heart, which should have been a secret from everyone.

At lunch he said that he had come to wish me many happy returns of the day and also, at the same time, to say goodbye, as he was going to Moscow the next day. As he was saying this he was looking at Katya, but then he glanced at me, and I saw that he was afraid of seeing me look concerned. But I was neither surprised nor alarmed, and did not even ask him if he would be away long. I had known that he would say this, and I knew that he would not go away. How I knew this I cannot now explain to myself, but on that memorable day I felt that I knew everything – what had been, and what was to be. It was as if I was in a happy dream in which it seemed that everything in the future had already happened, and that I had known about it for a long time, and yet I felt that it would happen again, and I knew that it would happen.

He wanted to leave immediately after lunch, but Katya, who was tired after mass, retired to lie down for a while, and he had to wait for her to wake up in order to take his leave of her. It was sunny in the ballroom, and we went out on the terrace. As soon as we sat down I began with complete calm to say the words which were to decide the fate of my love. I began to speak not a minute before or after, but at the very instant we sat down and before anything had been said, so that the conversation had, as yet, no tone or character whatsoever which might have prevented my saying what I wanted to say. I cannot understand myself how I was able to muster so much calmness, such determination and accuracy of expression. It was as if something independent of my will, rather than myself, was speaking within me. He sat opposite me, leaning on the balustrade and plucking the leaves off a branch of lilac which he had pulled towards him. When I began to speak he let go of the branch and leaned his head on his hand. It could have been the attitude either of a man who was completely calm, or of someone feeling extremely nervous.

"Why are you going away?" I asked, pausing significantly and looking straight at him.

He did not answer for a moment.

"Business!" he said, and looked down.

I realized how difficult it was for him to lie to me, especially in answer to a question which had been put so frankly.

"Listen," I said. "You know what this day means to me. It's a very important day for many reasons. If I ask you such a question, it is not merely to show my interest (you know how used I am to you and how much I love you). I ask you because I must know. Why are you going away?"

"It's very difficult for me to tell you truthfully why I am going away," he said. "I have thought about you a good deal this week, and about myself, and I have decided that I must go away. You understand why, and if you love me you won't ask me." He brushed his forehead with his hand and covered his eyes. "It's very hard for me – and clear to you."

My heart began to beat fast.

"I don't understand," I said. "I *can't*. You tell me, for God's sake, for the sake of today, tell me. I can listen to it all calmly," I said.

"All right, then," he said, pausing a little, and in a voice which he tried in vain to make hard. "Although it's silly and impossible to put it into words, although it's very painful for me, I'll try to explain to you," he added, frowning as if from physical pain.

"Well?" I said.

"Imagine that there was a certain Mr A. – imagine," he said, "that he was old and spent – and a certain Miss B., young, happy, who as yet did not know anyone or anything. For various family reasons he loved her as a daughter, and was not afraid he might love her in any other way."

He paused, but I did not interrupt him.

"But he forgot that B. was so young that life for her was still a plaything," he suddenly went on, quickly and resolutely, without looking at me, "and that it would be easy to love her in a different way, and that that would be fun for her. And he was mistaken, and suddenly became conscious of another feeling, as heavy as repentance, creeping into his heart, and was frightened. He was afraid that their former friendly relations would be destroyed, and decided to go away before that should happen." As he was saying this he began to wipe his eyes, as if carelessly, with his hand, and closed them.

"But why was he afraid of loving her differently?" I said in a barely audible whisper, and keeping my emotions under control; my voice was even, but to him it probably appeared to have a bantering tone. He answered as if he had taken offence.

"You're young," he said. "I am not young. You want to play, but I want something else. Play, but not with me, or I will take you seriously and be unhappy, and you will feel ashamed. That's what A. said," he added, "that's all nonsense, anyway, but you understand why I am going away. Don't let's talk about it any more – please!"

"Oh! yes, we shall talk about it," I said, and tears made my voice tremble. "Did he love her, or not?"

He did not answer.

"But if he did not love her, why did he play with her, as if she was a child?" I said.

"Oh, yes, A. was to blame," he answered, hurriedly interrupting me, "but it was all finished, and they parted... friends."

"But that's dreadful! Is there really no other ending?" I scarcely managed to say, and was frightened by what I had said.

"Yes, there is," he said, uncovering his face, which showed signs of emotion, and looking straight at me. "There are two different endings. Only for goodness' sake don't interrupt, and take in calmly what I have to say. Some say," he began, getting up and painfully smiling a forced smile, "some say that A. went out of his mind, fell madly in love with B. and told her so... But she only laughed. She took it as a joke, but for him life itself was at stake."

I started, and wanted to interrupt him to say that he should not presume to speak for me, but he stopped me, putting his hand on mine.

"Wait a moment," he said, with a trembling voice. "Others say that she took pity on him, and that she imagined, poor thing, without ever having met anyone else, that she could really love him – and she agreed to become his wife. And he was crazy and believed her – believed that his whole life would begin anew, but she herself realized that she had deceived him and that he had deceived her… Don't let's talk about it any more," he concluded, suddenly unable to continue, and he began to pace up and down in front of me, in silence.

He had said: "Don't let's talk about it," but I saw that he was waiting for my words with all his being. I wanted to speak, but could not; something was pressing on my heart. I looked at him. He was pale, and his lower lip was trembling. I felt sorry for him. Making an effort and breaking the silence that was fettering me, I began to speak in a quiet, even voice which I feared would break at any moment.

"And the third ending…" I said, and stopped, but he remained silent. "The third ending is that he did not love her, but hurt her, hurt her and thought it right, went away and was even proud of something. To you it's a joke – to you, but not to me. I loved you from the first day, *loved* you," I repeated, and at the world "loved" my voice changed involuntarily from a quiet, even one into a wild shriek which frightened even me.

He stood before me, pale, his lower lip trembling more and more, while two tears rolled down his cheeks.

"That's very wrong," I almost shouted, feeling that angry, unshed tears were stifling me. "Why do you do it?" I went on, and stood up to leave him.

But he did not let me. His head lay on my knees, his lips kissed my trembling hands, and his tears moistened them.

"Oh God, if only I had known!" he said.

"Why did you do it – why?" I still repeated, but in my heart there was happiness – the happiness that had almost escaped me, but that had now returned again.

Five minutes later Sonya was running upstairs to Katya and shouting all over the house that Masha wanted to marry Sergey Mikhailovich.

5

THERE WAS NO REASON for postponing our marriage, and neither of us wished to do so. Katya, it is true, would have liked to go to Moscow and buy or order things for a trousseau, and his mother tried to insist that he should get a new carriage and furniture before he married, and have all the rooms in the house newly papered, but we both insisted – successfully – that if it was really so necessary all this should be done afterwards, and that we should marry a fortnight after my birthday, without a trousseau, without guests, without ushers or a reception or champagne and all the other conventional paraphernalia of weddings. He told me how displeased his mother was that the wedding would be without music, without mountains of trunks and without the whole house being redecorated – unlike her wedding, which had cost thirty thousand roubles – and how, while going through the trunks in the box-room, she had been consulting gravely and surreptitiously with Maryushka the housekeeper, so that he would not know, about some carpets and curtains and trays absolutely essential to our happiness. On my side Katya was doing the same with nanny Kuzminishna, and the matter could not be treated lightly in her presence. She was absolutely convinced that when we discussed our future together we were just being sentimental and frivolous, as was characteristic of people in such a state, but that, in fact, our future happiness would depend entirely on the correct cut and stitching of chemises, and the hemming of tablecloths and table-napkins. Several times each day secret information was exchanged between Pokrovskoye and Nikolskoye as to what was being prepared, and although outwardly Katya and his mother seemed to be on the tenderest of terms, one could already feel that relations between them were based on a hostile, even if extremely fine diplomacy. Tatyana Semyonovna, his mother, whom I now got to know better, was a dour, strict housewife, and a lady of the old school. He loved her not only as a son, in duty bound, but as a man, by inclination, and he considered her the best, most intelligent, kindest and most affectionate woman in the world. Tatyana Semyonovna was always kind to us and especially to me, and was pleased that her son was getting married, but when I went to see her as a fiancée I felt that she wanted to make me feel that, as a match for her son, I could be better, and that no harm would be done if I were always to remember this. And I quite understood and agreed with her.

We saw each other every day during this last fortnight. He used to come to dinner and would stay on till midnight. But although he said that without me he could not live – and I knew that he was speaking the truth – he never spent the whole day with me, but tried to carry on with his work as usual. On the face of it our relations remained the same as before right up to the very wedding; we continued to say *vous* to each other, he did not even kiss my hand, nor did he seek opportunities for remaining alone with me – indeed, he even avoided them. It was as if he were afraid to succumb to all the tenderness which was in him, which was too great and was even harmful. I do not know which of us changed, but I now felt myself to be completely his equal. I now no longer found in him the pretence of simplicity which I had previously disliked, and often I was delighted to see before me, instead of a man inspiring awe and respect, a child meek and lost with happiness. "So that's all there ever was in him!" I would often think. "He's just the same sort of person as I am – no better." I felt that now I saw him as he really was and that I knew him completely, and all that I was discovering in him was so simple, and so much in tune with my own feelings. Even his plans for our future life together were the same as my own, only clearer and better expressed.

The weather was bad then, and we spent most of our time indoors. Our best and most heart-to-heart conversations took place in the corner behind the piano and the little window. The dark window reflected the light of the candles and drew it near to us, raindrops would occasionally beat against the shiny glass and run down it. Outside, rain pattered on the roof and splashed in the pool under the water-pipe; the damp came in through the window, and somehow our corner seemed all the lighter and warmer and more cheerful.

"You know, I've been wanting to tell you something for a long time," he said once, when we were sitting up late by ourselves in this corner. "I was thinking about it while you were playing the piano."

"Don't say a word. I know everything," I said.

"All right, we won't talk about it."

"No, do tell me. What?" I asked.

"Well, you remember when I told you that story about A. and B.?"

"As if I could ever forget that stupid story! It's a good thing it ended as it did…"

"Yes, a little longer, and I would have destroyed my own happiness. You saved me. But the most important thing is that I lied to you then and I'm ashamed of it, and I want to tell you now all I had on my mind."

"Oh! Please don't!"

"Don't be nervous," he said, smiling. "I only want to justify myself. When I started to speak I wanted to reason things out."

"Why reason things out?" I said. "One never should."

"Yes, my reasoning was at fault. After all my disappointments and mistakes in life, when I came to the country this year I said to myself so firmly that, as far as I was concerned, love was finished with, and that my only remaining duty was that of finishing my span of life, that for a long time I didn't realize what kind of feeling I had for you, and where it might lead me. I hoped, and yet I didn't hope; sometimes it seemed to me that you were just flirting, sometimes I believed in you, and I didn't know myself what I should do. But after that evening, you remember, when we walked in the garden at night, I was afraid: my happiness seemed too great and impossible. And what would have happened if I had allowed myself to hope in vain? But of course I only thought about myself, because I'm a horrid egoist."

He paused, and looked at me.

"However, what I said then wasn't really entirely nonsense. It was both right and proper for me to be afraid. I am taking so much from you, and can give you so little. You're still a child, you're a bud which has not opened yet, you love for the first time; whereas I…"

"Yes, tell me truthfully," I said, but suddenly I was afraid of his answer. "No, better not," I added.

"Have I ever loved anyone before? Is that what you mean?" he said, guessing my thought immediately. "I can tell you that. No, I have never been in love. Never anything approaching this feeling…" But suddenly it seemed as if some painful memory flashed across his mind. "No, and in this too I need your heart to have the right to love you," he said sadly. "Well, then, didn't I have to think things out before telling you that I loved you? What am I giving you? Love – that's true enough."

"Is that so little?" I said, looking into his eyes.

"It's little, my dear, for you it's little," he went on. "You have beauty and youth! I often don't sleep at night now from sheer happiness, thinking how we shall live together. I have lived through a great deal, and I think I have found what is needed for happiness. A quiet, secluded life in our country backwater, with the possibility of doing good to people whom it is easy to do good to because they are not used to it; then work – work which one thinks is useful, then rest, nature, books, music, love for the person who is close to you – that's my idea of happiness. I never dreamed of anything better. And now, on top of all this, I get a friend like you, a family perhaps, and everything that a man can desire."

"Yes," I said.

"For me, whose youth is over, that is, but not for you," he went on. "You haven't lived yet. You may want to look for happiness elsewhere perhaps, and perhaps it is elsewhere that you will find it. You think that this is happiness now because you love me."

"No, all I have ever wanted and loved was a quiet family life," I said. "You're only putting my thoughts into words."

He smiled.

"It only seems like that to you, my dear. But such a life doesn't hold much for you. You have beauty and youth," he repeated thoughtfully.

But I was annoyed that he did not believe me, and that he seemed to reproach me for my beauty and youth.

"What do you love me for, then?" I said crossly. "For my youth, or for myself?"

"I don't know, but I love you," he answered, and as he looked at me his gaze was steady and magnetic.

I did not answer, and looked involuntarily into his eyes. Suddenly something strange happened to me: first I ceased to see all my surroundings, then his face disappeared and only his eyes seemed to shine immediately in front of mine; then I felt that those eyes were inside me and everything became blurred, I could not see anything and had to close my eyes tightly in order to tear myself away from the feeling of delight and fear which this gaze produced in me...

The weather cleared up on the eve of the wedding. After the summer rains the first cold and bright autumn evening broke through. Everything was wet, cold and clear, and in the garden the spaciousness, the motley colours and bareness of autumn were apparent for the first time. The sky was clear, cold and pale. I went to bed happy with the thought that tomorrow, our wedding day, the weather would be fine. The next day I awoke at sunrise, and the thought that today... somehow frightened and surprised me. I went out into the garden. The sun had just risen, and shone in patches through the falling, yellowing leaves of the lime avenue. The path was strewn with rustling leaves. The bright clusters of wrinkled rowanberries reddened on the branches which were covered with rare shrivelled leaves caught by the frost, the dahlias had withered and turned black. For the first time frost lay silver on the pale-green grass and on the broken burdocks around the house. In the clear, cold sky there was not – could not be – a single cloud.

"Is it really today?" I asked myself, not believing my happiness. "Will I really wake up tomorrow no longer here, but in Nikolskoye, in a strange house with pillars? Will I really no longer wait for him and go to meet him, and no longer talk to Katya about him in the evenings and at night? No longer sit with him at the piano in the ballroom at Pokrovskoye? No longer see him off, and worry about him on dark nights?" Then I would remember that he had said yesterday he had come for the last time, and that Katya had made me try on my wedding dress, saying: "For tomorrow" – and I would believe it all for a moment, and then begin to doubt it again. "Will I really, from this very day, live there with my mother-in-law, without Nadyozha, without old Grigory, without Katya? Will I really not kiss nurse goodnight any more, and hear her say from long habit 'Goodnight, miss' as she makes the sign of the cross over me? Will I really no longer give lessons to Sonya and play with her and knock on the wall to her in the morning and hear her resounding laughter? Will I really today become a stranger to myself, and is a new life, the realization of my hopes and wishes, opening up before me? Is it really for ever, this new life?" I waited for him impatiently, for I felt depressed alone with these thoughts. He arrived early, and it was only when he was with me that I fully believed that I would that day become his wife, and that this thought ceased to terrify me.

Before lunch we went to our church for a commemoration service for my father.

"If only he were alive now!" I thought, as we were walking home, and I was silently leaning on the arm of the man who had been his best friend. During the prayers, resting my forehead on the cold stone floor of the chapel, I saw my father so clearly in my imagination and believed so strongly that his spirit understood me and blessed my choice, that it seemed to me as if it were hovering over us and I felt his blessing on me. Memories and hopes and happiness and sadness blended within me into one solemn and pleasant feeling which was matched by the still, fresh air, the silence, the bareness of the fields, and the pale sky from which bright but weak rays fell on everything, trying to burn my cheeks. It seemed to me that the man walking by my side understood and shared my feeling. He walked slowly and in silence, and on his face, which I looked at from time to time, I perceived the same solemn sadness mixed with joy which was in nature and in my heart.

Suddenly he turned to me; I saw that he wanted to say something. The question: "What if he should speak of something else, and not of what I am thinking?" came into my head. But he spoke of my father, without even naming him.

"Once he said to me, without meaning it seriously: 'Marry my Masha!'" he said.

"How happy he would be now," I said, squeezing tighter the hand that was holding mine.

"Yes, you were still a child," he went on, looking into my eyes. "I used to kiss those eyes then, and loved them only because they were like his, and never thought that they would be so dear to me for their own sake. I used to call you 'Masha' then."

"Do say *tu* to me," I said.

"I just wanted to say *tu* to you," he said. "It seems to me only now that you are entirely mine." And his calm and happy magnetic gaze fell on me.

We went on walking quietly along the untrodden field path through the trampled, beaten stubble, and we heard only our own footsteps and voices. On one side, stretching away across the ravine to a distant bare copse, lay the brownish stubble through which, some distance away, a peasant was soundlessly cutting out with his plough a gradually widening black strip. A drove of horses, scattered beneath the hill, seemed quite near. On the other side and ahead of us, right up to the garden and our house visible beyond it, lay a field sown to winter corn, black now that the frost had melted, and yet already streaked with green in places. A sun without warmth shone on everything, long fibrous spider-webs lay everywhere. They flew in the air around us and lay on the stubble which was withering because of frost, they fell in our eyes, on our hair, on our clothes. When we spoke our voices sounded and were arrested above us in the still air, as if no one but us alone existed in the whole world, alone under this blue vault in which the weak sun was shining and occasionally flaring up and shimmering.

I too wanted to say *tu* to him, but I felt shy.

"Why do you walk so fast?" I said, using the *tu* very quickly, almost in a whisper, and blushed in spite of myself.

He walked more slowly and looked at me even more tenderly, gaily and happily.

When we reached home his mother and some guests with whom we had been unable to dispense were already there, and I was not alone with him again until the very moment when we left the church and got into the carriage to drive to Nikolskoye.

The church was almost empty; out of the corner of my eye I saw only his mother, standing erect on the little carpet by the choir, Katya, wearing a black lace cap with lilac-coloured ribbons, and with tears rolling down her cheeks, and two or three servants looking at me with curiosity. I did not look at him, but felt his presence there beside me. I listened to the words of the prayers and repeated them, but there was no response in my heart. I could not pray, and looked dully at the icons, at the candles, at the embroidered cross of the chasuble on the priest's back, at the iconostasis, at the window of the church – and did not understand anything. I felt only that something unusual was being performed over me. When the priest turned towards us with the cross, congratulated us and said that he had baptised me, and that now it had been God's will that he should marry me, when Katya and his mother kissed us and Grigory's voice was heard calling for the carriage, I was surprised and alarmed that it was all over already, and that nothing extraordinary corresponding to the mystery just performed over me had happened within me. We kissed each other, and that kiss was so strange and alien to our feelings. "So that's all there is to it," I thought. We went out into the porch; the wheels echoed hollowly under the vault of the church; the smell of fresh air struck our faces. He put on his hat and helped me into the carriage. From the carriage window I saw a frosty, ringed moon. He sat down beside me and shut the door behind him. Something stabbed my heart. The sureness with which he did this somehow seemed offensive to me. Katya's voice called out to me to cover my head, the wheels rattled over the stones, then on the soft road, and we had gone. Squeezing myself into one corner, I looked out of the window at the distant, light fields, and at the road disappearing in the cold moonshine. And, without looking at him, I felt him there beside me. "What, is that all that this moment, from which I expected so much, has given me?" I thought, and somehow I felt that it was humiliating and offensive to be sitting there alone, so close to him. I turned towards him with the intention of saying something. But the words would not come, as if I no longer had my former feeling of tenderness, but in its stead a feeling of offence and fear.

"Till this minute I couldn't believe it was possible," he quietly answered my look.

"Yes, but for some reason I'm frightened," I said.

"You're frightened of me, my dear?" he said, taking my hand and bending his head over it.

My hand lay lifeless in his, and the cold made my heart ache.

"Yes," I whispered.

But at that very moment my heart suddenly began to beat faster, my hand trembled and pressed his hand, I began to feel hot, my eyes sought his in the dusk, and I suddenly felt that I was not afraid of him – that this fear was love, a new kind of love, a tenderer and stronger love than before. I felt that I was entirely his, and that I rejoiced in his power over me.

6

DAYS, WEEKS, two months of secluded country life passed – imperceptibly, it seemed at the time, and yet the feelings, emotions and happiness of those two months were enough to fill a lifetime. Our dreams of life in the country turned out quite different to what we had expected. But our life was no worse than our dreams. There was none of the unremitting toil, the fulfilment of duty, the self-sacrifice and living for others which I had imagined when I was engaged; there was, on the contrary, only a selfish feeling of love for each other, the desire to be loved, unreasoning, constant gaiety, and oblivion to everything else in the world. Sometimes, it is true, he would go off and work in his study, sometimes he would go into town on business or go round the estate, but I saw what an effort it cost him to tear himself away from me. He would himself admit afterwards that in my absence everything in the world seemed such sheer nonsense that he could not understand how one could have anything to do with it. I felt the same. My time was taken up with reading and music, with his mother and the school, but I did all this only because each of those tasks was connected with him and would gain his approval, but whenever anything I was doing had no connection with him, I would lose interest in it, and it would seem odd to me to think that anything existed in the world apart from him. Perhaps it was wrong and selfish of me to feel like that, but it made me happy and I felt on top of the world. He was the only man who existed for me, and I thought him the finest and most infallible person in the world, and therefore all I could live for in the world was him, my sole aim was to appear in his eyes such as he believed me to be. He too thought that I was the first and most perfect woman in the world, endowed with every possible virtue, and I tried to be just such a woman in the eyes of the first and best man in the whole world.

Once, he came into my room as I was saying my prayers. I looked round at him and went on praying. He sat down at the table so as not to disturb me, and opened a book. But I felt that he was looking at me, and turned my head. He smiled. I laughed and could not go on praying.

"Have you said your prayers already?" I asked.

"Yes. You go on, I'll go away."

"You do say your prayers, I hope?"

He did not answer, and wanted to leave me, but I stopped him.

"Darling, please, do read my prayers with me, for my sake." He came and stood beside me; with his arms hanging awkwardly at his sides, and with a serious expression on his face, faltering, he began to read. Occasionally he would turn towards me, looking for approval and help in my face.

When he had finished, I laughed and hugged him.

"It's all your fault, all your fault! I feel exactly as if I were ten years old again," he said, blushing and kissing my hands.

Ours was one of those old country houses in which several generations of the family had lived, loving and respecting one another. There was an odour of good, honest family memories which, as soon as I entered the house, suddenly somehow became my memories too. The house was furnished and the routine set by Tatyana Semyonovna in the old-fashioned way. It could not be said that everything was elegant and beautiful, but, from the servants down to the furniture and food, there was plenty of everything, and it was all tidy, solid, neat, and inspired respect. In the drawing room the furniture and portraits were symmetrically arranged, as were the carpets and rugs on the floor. There was an old grand piano in the morning room, two tallboys of different styles, sofas, and little tables inlaid with brass. In my study, which Tatyana Semyonovna had furnished herself, stood the very best furniture of different centuries and styles and, amongst other things, an old cheval-glass which at first I simply could not look at without embarrassment, but which subsequently became as dear as an old friend to me. Tatyana Semyonovna could not be heard, but everything in the house went like clockwork, in spite of many superfluous servants. But all the servants – wearing soft, heel-less boots because Tatyana Semyonovna considered squeaking soles and clattering heels the most disagreeable things in the world – all the servants seemed proud of their calling, trembled in front of their old mistress, looked at me and at my husband with patronizing affection, and seemed to perform their tasks with particular pleasure. Regularly every Sunday the floors of the house were washed and the carpets beaten; on the first of each month mass was said in the house and water consecrated, and a banquet was given for the whole neighbourhood on every name-day – on Tatyana Semyonovna's, on her son's, (and on my own for the first time that autumn). All this had gone on unchanged ever since Tatyana Semyonovna could remember. My husband did not interfere with the domestic arrangements, and dealt only with farming and the peasants, and this gave him a great deal of work. Even in the winter he got up very early, and was out by the time I woke up. He usually came back to tea, which we had by ourselves, and it was then, after all the trouble and difficulties occasioned by his work, that he was almost always in that particularly gay frame of mind which we called "wild delight". I often insisted that he should tell me what he had done in the morning, and he used to tell me such nonsense that we would die of laughter; sometimes I insisted on a serious account and he, restraining a smile, would give it me. I would look at his eyes, his moving lips, and not understand a word, but was simply glad to see him and to hear his voice.

"Well, what did I say? Repeat it," he would ask. But I could not repeat a word. It seemed so funny that *he* should be telling *me*, not about himself and myself, but about something else. As if I cared what was going on! It was only much later that I began to understand his preoccupations a little, and to take an interest in them. Tatyana Semyonovna did not appear before dinner, had tea by herself, and only greeted us through ambassadors. In our peculiar, extravagantly happy little world, this voice from her staid and orderly corner of it sounded so odd that I often could not contain myself, and would only laugh in reply to the maid who, with her hands folded, would report in measured tones: "Tatyana Semyonovna has told me to enquire if you are rested after yesterday's walk. And I am to tell you that her side ached all night, and that some silly dog barked outside and would not let her rest. And I am to ask you how you liked the cake this morning. Tatyana Semyonovna would have you note that it was not Taras who baked them this morning, but Nikolasha, and for the first time, just to give him a trial, and, she said, he hasn't done it at all badly – especially the pretzels – but the rusks were overdone."

We were not much together before dinner.* I played the piano or read alone, he read or went out again, but at dinner time, which was at four o'clock, we assembled in the drawing room, his mother sailed out of her room, and the distressed gentlewomen – roving souls of whom there were always two or three living in the house – would appear. Regularly every day, my husband would give his arm to his mother to take her in to dinner as he used to, but she insisted that he should give me the other arm, and regularly every day we got into a muddle at the door. At dinner, too, it was his mother who presided, and a decorously reasonable and somewhat solemn conversation was carried on. The simple words of my husband and myself agreeably destroyed the solemnity of these dinner sessions. Sometimes mother and son would argue together and tease each other; I particularly loved this banter and their arguments because it was in them that the tender and firm love linking mother and son was most strongly expressed. After dinner Maman sat in a large armchair in the drawing room and would make snuff or cut the pages of books which had just arrived, while we read aloud or went into the morning room to the piano. At that time we read together a great deal, but music was our favourite and greatest pleasure, striking new chords each time in our hearts and making us, as it were, discover each other anew. When I played his favourite pieces he would sit on a sofa some way off where I could scarcely see him and, too embarrassed to show it, would try to hide the impression which the music made on him, but I would often get up from the piano when he was least expecting it, come up to him and try to catch the traces of emotion on his face, the unnatural glitter and moisture in his eyes, which he would try in vain to hide from me. His mother often wanted to have a look at us in the morning room, but she was probably afraid to embarrass us, and she would sometimes walk through the morning room pretending not to look at us, with a pseudo-serious and indifferent expression on her face, but I knew that she had no reason for going to her room and coming back so quickly. I poured out tea in the evenings in the large drawing room, and once more the whole household would gather round the table.

For a long time that solemn session, with the samovar like a symbol of office and the distribution of cups and glasses, made me nervous. I felt that I was not yet worthy of this honour, and that I was too young and frivolous to turn the tap of such a large samovar and to put a glass on Nikita's tray, saying "For Pyotr Ivanovich and Marya Minichna", to ask "With sugar?" and to leave lumps of sugar for the nurse and other old retainers. "Splendid, splendid," my husband would frequently say, "just like a grown-up" – and this would make me all the more nervous.

After tea Maman would play patience, or listen to Marya Minichna's fortune-telling; then she would kiss us and make the sign of the cross over us both, and we would retire to our rooms. Mostly, however, we would sit up together till after midnight, and this was the best and most pleasant time of the day. He would tell me about his past life, we would make plans, sometimes we philosophized, and we would try to talk as quietly as possible so as not to be overheard upstairs and reported to Tatyana Semyonovna, who insisted that we should go to bed early. Sometimes, feeling hungry, we would creep to the larder and get a cold supper through the good offices of Nikita, and would eat in my study by the light of a single candle. We lived like strangers in the big old house, in which everything was dominated by the stern spirit of the past and of Tatyana Semyonovna. Not only her, but the servants, the old housemaids, the furniture, the pictures – all inspired me with respect, with a certain amount of awe, and also with the consciousness that he and I were not quite in our right place, that we had to be very careful and considerate in our manner of living. Looking back on it now, I can see that much in our house was inconvenient and difficult – both the binding, unchanging order, and the countless idle and inquisitive servants, but at that time this very restriction put all the more life into our love. He never showed – and neither, of course, did I – that there was anything that he did not like. He even managed to avoid confronting it. My mother-in-law's footman, Dmitry Sidorov, who was a great pipe-smoker, used to go regularly every day after dinner, when we were in the morning room, into my husband's study to take his tobacco from the drawer, and it was a sight to see with what hilarious alarm Sergey Mikhailovich would tiptoe towards me, shaking his finger, winking and pointing at Dmitry Sidorov, who had no idea that anyone was watching him. And when Dmitry Sidorov would go away, delight at his success making him quite oblivious to us, my husband would kiss my hand and tell me, as on every other occasion, that I was charming. At times I disliked this imperturbability of his, his all-forgivingness and almost indifference to everything; I did not notice that I was the same myself, and considered it to be weakness on his part. "Just like a child who doesn't dare to stand up for himself," I thought.

"Ah, my dear," he once replied, when I had told him that his weakness surprised me. "Can one really feel annoyed about anything, when one is as happy as I am? It is easier to yield than to impose one's will; I reached that conclusion long ago. There's no situation in which it's impossible to be happy – and we are so happy together! I can't be angry; nothing seems bad to me now, things seem only pitiful or amusing. The main thing to remember is – *le mieux est l'ennemi du bien*.* And would you believe it… when I hear a bell, get a letter, simply when I wake up, I am terrified – terrified that life must go on, that something will change, when nothing can be better than the present."

I believed him, but did not understand him; I was happy, but felt that everything should be just like that and in no way different, and that it should always be like that for everyone, and I felt too that there existed, somewhere, another happiness – not greater, perhaps, but different.

Thus two months went by, winter came with its cold and snowstorms and, even though I had him with me, I was beginning to feel that life was repeating itself, and that neither of us had anything new to give – but that we seemed rather to be going back to things as they had been before. He now spent more time without me attending to business than he had before, and I again began to feel that there was some special world within him to which he did not want to admit me. His perpetual calmness irritated me. I loved him no less than before, and was no less happy in his love than I had been, but my love stood still and ceased to grow and, apart from love, some new restlessness began to creep into my heart. Once I had experienced the happiness of falling in love with him I could not rest content with affection. I wanted movement, not the calm flow of life. I wanted emotion, danger, and self-sacrifice for the sake of feeling. I had a superabundance of strength which found no outlet in our quiet life. I suffered from bouts of nostalgia, which I tried to hide from him as if it were something bad, and transports of violent tenderness and hilarity which frightened him. He noticed my condition even before I did myself, and proposed that we should move to town, but I asked him not to do so, not to change our way of life, not to destroy our happiness. And I really was happy, but I was tormented by the fact that this happiness did not cost me any effort or sacrifice, while my capacity for effort and sacrifice consumed me. I loved him, and saw that I meant everything to him, but I wanted everyone to see our love, I wanted some obstacle to our love so that I could love him in spite of it. My mind and even my feelings were engaged, but there was a different feeling of youth, of the necessity for movement, which found no satisfaction in our quiet life. Why had he told me that we could move to town whenever I wanted to? Had he not told me this, perhaps I would have understood that the feeling oppressing me was pernicious nonsense, was my own fault, that the very sacrifice which I was seeking was there in front of me – in the suppression of that feeling. The thought that I could only save myself from my longings by moving to town involuntarily came into my head, yet at the same time I was ashamed and sorry to drag him away from everything he loved. But time passed, snow rose higher and higher round the walls of the house, and we were still alone and were just the same to each other; while somewhere far away from us, in glitter and noise, crowds of people thrilled, suffered and rejoiced, not thinking of us and of our existence which was ebbing away. Worst of all, I felt that, with each day, the habits of life were moulding our life into a definite pattern, that our feeling was ceasing to be free and was being subjected to the even, passionless flow of time. In the morning we were gay, at dinner – respectful, in the evening – tender.

"Good!…" I said to myself. "It's all very well to do good and to live honestly, as he says, but we have plenty of time for that yet, and there is something which I only have the strength for now." This was not what I wanted. I wanted a challenge; I wanted feeling to direct us in life, and not life to direct our feeling. I dreamed of going up to the edge of a precipice with him, saying: "One more step, and I'll throw myself over the edge; one more move, and I shall perish!" And then he would turn pale as he stood on the edge of the precipice, take me in his strong arms and hold me over it a moment so that my heart would stop beating, and then take me away – wherever he wished.

This state of mind even affected my health, and my nerves were now on edge. One morning I felt worse than usual. He came back from his office in a bad mood, which was rare for him. I noticed this at once and asked him what the matter was. But he did not want to tell me, saying that it was not worth it. As I afterwards learnt, the district police officer had summoned our peasants and, because he disliked my husband, had made unlawful demands on them and used threats. My husband – who was still unable to digest this and see only the amusing or pathetic side of it – was upset, and therefore did not want to talk to me. But I thought that he did not want to talk to me because he thought me a child who could not understand his preoccupations. I turned away from him in silence, and sent a servant to ask Marya Minichna, who was staying with us, to come to tea. After tea, which I finished particularly quickly, I took Marya Minichna into the morning room and began talking to her very loudly about some nonsense which had no interest for me. He walked up and down the room, occasionally glancing at us. For some reason these glances made me want to talk and laugh all the more; everything I said and that Marya Minichna said seemed funny to me. Without a word, he went to his study and shut the door behind him. As soon as I could no longer hear him all my gaiety suddenly disappeared, to the surprise of Marya Minichna, who kept asking me what the matter was. Without replying, I sat down on the sofa and felt like crying. "What's he thinking up, anyway?" I thought. "Some sort of nonsense, which seems important to him, but just let him try and tell me about it, I'll show him that it's all rubbish. Oh, no, he wants to think that I won't understand, wants to humiliate me by his lofty calm, wants to be always in the right. But then I'm right too, when I feel bored and empty, when I want to live, to move about," I thought, "and not stay in one place and feel time passing me by. I want to move forwards, and every day, every hour I want something new, but he wants to stay still and to hold me back with him. Yet how easy it would be for him! He need not take me to town to achieve this, he should just be like me, not try to change himself, not hold himself back, but live simply. That's what his advice is to me, but he's not simple himself. So there!"

I felt tears welling up, and was irritated with him. The fact that I was irritated frightened me, and I went to him. He was sitting writing in his study. Hearing my footsteps, he looked round indifferently and calmly, and went on writing. I did not like the look he gave me; instead of coming up to him I stood at the table at which he was writing, opened a book and began looking at it. Once again he interrupted his work and looked at me.

"Masha, are you in a bad mood?" he said.

I replied with a cold glance, which said: "There's no need to ask – what's all this politeness for?" He shook his head and smiled timidly, tenderly, but, for the first time, I gave him no answering smile.

"What was the matter today?" I asked. "Why didn't you tell me?"

"Oh, nothing! Just a little unpleasantness," he answered. "However, I can tell you now. Two of our men set out for town…"

But I did not let him finish.

"Why didn't you tell me before, when I asked at tea?"

"I would have said something stupid. I was angry then."

"But it was just then that I wanted you to tell me."

"Why?"

"Why do you think that I can never help you about anything?"

"Think, indeed!" he said, throwing down his pen. "I think that I couldn't live without you. You not only help me in everything, everything, but you do everything. What an idea!" he laughed. "I live only through you. I think all goes well only because you're here, because you are needed…"

"Yes, I know that; I'm a nice child, who must be calmed down," I said in a voice which made him look up at me in surprise as if he were seeing something for the first time. "I don't want any calm, you've got enough of it yourself – quite enough," I added.

"Well now, you see, it was like this," he started, hurriedly interrupting me, apparently afraid to let me say all that was on my mind. "What would you have done about it?"

"I don't want to talk about it now," I answered. Although I did want to listen to him, I found it so pleasant to destroy his calm. "I don't want to play at life, I want to live," I said, "just like you."

His face – on which everything was so quickly and vividly reflected – showed pain and increasing attention.

"I want to live as your equal, as your…"

But I could not say any more; such sadness, deep sadness showed in his face. He was silent for a little.

"But in what way are you not my equal?" he said. "Because I, and not you, have to bother with the police officer and drunken peasants?…"

"It's not only that," I said.

"For God's sake understand me, darling," he went on. "I know that worries always hurt us, I have lived and found this out. I love you and, consequently, cannot help wishing I could spare you all the worry. That's what my life is made up of, of love for you – so let me live it."

"You're always right," I said, not looking at him.

I was annoyed that, once again, everything was clear and calm in his mind, whereas I was filled with vexation and a feeling akin to repentance.

"Masha, what's the matter?" he said. "It isn't a question of whether I'm right or you're right, but of something quite different: what have you got against me? Don't speak at once; think a little, and tell me all that's on your mind. You are angry with me – and probably you are right – but tell me what it is I am guilty of."

But how could I tell him what was in my heart? The fact that he had immediately understood me, that I was once again a child before him, that I could not do anything which he did not understand and foresee, upset me all the more.

"I haven't anything against you," I said. "It's simply that I'm bored, and wish I wasn't bored. But you say that it should be like that, and again you're right!"

I said this, and looked at him. I had achieved my purpose; his calmness had disappeared, his expression showed fear and pain.

"Masha," he said, in a quiet voice filled with emotion, "what we're doing now is no joke. Our fate is now being decided. I ask you not to answer me and to listen. Why do you want to cause me pain?"

But I interrupted him. "I know, you'll be right. It's better not to say anything; you're right," I said coldly, as if not I but some evil spirit were speaking within me.

"If only you knew what you're doing!" he said, and his voice trembled.

I began to cry, and felt better. He was sitting beside me and was silent. I was both sorry for him, and ashamed of myself and vexed at what I had done. I did not look at him. I felt that he must be looking at me at that moment either sternly or perplexed. I looked round: a mild, tender gaze was fixed on me, as if asking forgiveness. I took his hand and said: "Forgive me! I don't know myself what I was saying."

"Yes, but I know what you said, and I know that you were right in what you said."

"What?" I asked.

"That we must go to Petersburg," he said. "There's nothing for us to do here now."

"As you like," I said.

He took me in his arms and kissed me.

"Forgive me," he said. "I am to blame."

That evening I played to him for a long time, while he walked up and down the room, whispering something. He had a habit of doing this; I would often ask him what it was he was whispering, and he would think about it for a moment and then would always answer me precisely what it had been; it was usually poetry, and sometimes complete nonsense, but nonsense from which I could gauge his mood.

"What are you whispering now?" I asked.

He stood still, thought a moment and, smiling, answered with two lines of Lermontov:

But it, demented, seeks a tempest,
As if in tempests peace is found...*

"No, he's more than a man; he knows everything!" I thought. "How can one help loving him?"

I got up, took him by the hand, and began walking up and down with him, trying to fall in step.

"Yes?" he asked, smiling and looking at me.

"Yes," I said in a whisper, and suddenly we were both overcome with a fit of gaiety. Eyes smiling, we made bigger and bigger steps and stood more and more on tiptoe. To the immense indignation of Grigory, and to the amazement of my mother-in-law who was playing patience in the drawing room, we went through all the rooms in this way till we reached the dining room, where we stopped, looked at each other, and burst out laughing.

Two weeks later, just before Easter, we were in Petersburg.

7

OUR TRIP TO PETERSBURG, the week in Moscow, his and my relatives, settling down in the new flat, the journey, new towns and faces – all this passed like a dream. It was all so varied, new and gay, and all of it was so brilliantly illuminated by his presence and his love, that our quiet country existence seemed far off and insignificant. To my great surprise, instead of the worldly pride and coldness which I had expected to find in people, everyone greeted me with such genuine kindness and pleasure (not only relatives, but also people I did not know), that it seemed they had all been waiting for me to be happy themselves. Nor had I expected to find that my husband had friends in what seemed to me to be the best possible social set – friends that he had never mentioned to me, and I often found it odd and unpleasant to hear him pass stern judgement on some of these people, who seemed to me to be so kind. I could not understand why he was so short with them, and why he tried to avoid people whom it seemed to me flattering to know. I thought that the more kind people one knew, the better, and everyone was kind.

"You see, we must arrange things in this way," he had said before we left the country. "Here we are little Croesuses, whereas there we shan't be at all rich, and so we must live in town only till Easter, and not lead a social life, otherwise we shall get into a mess; besides, I wouldn't like it for your sake…"

"What do we want a social life for?" I answered. "We'll just go to a few theatres, see relatives, visit the opera and hear good music, and then come back to the country before Easter."

But as soon as we arrived in Petersburg these plans were forgotten. I suddenly found myself in such a new and happy world, I was so overwhelmed with joy, so many new interests opened up before me, that immediately – if unconsciously – I renounced my past and all its plans. "That was nothing – child's play; the real thing had not started yet, but this is real life! And surely, it's nothing to what it will be?" I thought. The uneasiness and the beginning of nostalgia which had disturbed me in the country disappeared suddenly and completely, as if by magic. My love for my husband became calmer, and the thought that he might love me less no longer occurred to me. Indeed, I could not doubt his love: my every thought was immediately understood, my feelings shared, my wishes fulfilled by him. His calmness either disappeared or else no longer irritated me. Besides, I felt that, apart from his love for me, he now also admired me. Often, after a visit to a new friend or after a party given by us in our house at which I, inwardly quaking for fear of making a mistake, fulfilled the duties of hostess, he would say: "Good girl! Fine! Don't be nervous. Really, very good!" – and I was very pleased. Soon after our arrival he wrote a letter to his mother; when he called me to add a postscript he did not want to let me read what he had written; in consequence I insisted, of course, and read it. "You won't recognize Masha," he had written, "and I can hardly recognize her myself. Where does she get that charming, graceful self-assurance, *affability*, even a social mentality and courtesy? And it's all so simple, charming, and good-natured. Everyone is delighted with her; even I can't admire her enough and – if it were possible – I would love her even more!"

"Ah! So that's what I'm like!" I thought, and I felt so gay and happy, and even had the feeling that I loved him all the more. The success I had with all our friends was quite unexpected for me. I was told from all sides that here an uncle liked me particularly, there an aunt had lost her heart to me, a man would tell me that there was not another woman like me in Petersburg, a woman would assure me that I had only to desire it to become the most sought-after woman in society. In particular a cousin of my husband's, Princess D., a society woman no longer young, suddenly became enamoured of me and told me more flattering things than anyone, quite turning my head. When this cousin asked me to go to a ball for the first time and I asked my husband about it, he turned to me and, with a scarcely noticeable sly smile, asked me whether I wanted to go. I nodded my head and felt myself blushing.

"She confesses to what she wants as if she were a criminal!" he said, laughing good-humouredly.

"But you said yourself that we shouldn't go out, and you don't like it," I answered, smiling and looking at him entreatingly.

"If you want to very much, then let's go," he said.

"Really, it's better not to."

"Do you want to? Very much?" he asked again.

I did not answer.

"A social life in itself is only a slight affliction," he went on, "but unrealized worldly desires – that's neither good nor pretty. We must certainly go, and we shall," he concluded determinedly.

"To tell you the truth," I said, "there's nothing in the world I want more than to go to this ball."

We did go, and I enjoyed myself beyond all my expectations. At the ball I felt even more than before that I was the centre around which everything revolved, that it was for my sake that the large ballroom was illuminated, the music played, and an admiring crowd had assembled. It seemed to me that everyone – from the hairdresser and maid to the dancers and old men who passed through the ballroom – told me or else made me feel that they loved me. The general opinion of me at that ball, as my cousin told me afterwards, was that I was quite unlike other women – that there was something special about me, a kind of countrified air, simple and delightful. This success so flattered me that I candidly told my husband that I wished to go to two or three more balls, "so as to get thoroughly fed up with them," I added insincerely.

My husband readily agreed, and at first was obviously pleased to go with me and delighted at my success. He seemed to have forgotten completely all he had said before or, at least, to have changed his mind about it.

Later on, the life we were leading obviously became both a bore and a burden to him. But I had no time to notice that, and even if I did sometimes become aware of his enquiring gaze, at once grave and searching, I failed to grasp its significance. I was so dazed by the spontaneous affection that I apparently evoked from all around me, and by the novel atmosphere of elegance and pleasure which I had never breathed before, his overwhelming moral influence disappeared so suddenly, I enjoyed so much being not only his equal but even his superior in that particular world – and hence loving him even more and in a more independent spirit than before – that I could not understand what he saw in social life that might be unpleasant for me. I experienced for the first time a feeling of pride and self-satisfaction when all eyes turned towards me as I entered a ballroom; whereas he would hasten to leave me and lose himself in a black crowd of tail-coats, as if ashamed to acknowledge his possession of me in front of the crowd. "You just wait!" I often thought, picking out his inconspicuous and sometimes bored figure at the other end of the ballroom. "Wait," I thought, "till we get home, and then you'll understand, and see for whom it was that I tried to be pretty and brilliant, and what it is I love best of all I see around me tonight." I sincerely imagined that my success gave me pleasure only because I would thus be in a position to offer it to him. The only way, I thought, in which social life could do me harm was in the possibility it offered of falling in love with one of the men I met at parties, and arousing my husband's jealousy, but he had such faith in me, seemed to be so calm and indifferent, and all those young people seemed to me so insignificant in comparison to him, that what I thought to be society's only danger did not frighten me. However, the attention paid me by many people of our social world pleased me, flattered my self-esteem, made me think there was some sort of merit in my love for my husband, and made me treat him in a way which was self-assured and almost casual.

"I saw you having a very animated conversation about something with N.N.," I said once on our way back from a ball, shaking my finger at him and naming a well-known Petersburg lady with whom he had indeed talked that evening. I said this to stir him up – he was particularly silent and bored.

"Oh! Why say things like that? And you, too, Masha!" he muttered through his teeth, frowning as if something pained him physically. "How little that sort of thing suits you and me! Let's leave it to other people; such a false relationship can spoil our real one, and I still hope that the real one will come back."

I felt ashamed, and was silent.

"Will it come back, Masha? What do you think?" he asked.

"It has never been spoilt, and it won't be," I said, and I really thought so then.

"I hope to God you're right; anyway, it's time for us to go back to the country," he went on.

But he only said this to me once; the rest of the time it seemed to me that he was just as happy as I was, and I felt so joyful and gay. "And even if he is bored sometimes," I consoled myself, "I was bored too for his sake in the country, and even if our relationship has changed a little, everything will come back again once we're alone again with Tatyana Semyonovna in the summer, at Nikolskoye."

And so the winter passed, without my noticing it, and contrary to our plans we even spent Holy Week in Petersburg. The week after Easter we were already preparing to leave, and everything was packed. My husband had already bought presents and such things as plants for our country house, and was in a particularly tender and cheerful frame of mind, when his cousin unexpectedly came to see us and begged us to stay on until Saturday in order to go to a party at Countess R.'s. She said that Countess R. was very anxious to have me, that a certain Prince M., who was then in Petersburg, had wanted to make my acquaintance ever since the last ball I had been at, that he was only going to the party for that reason, and that he said I was the prettiest woman in Russia. Everyone was going to be there and, in short, it would be disgraceful if I did not go.

My husband was at the other end of the drawing room, talking to someone.

"Well then, Marie, are you coming?" his cousin said.

"We wanted to leave for the country the day after tomorrow," I answered indecisively, looking at my husband. Our eyes met; he hurriedly turned away.

"I'll persuade him to stay," his cousin said, "and on Saturday we'll go and turn people's heads! All right?"

"That would upset our plans, and we've already packed," I answered, beginning to give in.

"It would be better for her to go and call on the prince this evening," my husband said from the other end of the room in a voice full of restrained irritation I had never heard before.

"Ah! He's jealous! There, that's the first time I've noticed it," his cousin laughed, "but I'm not trying to persuade her for the prince's sake, Sergey Mikhailovich, but for the sake of all of us. How Countess R. begged her to come!"

"It's up to her," my husband said coldly, and went out.

I saw that he was more than usually upset: this worried me, and I did not promise his cousin anything. As soon as she had left, I went to see my husband. He was walking up and down the room deep in thought, and neither saw nor heard me as I tiptoed in.

"There he is – thinking of our dear house in Nikolskoye," I said to myself as I looked at him, "and of morning coffee in the light drawing room, and of his fields and peasants, and of evenings in the study, and of secret midnight feasts... No!" I inwardly decided. "I'll never go to another ball again and I'll give up the flattery of all the princes in the world for the sake of his happy confusion, of his quiet caress." I wanted to tell him that I would not go and did not want to go to the party, when he suddenly looked round and frowned as he saw me, and the gentle and thoughtful expression of his face changed. Once more his look expressed perspicacity, wisdom, and patronizing calm. He did not want me to see him as an ordinary person: he had always to be a demi-god on a pedestal to me.

"What's the matter, my dear?" he asked, casually and calmly turning towards me.

I did not answer. I was annoyed that he should conceal his true self from me, and not want to remain the person I loved.

"You want to go to the party on Saturday?" he asked.

"I wanted to," I answered, "but you don't like it. And anyway, everything is packed," I added.

Never had he looked at me so coldly, never had he spoken so coldly to me.

"I shall not leave before Tuesday, and will order the things to be unpacked," he went on, "so you can go, if you want to. Do me a favour, and go. I shall not be leaving."

As always, when he was upset, he took to pacing up and down the room irritably, not looking at me.

"I simply don't understand you at all," I said, staying where I was but following him with my eyes. "You say you are always so calm," (He had never said this.) "Why do you talk to me in this odd way? I'm ready to sacrifice this pleasure for your sake, while you, ironically somehow, insist that I should go, in a way you never usually speak to me."

"Well, really! You make *sacrifices*" – he particularly stressed the word – "and I make sacrifices. What could be better? It's a struggle for magnanimity. What greater family happiness can there be?"

It was the first time that I had heard such bitterly mocking words from him. His mocking did not shame me, but offended me, and his bitterness did not frighten me, but was transmitted to me. Had he, who was always so afraid of empty phrases in our relationship, who was always sincere and simple, really said this? And why? Precisely because, for his sake, I wanted to sacrifice a pleasure in which I could see nothing bad, and because a minute before I had so well understood and loved him. Our roles were changed – he avoided straightforward and simple words, whereas I sought them.

"You have changed a great deal," I said, with a sigh. "What am I guilty of? It's not the party you have against me deep down in your heart; it's something else, something long-standing. Why be insincere? Weren't you yourself afraid of insincerity before? Tell me straight out: what have you got against me?" "What will he say?" I thought, remembering with self-satisfaction that he had had nothing with which to reproach me all the winter.

I came out into the middle of the room, so that he had to pass close by me, and I looked at him. The thought 'He will come up to me, take me in his arms, and it will be finished with', came into my head, and I even began to feel sorry that I would not have to prove him to be in the wrong. But he stopped at the other end of the room and looked at me.

"You still don't understand?" he asked.

"No."

"Well then, I'll tell you. I am disgusted, disgusted for the first time, at what I feel and cannot help feeling." He stopped, visibly alarmed at the harsh sound of his own voice.

"But what is it?" I asked, with tears of indignation in my eyes.

"It's disgusting, that the prince should think you pretty, and that therefore you should run after him, forgetting your husband and yourself, and your womanly dignity. It's disgusting that you should not want to understand what your husband must feel for you, if you yourself have no feeling of self-respect; on the contrary, you come and tell your husband that you are making a *sacrifice* – in other words: 'It would be a great pleasure for me to show myself to His Highness, but I am making a *sacrifice* of it!'"

The longer he spoke, the more the sound of his own voice inflamed him, and his voice sounded venomous, cruel and harsh. I had never seen nor expected to see him like that. My heart thumped, I was afraid, but at the same time feelings of undeserved shame and injured pride surged up in me, and I wanted to take my revenge on him.

"I've expected this for a long time," I said. "Go on, go on."

"I don't know what you were expecting," he continued. "I could expect the worst, seeing you every day in the filth, idleness and luxury of that idiotic society, and I got what I expected... so that now I'm ashamed and hurt, as I've never been before; hurt for myself, when your friend tried to probe my heart with her filthy hands and began talking about jealousy – about my jealousy, and of whom am I supposed to be jealous? Of a man whom neither you nor I know. While you, as if on purpose, refuse to understand me, and wish to sacrifice to me... what, indeed? I'm ashamed of you, I'm ashamed of your humiliation... Sacrifice!" he repeated.

"Ah! So that's what a husband's power is like!" I thought. "To insult and humiliate a woman who is not guilty of anything – that's what a husband's rights consist of, but I won't subject myself to them."

"No, I'm making no sacrifice to you," I went on, feeling my nostrils dilate unnaturally and the blood leaving my face. "I will go to the party on Saturday. I will most certainly go."

"And I wish you joy of it – only all is over between us!" he shouted in a burst of uncontrolled fury. "But you won't torment me any more. I was a fool to..." he started again, but his lips began to tremble and with a visible effort he refrained from finishing what he had started to say.

At that moment I was afraid of him, and hated him. I wanted to say a great deal and to take my revenge for all his insults: but if I had opened my mouth I would have burst into tears, and would have lowered myself in his eyes. I left the room in silence. But no sooner had I ceased to hear his footsteps than I was horrified at what we had done. I was afraid that the bond, of which all my happiness consisted, would indeed snap for ever, and I wanted to go back to him. "But will he have regained his calm sufficiently to understand me if I stretch out my hand in silence, and look at him?" I thought. "Will he understand my generosity? What if he should call my grief a pretence? Or if, with conscious righteousness and proud calm, he should accept my repentance and forgive me? And why, why has he, whom I love so much, so cruelly insulted me?"

I went, not to him, but to my own room, where I sat alone for a long time, weeping and recalling with horror every word of the conversation which had taken place between us; I replaced those words by others, adding different, kind words – and the memory of what had happened would again overwhelm me with its horror, and my feelings would be outraged. In the evening when I went down to tea and met my husband in the presence of S., who had called on us, I felt that from that day a whole abyss had opened up between us. S. asked me when we were leaving. I did not have time to answer.

"On Tuesday," my husband answered. "We have still to go to a party at Countess R.'s. You are going, aren't you?" he turned to me.

I was frightened by the sound of that ordinary voice, and looked round timidly at my husband. His eyes were looking straight at me, their expression was malicious and mocking, his voice was even and cold.

"Yes," I answered.

In the evening, when we were by ourselves, he came up to me and held out his hand.

"Please forget what I said to you," he said.

I took his hand with a trembling smile and with tears ready to flow, but he took his hand away and, as if afraid of a sentimental scene, sat down in an armchair some distance away from me. "Does he really still believe he was right?" I thought – and the explanation which I had ready and the request that we should not go to the party remained unsaid.

"We must write and tell Mamma that we have put off our departure," he said, "or she will be worried."

"When were you thinking of leaving?" I asked.

"On Tuesday, after the party," he answered.

"I hope it's not for my sake," I said, looking at him straight in the eyes, but his eyes only looked back at me, and said nothing, as if they were somehow shrouded from me. His face suddenly seemed old to me, and unpleasant.

We went to the party, and it seemed that a good, amicable relationship had been re-established between us, but this relationship was quite different to what it had been before.

I was sitting with the ladies at the party when the prince came up to me, so that I had to stand up in order to speak to him. As I got up I instinctively looked for my husband, and saw him look at me from the other end of the ballroom, and turn away. I suddenly felt so ashamed and hurt that I became painfully shy, and blushed all over my face and neck under the gaze of the prince. But I had to go on standing and listening to what he was saying as he looked down at me. Our conversation did not last long – there was nowhere for him to sit beside me, and he probably sensed that I felt very ill at ease with him. Our conversation was about a previous ball, of where I spent the summer, and so on. Taking leave of me, the prince expressed a wish to make the acquaintance of my husband, and I saw them meet and talk at the other end of the ballroom. The prince must probably have said something about me, for in the middle of their conversation he looked round smiling in our direction.

My husband suddenly blushed, bowed low, and was the first to take his leave. I blushed too: I felt ashamed of the impression which I – and especially my husband – must have made on the prince. It seemed to me that everyone had noticed my awkward shyness when I was talking to the prince, and had noticed my husband's strange behaviour; goodness knows how they could explain it – did they perhaps know about my conversation with my husband? His cousin took me home, and on the way she and I spoke of my husband. I could not refrain from telling her all that had happened between us because of this unfortunate party. She reassured me by saying that that kind of thing meant nothing, and that it was a very usual misunderstanding which would not leave any trace. She explained to me my husband's character as she understood it, and said that she thought he had become very uncommunicative and proud. I agreed with her, and felt that I now understood him better and more dispassionately myself.

But later, when he and I were alone together, the fact of having discussed him lay heavy on my conscience like a crime, and I felt that the gulf which now separated us had widened still further.

8

FROM THAT DAY our life and our relationship changed completely. We were no longer as happy when we were alone as we had been. There were questions which we avoided, and we could talk more easily in the presence of a third person than we could by ourselves. As soon as we started to talk about life in the country or about the ball our eyes betrayed an uneasy conscience, and we felt awkward when we looked at each other. We both seemed to feel exactly where the gulf was that separated us, and were afraid to approach it. I was convinced that he was proud and touchy, and that one had to be very careful not to offend his susceptibilities. He was convinced that I could not live without parties, that country life was not for me, and that he had to submit to this unfortunate taste. We both avoided speaking directly about these subjects, and each judged the other wrongly. We had each long since ceased to regard the other as the most perfect person in the world, but made comparisons with others and secretly passed judgement on each other.

I fell ill before our departure, and instead of going to the country we went to our summer villa, whence my husband went on alone to his mother. When he left I was sufficiently recovered to go with him, but he persuaded me to stay behind on the pretext that he was worried about my health. I felt it was not my health that worried him, but the thought that we would not be happy in the country; I did not much insist on going with him, and remained behind. Without him I felt empty and lonely, but when he came back I saw that he no longer added something to my life, as he had done before. Our relationship was no longer what it used to be when, as would sometimes happen, every thought, every impression not shared with him would weigh on me like a crime, when his every word and deed seemed to me models of perfection, when we felt like laughing for joy as we looked at each other; that relationship so imperceptibly changed into another that we did not even notice that it was no longer there. We each of us acquired our separate interests and worries, which we no longer even tried to share. We even ceased to be embarrassed by the fact that we each had our own separate world, foreign to the other. We became accustomed to this idea and, after a year's time, our eyes no longer betrayed an uneasy conscience when we looked at each other. His bouts of gaiety when he was with me and his childish pranks disappeared completely, as did his all-forgivingness and indifference to everything, which had formerly aroused my indignation. He no longer had that penetrating look which used to confuse and gladden me, there were no more prayers, no more transports of joy together, we did not even see each other very often – he was constantly away, and was neither afraid nor sorry to leave me alone; I constantly went to parties, where I did not need him.

There were no longer any scenes or quarrels between us; I tried to please him, he fulfilled all my wishes, and we appeared to love each other.

When we were by ourselves – which rarely occurred – I experienced neither joy, nor emotion, nor confusion, just as if I were by myself. I knew very well that he was my husband and not some other, unknown person, but a good man – my husband, whom I knew as well as I knew myself. I was convinced that I knew everything he would do or say, how he would look, and if he acted or looked differently to what I expected I felt that it was he who had made a mistake. I expected nothing from him. In a word, he was my husband and nothing more. It seemed to me that it was exactly as it should be, that there could be no other relationship, and that between us there had never even been any other. When he went away, especially at first, I felt lonely and frightened – without him I felt all the more strongly how important his support was to me; when he came back I would throw my arms round his neck from joy, although two hours later I would completely forget my joy and have nothing to say to him. It was only in moments of quiet, restrained tenderness which we sometimes had that I felt something was wrong; something made my heart ache, and in his eyes I seemed to read the same thing. I sensed the limit of tenderness which he did not seem to want to, and which I could not, cross. Sometimes this made me sad, but I had not time to think about anything, and I tried to forget the sadness that these dimly felt changes caused me, in the amusements which were constantly waiting for me. Social life, which at first had dazzled me with its glitter and its flattery to my pride, soon completely took possession of me, became habit, fastened its fetters on me, and occupied in my heart all the place which rightly belonged to feeling. I now never remained alone with myself, and was afraid to think too deeply about my way of life. All my time was occupied, from late morning till late at night, and no longer belonged to me, even if I did not go out. I was no longer either amused or bored by this, but it seemed to me that it must always have been just like that, and in no way different.

So passed three years, during which time our relationship remained the same, as if it had stood still, become set, and could not become either worse or better. During these three years two important events occurred in our family life, but neither of them altered my life. These events were the birth of my first child, and the death of Tatyana Semyonovna. At first a maternal feeling seized me with such force and filled me with such unexpected joy that I thought a new life would begin for me, but after two months, when I started to go out again, this feeling grew weaker and weaker, and was finally transformed into a habit and the cold fulfilment of a duty. My husband, on the contrary, with the birth of our first son became the gentle, calm home-lover he used to be, and transferred his former tenderness and gaiety to the child. Often, when I went into the nursery in evening dress to say goodnight to the child and found my husband there, I noticed his seemingly reproachful and sternly thoughtful gaze fixed on me, and I would feel ashamed. I would suddenly be horrified at my indifference to the child, and would ask myself: "Am I really worse than other women? But what can I do?" I thought. "I love my son, but I simply can't sit with him all day, it bores me, and I refuse to pretend about it."

His mother's death was a great grief to him; it was hard for him, as he said, to go on living at Nikolskoye without her, but although I was both sorry about her and sympathized with my husband's grief, life in the country was now pleasanter for me and I felt more at ease there. During these three years we spent most of our time in town. I only went to the country once every two months, and in the third year we went abroad.

We spent the summer at a spa.

I was then twenty-one years old; our financial situation was, I thought, flourishing; I did not demand anything more from family life than it gave me; it seemed to me that everyone I knew loved me; my health was good, I was the best-dressed woman at the spa, I knew I was pretty, the weather was wonderful, an atmosphere of beauty and elegance surrounded me, and I felt very gay. I was not as gay as I had been at Nikolskoye, when I had felt that I was happy within myself, that I was happy because I deserved happiness, that my happiness was great but that it must become still greater, that I wanted more and more happiness. Then it was different, but that summer, too, I was content. I desired nothing, hoped for nothing, feared nothing, and I felt that I had a full life and a clear conscience. Among the young people that season there was not one man that I preferred to any of the others in any way – even old Prince K., our minister, who paid me marked attention. One was young, another old, one a fair-haired Englishman, another a Frenchman with a little beard – they were all the same to me, but they were all essential to me. They were all equally indifferent faces making up the joyful atmosphere of the life surrounding me. Only one of them, an Italian, Marquis D., attracted my attention more than the others by the daring way he expressed his admiration for me. He never missed an opportunity of being with me – of dancing, riding, going to the casino and so on – and of telling me that I was beautiful. From the window I saw him several times outside our house, and often the unpleasant, intent gaze of his bright eyes would make me blush and look round. He was young, good-looking, elegant and, above all, in his smile and the shape of his forehead he resembled my husband, but was much better-looking. I was struck by this similarity, although his general appearance – his lips, the expression of his eyes, his long chin – all had something coarse and animal in place of the charm radiated by my husband's expression of kindness and ideal charm. At that time I supposed that the Marquis loved me passionately, and I occasionally thought of him with proud compassion. I sometimes wanted to calm him, to bring him round to a tone of half-friendly, quiet trust, but he sharply rejected these attempts and continued to disconcert me unpleasantly with his passion – unexpressed, but ready to express itself at any moment. I was afraid of that man, and often thought of him in spite of myself. My husband knew him, and was even colder and haughtier with him than with our other acquaintances, for whom he was only his wife's husband.

Towards the end of the season I fell ill and did not leave the house for a fortnight. When I went out in the evening to a concert for the first time after my illness, I learned that in my absence Lady S., who had long been expected and was famed for her beauty, had arrived. There was a crowd round me, people greeted me with pleasure, but there was a still greater crowd around the newly-arrived lioness. Everyone around me was talking only of her and of her beauty. She was pointed out to me, and she really was lovely, but I was unpleasantly struck by the expression of self-satisfaction on her face, and I said so. That day everything which had formerly been so amusing I now found boring. Another day Lady S. arranged an excursion to a castle, which I declined to join. Practically no one remained with me, and everything finally changed for me. Everything and everyone seemed stupid and boring. I wanted to cry, to finish the cure quickly and to go back to Russia. There was some sort of unpleasant feeling in my heart, but I did not acknowledge it to myself as yet. I pleaded convalescence, and ceased to appear on grand occasions, and only sometimes went out alone in the mornings and to take the waters, or went out driving in the neighbourhood with L.M., a Russian lady of our acquaintance. My husband was not there at that time; he had gone to Heidelberg for a few days, waiting for the end of my cure to go back to Russia, and he rarely came to see me.

One day Lady S. had persuaded everyone to go to a shooting party, and L.M. and I went to the castle after dinner. While we drove in the carriage at walking pace along the winding avenue flanked by ancient chestnut trees, through which could be seen the attractive, elegant suburbs of Baden-Baden lit up by the rays of the setting sun, our conversation took a serious turn such as it had never taken before. L.M., whom I had known for a long time, now for the first time appeared to me as a good, intelligent woman with whom one could talk about everything, and whom it was pleasant to have as a friend. We spoke of our families, our children, about the emptiness of life in Baden, we suddenly had a longing to go back to Russia, to the country, and somehow we felt sad and yet we felt better. We went into the castle, still under the influence of the same grave mood. Inside it was shady and cool, sunshine played on the ruins above us, and the sounds of footsteps and voices could be heard. The door served as a frame through which could be seen a typical Baden view – charming, though cold to us Russians. We sat down to rest and gazed silently at the setting sun. The sound of voices became more distinct, and I thought I heard someone mention my name. I began to listen, and involuntarily overheard every word. The voices were familiar: it was the Marquis D. and a Frenchman, his friend, whom I also knew. They were talking about me and about Lady S. The Frenchman compared her to me, and analysed the beauty of both of us. He did not say anything offensive, but my heart thumped as I overheard his words. He explained in detail what my good points were, and what were those of Lady S. I had a child already, whereas Lady S. was only nineteen; my hair was more luxuriant, but Lady S. had a more graceful figure; Lady S. was more of a *grande dame*, "whereas yours," he said, "is so-so, one of those little Russian princesses who are beginning to appear here so often." He concluded by saying that I was quite right not to try to compete with Lady S. and that I was definitely finished in Baden.

"I'm sorry for her."

"Unless she feels like consoling herself with you," he added, with a gay, hard laugh.

"If she goes away, I shall go after her," said the voice with the Italian accent roughly.

"Happy mortal! He can still love!" laughed the Frenchman.

"Love!" said the voice, and was silent for a moment. "I cannot help loving; there's no life without it. The only thing worth doing is to make a novel out of life. My novels never stop halfway, and I shall bring this one to a conclusion."

"*Bonne chance, mon ami*," said the Frenchman.

We did not hear any more, because they went round the corner and we heard their footsteps from the other side. They went down the stairs and, a few minutes later, came through the side door; they were very surprised to see us. I blushed when the marquis came up to me, and was terrified when he gave me his arm as we left the castle. I could not refuse, and we walked to the carriage behind L.M., who was walking with his friend. I felt insulted by what the Frenchman had said about me, although I had to acknowledge that he had only expressed my own feelings, but the marquis's words had surprised me and roused my indignation by their coarseness. I was tormented by the thought that I had heard what he had said and that, in spite of it, he was not afraid of me. It was unpleasant to feel him so close and, without looking at him or answering him, and trying to hold his arm so as not to hear what he was saying, I hurriedly followed L.M. and the Frenchman. The marquis was saying something about the beautiful view, about the unexpected pleasure of meeting me, and so on – but I was not listening to him. I was thinking then about my husband, about my son, about Russia; I felt ashamed about something, sorry about something, I wanted something, and I was in a hurry to get home as quickly as possible to my lonely room in the Hôtel de Bade so as to be able to think at leisure about all the feelings surging up in me. But L.M. walked slowly, the carriage was still a long way off, and my partner seemed intent on walking more and more slowly, as if trying to hold me back. "It's impossible!" I thought, and walked faster with determination. But he was definitely trying to hold me back, and was even pressing my arm. L.M. disappeared round the corner of the road, and we were quite alone. I was afraid.

"Excuse me," I said coldly, and tried to free my arm, but my lace sleeve got caught on a button of his coat. Bending towards me, he started to disentangle the sleeve, and his gloveless fingers touched my hand. A new kind of feeling, terror mingled with pleasure, ran like a shiver down my spine. I looked at him, trying to express with one cold glance all the contempt that I felt for him, but my glance expressed something different: it expressed fear and agitation. His burning, moist eyes close to my face looked at me strangely, at my neck, at my breast; both his hands held mine above the wrist; his open lips were saying something – were saying that he loved me, that I meant everything to him, and his lips came closer to me, and his hands pressed mine harder, burning me. Fire ran in my veins, everything became blurred, I was trembling, and the words with which I wanted to stop him dried in my throat. Suddenly I felt a kiss on my cheek and, trembling and growing cold all over, I looked at him. Without strength to speak or move, terrified, I waited and wanted something. All this lasted for an instant, but that instant was terrible. In the course of it I saw the whole of him so clearly. I so well understood his face, the abrupt, low forehead – so similar to my husband's – visible under a straw hat; the beautiful, straight nose with distended nostrils; the long, finely pomaded moustache and the little beard; the smoothly shaved cheeks and sunburnt neck. I hated, I feared him; he was so alien to me, but at that instant the emotion and passion of that hated stranger found such a powerful response in me! I irresistibly longed to give myself up to the kisses of that coarse and beautiful mouth, to the caresses of those white hands with fine veins and rings on the fingers; I felt impelled to throw myself headlong into the abyss of forbidden delights thus suddenly opening up in front of me!

"I'm so unhappy," I thought. "What does it matter if more and more unhappiness falls to my lot?"

He embraced me with one arm and bent down towards my face. "Let it be, let me be covered with still more shame and sin," I thought.

"*Je vous aime*," he whispered, in a voice that was so like my husband's. I remembered my husband and child as if they were dear things that had existed long ago, and as if all was over between them and me. But at that very moment, from round the bend in the road, came the sound of L.M.'s voice calling me. I recovered myself, tore my hands away and, without looking at him, almost ran after L.M. We sat down in the carriage, and it was only then that I looked at him. He took off his hat and asked me something, smiling. He did not understand the inexpressible disgust that I felt for him then.

My life seemed so unhappy to me, the future so hopeless, the past so black! L.M. talked to me, but I did not understand what she was saying. I thought that she only spoke to me because she was sorry for me, to hide the contempt that I aroused in her. In every word, in every look I imagined her contempt and wounding pity. His kiss burned my cheek with shame, and I could not bear the thought of my husband and child. When I was alone in my room I hoped to think over my position, but I was afraid to be alone. I did not finish the tea which was brought me and, for no reason that I could explain, started feverishly then and there to make ready to catch the evening train to Heidelberg, to rejoin my husband.

My maid and I sat down in an empty carriage, the train moved off, I felt the coolness of the air through the open window, and began to recover and to have a clearer vision both of my past and my future. I suddenly saw all my married life, from the day of our move to Petersburg, in a new light, and I felt it lie heavily like a reproach on my conscience. For the first time I vividly recalled our early days in the country and our plans, and for the first time the question: what sort of happiness did he have, all this time? – came into my head. And I felt guilty. "But why didn't he stop me, why did he play the hypocrite, why did he avoid explanations, why did he hurt me?" I asked myself. "Why did he not make use of the power of his love over me? Perhaps he did not love me?" But however much he might be to blame, the kiss of another man was imprinted on my cheek, and I felt it. The nearer I got to Heidelberg, the clearer became the image I had of my husband and the more terrifying the forthcoming meeting. "I'll tell him everything, everything, I'll sob it all out with tears of repentance," I thought, "and he will forgive me." But I did not know myself what that "everything" was, and did not myself believe that he would forgive me.

But as soon as I entered my husband's room and saw his calm, if surprised, face, I felt I had nothing to tell him, nothing to confess, and no reason to ask for his forgiveness. Unexpressed grief and repentance had to remain locked within me.

"Why did you take it into your head to come here?" he said. "I had planned to go to you tomorrow." But he was obviously alarmed when he looked more closely at my face. "What's happened? What's the matter with you?" he went on.

"Nothing," I answered, scarcely holding back my tears. "I've come for good. Let's go back to Russia – tomorrow, if possible."

He was silent for a time and looked at me thoughtfully.

"Come now, tell me what has happened to you," he said.

I blushed involuntarily, and looked down. Injured pride and anger flashed in his eyes. I was afraid of what he might think, and with a wealth of hypocrisy which I never suspected in me, I said: "Nothing has happened. I just got bored and sad living by myself, and thought a great deal about our life and about you. I have been to blame for so long now! Why do you accompany me to places you don't want to go to? I have been to blame for so long," I repeated, and once more I felt tears welling up. "Let's go back and live in the country, and for good."

"Oh, my dear, spare me sentimental scenes," he said coldly. "It's fine that you should want to go back and live in the country, because we haven't much money; as to going there for good – that's a myth. I know you would never be able to settle down there. There now, have some tea and you'll feel better," he concluded, getting up to ring for the servant.

I imagined all he might think of me, and felt outraged by the dreadful thoughts that I attributed to him as I met his uncertain and seemingly self-conscious gaze. "No, he doesn't want to and can't understand me!" I said I was going to look at the child, and left him. I wanted to be alone, and to cry and cry and cry…

9

OUR HOUSE AT NIKOLSKOYE, long unheated and empty, revived again, but that which had lived in it did not revive. His mother was no more, and we lived alone, face to face. Now we not only had no need for solitude, but it even embarrassed us. The winter was all the more difficult for me as I was ill, and recovered only after the birth of my second son. I continued to have the same cold but friendly relationship with my husband as we had had during our life in town, but in the country every floorboard, every wall, every sofa reminded me of what he had been for me and of what I had lost. It was as if we were divided by some unforgiven offence – as if he was punishing me for something while pretending not to notice it himself. There was nothing to ask forgiveness for, there was no reason to ask for mercy: he punished me only by not giving me his whole self, his whole heart, as he had done before: but he gave it to no one and to nothing, as if he no longer had it to give. Sometimes I thought that he was pretending to be like that only in order to torment me, but that his former feeling was still alive within him, and I would try to arouse it. But, each time, he seemed to avoid frankness, seemed to suspect me of hypocrisy and seemed to be afraid of sentimentality as of something ridiculous. His look and his tone said: "I know everything, everything; there's nothing more to be said, and I know all you want to say. I know, too, that you will say one thing and do another." At first I was hurt by this avoidance of frankness, but then I became used to the idea that it was not the avoidance of frankness, but the absence of the need for frankness that I was hurt by. My tongue would no longer suddenly form the words to tell him that I loved him, or to ask him to read prayers with me, or to call him to hear me play the piano. Certain rules of propriety were now felt between us. We each lived apart: he, with his occupations in which I could not and no longer wished to take part; I, with my idleness, which no longer worried or saddened him as it used to do. The children were still too small and could not yet unite us.

But spring came. Katya and Sonya came to live with us in the country for the summer, but our house at Nikolskoye was being rebuilt, and we moved to Pokrovskoye. It was the same old house with its terraces, with the folding table and the piano in the light drawing room, and my old room with white curtains and my girlhood's dreams, which had somehow been forgotten there. There were two beds in this room: one – which had been mine – in which I would make the sign of the cross over sprawling, chubby Kokosha in the evenings, and the other, a small bed in which Vanya's little face peeped out from under the shawls. When I was saying goodnight to them I would often stop in the middle of the quiet little room, and suddenly, from every corner, from the walls, from the curtains, the old, forgotten visions of youth would creep out, the old voices of my girlhood's songs would begin to sing. And what had become of these visions, of those dear, sweet songs? All I had hardly dared hope had been realized. What had been vague, intermingled dreams had turned into reality, and reality had turned into a hard, difficult and joyless life. And yet everything was just the same: the same garden could be seen from the window, the same lawn, the same path, the same bench over there above the ravine, the same sound of nightingales' song came across from the pond, the same lilac all in flower, and the same moon stood over the house – and yet, everything had so terribly, so impossibly changed. Everything was so distant that could have been so near and dear! Just as of old, I would sit quietly in the drawing room talking to Katya, and talking quietly about him. But Katya had become wrinkled and yellow, her eyes no longer shone with joy and hope, but expressed sympathetic sorrow and pity. We no longer praised him, as of old, we analysed him; we no longer marvelled and wondered why and wherefore we were so happy, and we no longer wanted, as we had done, to tell the whole world what we were thinking; like conspirators, whispering to each other, we would ask each other a hundred times why everything had so sadly changed. And he was just the same too, only with deeper furrows between his eyebrows, with more grey hair on his temples, but his profound and thoughtful gaze was always shrouded from me as by a cloud. And I, too, was just the same, only I no longer had any love within me, or any desire for love. I felt no necessity to work, no satisfaction with myself. My former religious ecstasy and the love I had once felt for him, the old fullness of life, now seemed so distant and impossible. I would not now have understood what had before seemed to me so obvious and right – the happiness of living for someone else. Why live for someone else when there is no desire to live for oneself?

I had completely given up my music ever since he had moved to Petersburg, but now the old piano and music books began to appeal to me once again.

One day I did not feel well, and stayed at home by myself. Katya and Sonya had gone to Nikolskoye with my husband to look at the new building. The table was laid for tea, I went downstairs and, while I was waiting for them, sat down at the piano. I opened the *Sonata quasi una fantasia* and started to play it. There was no one about, the windows were open on to the garden, and the well-known, sadly solemn notes resounded through the room. I finished playing the first movement and, quite unconsciously, from long habit glanced at the corner in which he once used to sit listening to me. But he was not there; the chair, long untouched, stood in its corner, and through the window a bush of lilac could be seen against a light sunset. The freshness of the evening poured in through the open window. I leant my arms on the piano, covered my face with both hands, and was plunged in thought. I sat like that for a long time, painfully remembering the old, irretrievable life, and timidly thinking out a new one. But nothing seemed to lie before me, no desire, no hope. "Is my life really finished?" I thought and, horror-struck, I raised my head and began to play the same *andante* all over again so as to forget and not to think. "Oh God!" I thought. "Forgive me if I am guilty, or give me back all that used to be so wonderful in my soul, or teach me what to do – how to live now." I heard the noise of wheels on the grass and in front of the porch, and from the terrace came the sound of careful, familiar footsteps, and then silence. But it was no longer the old feeling that responded to the sound of those familiar footsteps. When I had finished playing I heard steps behind me, and a hand was laid on my shoulder.

"How clever of you to have played that sonata," he said.

I was silent.

"You haven't had tea?"

I shook my head and did not look round at him, in order not to disclose the traces of emotion remaining on my face.

"They will be coming in a moment; the horse played up and they continued on foot from the main road," he said.

"Let's wait for them," I said and went out on the terrace, hoping that he would follow me, but he asked about the children, and went to see them. Once more his presence, his simple, kind voice convinced me that I was wrong in thinking that something was lost to me. What more could one want? He was kind, gentle, a good husband, a good father. I did not know myself what else I needed. I went out on the balcony and sat down under the awning of the terrace on the very bench on which I had sat on the day of his proposal. The sun had already set, night was drawing on, and a dark springtime cloud hung over the house and garden. Only one clear patch of sky, with the dying sunset and an evening star which had just broken through, could be seen from behind the trees. The shadow of the little cloud lay over everything, and everything was waiting for the gentle summer rain. The wind dropped; not a leaf stirred, not a blade of grass. The scent of lilac and cherry blossom filled the garden and the terrace, as if all the air was in bloom; it came in waves, now stronger, now weaker, so that one wanted to close one's eyes and see nothing, hear nothing apart from that sweet scent. The dahlias and rose bushes, not yet in bloom, stretched out motionless along the dark, furrowed flower-beds, and seemed to be slowly growing up their white supports of whittled wood. From the ravine came the sound of frogs as if in a final outburst before the rain that would drive them into the water. All that could be heard above this clamour was a thin, uninterrupted sound of water. Nightingales called to each other in turn, and could be heard anxiously flying from place to place. That spring a nightingale had once again tried to make its home in a bush under the window, and when I went out on the terrace I heard it flit across to the other side of the drive, from where it clucked once and was silent, waiting too.

Vainly I tried to reassure myself; I was waiting and hoping for something.

He came down and sat down beside me.

"It looks as if they will get wet," he said.

"Yes," I said, and we were both silent for a long time. There was no wind and the cloud came lower and lower; everything became quieter, stiller, and more fragrant. Suddenly a raindrop fell and seemed to bounce on the canvas awning of the terrace, another fell on the gravel path; drops splashed on the burdocks and heavy, cool rain came down harder and harder. The nightingales and frogs became quite silent, only the thin sound of falling water continued to fill the air – although it, too, sounded further away because of the rain – and a bird, probably hiding in the dry leaves not far from the terrace, evenly gave out its two uniform notes. He stood up, and wanted to leave.

"Where are you going?" I asked, holding him back.

"I must have an umbrella and galoshes sent out to them," he answered.

"It's not worth it; it will soon be over."

He agreed with me, and we remained together by the balustrade of the terrace. I leaned my arm against the slippery wet rail and put my head out. The fresh rain spattered my hair and neck. The little cloud, growing lighter and smaller, emptied itself over us; the even sound of the rain gave way to rare drops falling from above and from the leaves. Below, the frogs began to croak again, the nightingales broke into song once more and began to answer each other out of the wet bushes, now from one side, now from the other. Everything was light again before us.

"How lovely it is!" he said, sitting down on the balustrade and stroking my wet hair with his hand.

This simple caress affected me like a reproach: I wanted to cry.

"And what more can a man want?" he said. "I am so content now that I don't need anything. I'm completely happy."

"You didn't always speak to me like that about your happiness," I thought. "No matter how great it was, you used to say that you wanted more and more of something. But now you are calm and content, whereas my heart is somehow full of unexpressed repentance and unshed tears."

"I feel all right, too," I said, "but sad, just because everything around me is so lovely. Inside me everything is so incoherent, so incomplete; I still feel I want something, but here it's so beautiful and peaceful. Don't you, too, have a feeling of nostalgia mixed with your delight in nature, as if you wanted something that is past?"

He took his hand off my head and was silent for a little.

"Yes, once I used to feel that too, especially in spring," he said, as if trying to recollect it. "And I too used to sit up at night, wishing and hoping – and how good they were, those nights!… But then, everything was before me, and now it is all behind me; now I am satisfied with what I have and feel content," he concluded – in such an assured and casual way that, however painful it was to hear him, I believed that he was speaking the truth.

"And you don't wish for anything?" I asked.

"Nothing that is impossible," he answered, guessing my feeling. "Look, you're getting your head wet," he added, stroking me like a child and passing his hand over my hair again. "You envy the leaves and the grass because the rain waters them; you would like to be both the leaves and the grass and the rain. Whereas I simply rejoice for them, as I do for everything in the world that is beautiful and young and happy."

"And you don't regret anything of the past?" I pressed him, feeling my heart grow heavy.

He thought a little, and was silent again. I saw that he wanted his answer to be absolutely sincere.

"No!" he answered shortly.

"It's not true! It's not true!" I said, turning towards him and looking him straight in the eyes. "You don't regret the past?"

"No!" he repeated once again. "I am grateful for it, but I don't regret the past."

"But would you really not like to bring it back?" I said.

He turned, and gazed into the garden.

"I don't wish to, in the same way as I don't wish to grow wings," he said. "It's impossible!"

"And you wouldn't like to change the past? You don't reproach yourself – or me?"

"Never! Everything was for the best."

"Listen!" I said, touching his hand to make him look round at me. "Listen! Why did you never tell me what you wanted, so that I would have lived just as you wished? Why did you let me have my freedom, which I didn't know how to use? Why did you stop being my mentor? If you had wanted to, if you had guided me differently, nothing, nothing would have happened," I said, in a voice which increasingly expressed cold vexation and reproach, and not my former love.

"What wouldn't have happened?" he said, turning round to me in amazement. "Nothing did. Everything is all right – very much all right," he added, smiling.

"Does he really not understand or – even worse – doesn't he want to understand?" I thought, and tears came into my eyes.

"I'll tell you what wouldn't have happened," I suddenly blurted out. "I wouldn't now be punished by your indifference, contempt even – without being guilty of anything. You wouldn't suddenly have deprived me of all that was dear to me – that's what wouldn't have happened!"

"What is the matter with you, my dear?" he said, as if not understanding what I was saying.

"No, let me speak… You took away from me your trust, your love, even your respect; because I don't believe you love me now, not after the way you loved me before. No, I must get it all off my chest now – all that has been tormenting me for so long." I interrupted him again. "Am I really to blame because I didn't know life, and because you left me to find it out for myself?… Am I really to blame because now, when I have understood what I must do, when, for almost a year now, I have been fighting to return to you, you push me away, as if you didn't understand what I want, and all in such a way that it is impossible to reproach you, whereas I am both guilty and unhappy! Yes, you want to throw ne back again into that life which could have been responsible for our unhappiness, both yours and mine."

"But how did I show you this?" he asked, with genuine alarm and amazement.

"Didn't you say to me only yesterday – and don't you always say that I won't be able to settle down here, and that for the winter we must again go to Petersburg, which I hate?" I went on. "Instead of giving me some support, you avoid all frankness, all sincerity or tenderness. And then, when my downfall is complete, you will reproach me and rejoice over it."

"Wait, wait," he said sternly and coldly. "What you are saying now is wicked. It only shows that you are ill-disposed towards me, that you don't…"

"That I don't love you? Say it!" I concluded, and tears streamed down my cheeks. I sat down on the bench and covered my face with a handkerchief.

"That's the way he understood me!" I thought, trying to hold back the sobs which were choking me. "But our old love is over, is over!" a voice in my heart was saying. He did not come towards me, did not comfort me. He had taken offence at what I had said. His voice was calm and dry. "I don't know what you are reproaching me for," he began. "If it's with no longer loving you as I did…"

"Did!" I said into my handkerchief, and bitter tears fell on it in still greater profusion.

"Then time and we ourselves are to blame. There is a season for every love…" He was silent for a moment. "And, to tell you the whole truth, if you still want frankness, just as that year when I first got to know you I spent sleepless nights thinking of you, and created my own love, and that love grew and grew in my heart, so, in Petersburg and abroad, I spent dreadful nights awake destroying, breaking up that love which tormented me. I did not destroy it, I only destroyed what was tormenting me; I regained my peace of mind and I love you all the same, but with a different love."

"Yes, you call that love, but it's torment," I said. "Why did you let me lead a social life if you thought it so harmful that you ceased to love me because of it?"

"Not because of a social life, my dear," he said.

"Why didn't you make use of your authority?" I went on. "Why didn't you restrain me, why didn't you kill me? I would be better off now than

I am, deprived of everything my happiness was made up of. I would be better off, and not feel ashamed."

I burst into sobs again and covered my face.

At that moment Katya and Sonya, gay and wet, loudly talking and laughing, came out onto the terrace, but, seeing us, grew silent and left immediately.

We were silent for a long time after they had gone. I had shed all my tears and began to feel better. I looked at him. He was sitting leaning his head on his hand, and wanted to say something in answer to my look, but only sighed heavily and put his head on his hand again.

I came up to him and took his hand away. He turned to look at me thoughtfully.

"Yes," he began, as if continuing his thoughts. "All of us – especially you women – must live through all the nonsense of life ourselves in order to come back to life itself, and one can never believe someone else. At the time, you were far from having lived through all that delightful and charming nonsense which I admired in you and I left you to live it out, feeling that I did not have the right to stand in your way, although – for me – the time for that sort of thing was already long past."

"Why, then, did you live through that nonsense with me and let me live through it, if you love me?" I said.

"Because, even if you had wanted to, you couldn't have believed me; you had to find out for yourself – and you did."

"You reasoned, you reasoned a great deal," I said. "You loved too little."

We were silent once more.

"It was cruel, what you just said, but it was true," he went on, suddenly getting up and walking up and down the terrace. "Yes, it's true. I was to blame," he added, stopping opposite me: "I should either not have allowed myself to love you at all, or I should have loved you more simply."

"Let's forget it all," I said timidly.

"No, what has passed cannot return again, you can never bring it back," and his voice softened as he said this.

"It has come back already," I said, putting my hand on his shoulder.

He took my hand away and pressed it. "No, I was not speaking the truth when I said that I didn't regret the past. I do; I regret, I weep for that old love which is no longer, and can no longer be. Who is to blame for this, I don't know. Love remains, but is not the same love; its place remains, but the old love has disappeared through suffering, and there's no strength or sap in the new one; memories and gratitude remain, but..."

"Don't talk like that," I interrupted. "Let everything be as it was before once more. It is possible, isn't it?" I asked, looking into his eyes. But his eyes were clear and calm, and did not look deeply into mine.

Even as I was speaking I felt that what I wished for and what I was asking of him was impossible. He smiled calmly, gently, with what seemed to me an old man's smile.

"How young you still are, and I am so old," he said. "I have no longer in me what you are looking for – why deceive yourself?" he added, continuing to smile in the same way.

I stood beside him in silence, and in my heart I began to feel calmer.

"Don't let's try to repeat life," he went on. "Don't let's lie to ourselves. And if the old worries and emotions no longer exist – well, thank God for that! We needn't seek anything nor worry about anything any more. We have already found it, and enough happiness has fallen to our lot. Now we must stand aside and give way to – look, to whom!" he said, pointing to the nurse who had come towards us with Vanya, and was standing at the door of the terrace. "So there, dear friend," he concluded, bending my head towards his and kissing it. Not a lover, but an old friend was kissing me.

From the garden the scented freshness of night was rising with increasing strength and sweetness, ever more solemn grew the sounds and the silence, ever more stars appeared in the sky. And suddenly, as I looked at him, I felt easier in my heart, as if the painful moral nerve which had made me suffer had been removed. I suddenly understood clearly and calmly that the feeling of that time had passed irrevocably away like that time itself, and that it was not only impossible to retrieve it, but that it would be painful and embarrassing to do so. And indeed, had it really been so perfect, that time which had seemed to me so happy? And it was all so long ago already!

"Well, it's time for tea!" he said, and we went into the drawing room together. At the doors we again met the nurse with Vanya. I took the child in my arms, covered up his little bare red legs, pressed him to me and kissed him, scarcely touching him with my lips. He stirred his little hands with spread-out, wrinkled fingers, as if in sleep, and opened dim eyes as if looking for or remembering something; suddenly those eyes came to rest on me, the spark of a thought shone in them, the fat, parted lips started to pucker and broke into a smile. "Mine, mine, mine!" I thought, pressing him to my breast with happy intensity in every limb, and with difficulty restraining myself from hurting him. I kissed his cold little legs, his tummy, his hands, and his downy head barely covered with hair. My husband came towards me, and I quickly covered up the baby's face and then uncovered it again.

"Ivan Sergeych!" said my husband, touching him under the chin with his finger. But I quickly covered Ivan Sergeych up again. No one but I should look at him for long. I glanced at my husband; his eyes were laughing as they met mine, and for the first time for many months, I looked at him light-heartedly and joyfully.

From that day my romance with my husband was over. The old feeling became a dear, irretrievable memory and a new feeling of love for my children and for the father of my children laid the foundation for another, this time completely different, happy life, which I am still living at the present moment...

Notes

p. 144, *en raccourci*: "Foreshortened" (French).

p. 164, *dinner*: This was clearly in this household the main meal of the day. In rural Russia, in the mid-nineteenth century, it was not uncommon to have the last proper meal of the day at four o'clock.

p. 166, *le mieux est l'ennemi du bien*: "The best is the enemy of the good" (French).

p. 171, *But it... is found*: Tolstoy misquotes Lermontov – the line should read: "But it, rebellious, seeks a tempest..." etc. In the poem "it" refers to the sail of a boat.